Army of Shadows

ORCS
Bad Blood II

Army of
Shadows

STAN NICHOLLS

GOLLANCZ

LONDON

Copyright © Stan Nicholls 2009
All rights reserved

The right of Stan Nicholls to be identified as the
author of this work has been asserted by him in accordance
with the Copyright, Designs and Patents Act 1988.

First published in Great Britain in 2009 by Gollancz
An imprint of the Orion Publishing Group
Orion House, 5 Upper St Martin's Lane, London WC2H 9EA
An Hachette UK company

A CIP catalogue record for this book is available
from the British Library.

ISBN 978 0 575 07805 5 (Cased)
ISBN 978 0 575 07806 2 (Trade Paperback)

1 3 5 7 9 10 8 6 4 2

Typeset at The Spartan Press Ltd,
Lymington, Hants

Printed and bound at CPI Mackays,
Chatham, Kent

The Orion Publishing Group's policy is to use papers that
are natural, renewable and recyclable products and
made from wood grown in sustainable forests. The logging
and manufacturing processes are expected to conform to
the environmental regulations of the country of origin.

www.stannicholls.com
www.orionbooks.co.uk

This Wolverines adventure is dedicated to
Elaine and Sam Clarke and Anna and Rod Fry,
with love and best wishes for the even greater
escapade they've embarked upon.

Of Omens, Revolts
and Legendary Heroes

After escaping Maras-Dantia, their chaotic birthplace, the survivors of orcs warband the Wolverines settled in Ceragan, a world populated solely by their own kind. Stryke, the band's leader, took native female Thirzarr as his mate, siring two male hatchlings. But by the time the oldest of Stryke's offspring was four, the band had grown restless with their bucolic life.

While hunting, Stryke and Wolverine sergeant Haskeer found themselves near the cave where the warband arrived in Ceragan, and were shocked when an unknown human emerged. But the man was mortally wounded, a dagger jutting from his back. A search of the corpse turned up an amulet bearing strange markings, and a gemstone.

The magical stone issued a message from Tentarr Arngrim, known to the Wolverines as Serapheim, the wizard who made possible their escape from Maras-Dantia. It included images of orcs in another world being cruelly subjugated by humans, and to Stryke and Haskeer's dismay they appeared not to be fighting back. Even more shocking, the architect of their oppression was shown as Serapheim's malevolent daughter, sorceress queen Jennesta, the warband's old enemy and once their ruler.

Arngrim's likeness asserted that it was in the Wolverines' power to help these fellow orcs and exact revenge on Jennesta. To do so they would have to use the five mysterious artefacts called instrumentalities – known to the orcs as stars – which Serapheim created and the warband still possessed. The instrumentalities allowed dimension-hopping, and perhaps more, and were the means by which the Wolverines were transported to Ceragan. Had someone not murdered him, Serapheim's messenger would have acted as the band's guide.

Wanting to accept the challenge, despite his suspicions of Arngrim's motives, Stryke guessed that the symbols on the amulet showed how the stars should be fitted together in order to travel to other worlds. Gathering the scattered members of the Wolverines, he found they were as keen on the mission as he was.

Stryke stood at the warband's head, as captain. Below him were two sergeants, one of whom was Haskeer. The other would have been the band's only dwarf, Jup, had he not elected to stay in Maras-Dantia. Under them came two corporals. Again, one was missing; but it was death, not the gulf between worlds, that separated Alfray from the Wolverines. The other corporal was Coilla, the sole female member, and their Mistress of Strategy. Beneath the officers were thirty privates. Or would have been if six hadn't fallen along the way.

To make up the strength, Stryke enlisted half a dozen native warriors, all tyros; and to replace Alfray as second corporal he chose an ageing orc called Dallog. None of which pleased Haskeer, who was even less happy when local chieftain Quoll forced Stryke to include his foppish offspring, Wheam, on the mission. Stryke decided that the band would go back to Maras-Dantia to try to find Jup, in hope of him resuming his role as sergeant. If he was still alive.

After an alarming transference, they found Maras-Dantia in an even worse state than when they left. The magical energy that coursed through the land had grown much weaker, and what remained was corrupted and malign.

Almost as soon as the Wolverines arrived they were attacked by human marauders. One new recruit, and Liffin, a seasoned member, were killed. As Liffin died defending Wheam, Haskeer's contempt for the youth increased. Stryke pushed the band onward to Quatt, the dwarfs' homeland, a journey fraught with peril.

An unknown number of instrumentalities exist, spread across the infinity of dimensions. Activation of the warband's set was detected by a covert group called the Gateway Corps. A multirace assemblage of great antiquity, dedicated to the task of keeping the portals between worlds sealed off, the Corps hunted down instrumentalities. Corps leader Karrell Rivers, a human, ordered his second-in-command, elf female Pelli Madayar, to recover the instrumentalities held by the Wolverines. Her unit armed with potent magical weaponry, Pelli's brief was to stop at nothing to achieve her mission.

The Wolverines battled their way to Quatt and found Jup, and were surprised to discover he had acquired a mate, Spurral. Wearied by Maras-Dantia's increasing deterioration, Jup agreed to rejoin the band, but insisted that Spurral went along too.

Before they could leave, the Wolverines encountered humans Micalor Standeven and Jode Pepperdyne, who warned them of an imminent raid by religious fanatics. Despite their loathing and distrust of humans, the orcs heeded them, and with the dwarfs beat off the attack. During the fight, Pepperdyne, a superb warrior, saved Coilla's life. Standeven proved less heroic.

The Wolverines weren't aware that Pepperdyne was little more than Standeven's slave. Nor did they know that the pair were on the run from a despot called Kantor Hammrik, to whom Standeven was in debt. Standeven and Pepperdyne only avoided being executed by Hammrik because Pepperdyne played on the tyrant's desire to possess the fabled instrumentalities. Convincing him that they could locate a set in the so-called barbarous lands of Maras-Dantia, Standeven and Pepperdyne were dispatched there by Hammrik under armed escort, but overcame their guards. The tale they told the Wolverines was that they were merchants wronged by Jennesta, and were seeking revenge on her. In reality, Standeven coveted the instrumentalities the Wolverines held, intending to use them as a bargaining chip with Hammrik.

Irate that the Wolverines had brought trouble to their settlement, the dwarfs turned on them. The band, along with Jup, Spurral and the two humans, found themselves cornered in a blazing longhouse. Realising the only way to escape was by using the stars, Stryke aligned them for what he hoped was the world of their mission.

The warband materialised in the verdant terrain of Acurial, whose indigenous population of orcs had lost their martial instincts. Exploiting this weakness, the human Peczan empire had invaded under the pretext that Acurial possessed destructive magical weapons, and their occupation was brutal.

The Wolverines soon tangled with the invaders in Taress, the capital, and were startled to discover that the humans, a race with no talent for sorcery in Maras-Dantia, commanded powerful magic in Acurial. They had another jolt on learning that not all the orcs of Acurial were docile. Facing overwhelming odds, they were rescued by a group of orc resistance fighters, and spirited away by them.

Outbreaks of native opposition were a thorn in the side of Kapple Hacher, General of the occupying army and Governor of what the Peczan empire considered a province. He shouldered the burden alongside Brother Grentor, the High Cleric of the Order of the Helix, custodians and practitioners of the magic.

The resistance group was headed by twins Brelan and his sister Chillder. The movement's leader in hiding was their mother, Sylandya, who before the invasion was Acurial's ruler, bearing the title Primary. Stryke persuaded them that he and his band had come from the wilderness of the far north, where some humans allied themselves with orcs, to explain Pepperdyne and Standeven, and where dwarfs, unknown in Acurial proper, were commonplace. The mythical northern orcs, he told them, had never lost their taste for combat. Sceptical of

Stryke's story, the resistance decided that the Wolverines could join them if they proved their mettle. Their task was to free resistance prisoners awaiting execution. With half the band held as hostages, under penalty of death for failure, Stryke liberated the prisoners.

The Wolverines set about helping to train and organise the rebels; and Coilla persuaded Brelan and Chillder to agree to her forming an all-female fighting unit dubbed the Vixens.

When the occupiers of Acurial sent a feared envoy to Taress to oversee the suppression of resistance, it turned out to be Jennesta. Having somehow survived her fate in Maras-Dantia, she had risen to a position of power and influence in the Peczan empire, and was also titular head of the Order of the Helix. The Gateway Corps secretly arrived in Taress too, and prepared to retrieve the instrumentalities, whatever the cost.

More than a century before, two chieftains had vied for leadership of Acurial. At the height of the crisis a comet appeared. It was taken as a portent, and the two agreed to rule in harness; a reign that proved beneficial. From old records the resistance discovered that the comet, named Grilan-Zeat in the chieftains' honour, returned at precise intervals, and that it was due back imminently. The resistance's hope was that the comet would be seen as an augury, and that, along with a rallying call from Sylandya, would inspire the populace to rise up. A prophecy connected to the comet stated that its arrival would be accompanied by a heroic band of liberators. To the Wolverines' astonishment, the resistance thought the warband might be these long-awaited saviours, or at least could be presented as such to inspire the masses.

The resistance stepped up their activity with the aim of provoking greater repression, in the hope that this would goad the placid majority of orcs into reacting. Sylandya's belief was that if pushed hard enough the orcs of Acurial would have their martial spirit rekindled.

A series of assaults on Peczan interests proved successful,

until an ambitious raid on one of the occupiers' garrisons went disastrously wrong. Upping the stakes, the Wolverines launched a bid to assassinate Jennesta. This, too, was foiled, and ended with the sorceress gaining possession of four of the five instrumentalities. Stryke began to speculate that there could a traitor in the resistance ranks, or perhaps nearer to home. Among those suspected were the humans Standeven and Pepperdyne, despite their apparent support for the rebellion.

Then the fifth star, which Stryke entrusted to Coilla, was stolen from a resistance safe house. The presumption was that it, too, had fallen into Jennesta's hands.

As the comet made its appearance, dim but unmistakable, the Wolverines faced the prospect of being stranded in an alien world.

1

Only five of them were left alive.

They were four privates and an officer, the latter a female. Several bore wounds. All were close to panic.

The defence had been tough and bloody. But the company's ranks had finally broken under the onslaught, forcing the handful of survivors to retreat. They fell back from the breached gates and dashed for refuge. Behind them, the savage creatures poured in on a wave of fear and destruction.

Sprinting across the parade ground the five headed for a barracks block, a building of wood and stone, windowless and with a single door. They piled in and frantically barricaded the entrance with cots and lockers. Outside, the commotion carried on.

'This is one hell of a bolthole,' an infantryman complained. 'There's no way out of here.' He was near the edge, and like the others, sweat-sheened and breathing hard.

'I don't get it,' a comrade said. 'These animals are supposed to be docile.'

'Docile?' another retorted. 'Like hell!'

'What we going to do?' the fourth wanted to know.

'Get a grip,' their captain told them, doing her best to sound calm. 'There'll be support. We just need to sit tight.'

'Reinforcements, ma'am?' the first queried. 'It'll be a while before we see any out here on the fringes.'

'The more reason to stand firm. Now let's get those wounds seen to. And stay alert!'

They ripped up bedding for dressings and set to binding their injuries. Their captain got them checking their weapons, and scouring the barracks for more. She had them further reinforce the door. Anything to keep them occupied.

'Hey,' one of the troopers said, halting the activity. 'It's gone really quiet out there.'

They listened to the silence.

'Could be they've gone,' a comrade offered, instinctively whispering.

'Maybe the back-up's arrived,' somebody added hopefully.

'So why can't we hear them?'

'Just the sight of reinforcements coming might've scared the creatures off.'

'Care for a wager on that?'

'Stow it!' the Captain snapped. 'Chances are the raiders have pulled out. All we have to do—'

A series of heavy thumps shook the door. They scrambled to it and threw their weight against the barricade. The pounding grew stronger, making the pile of furniture blocking it shudder. Fine clouds of dust began falling from the beamed ceiling.

Something hit the door with a tremendous crash, the shockwave jolting the defenders and sending part of the barricade tumbling. They hardly had time to brace themselves again when there was a second hefty impact. A cabinet toppled. Something made of pottery shattered.

The blows took on a regular, almost rhythmic pattern, each more jarring than the last. The door started to warp and splinter. The remains of their makeshift fortifications were weakening under the assault.

'We . . . can't hold . . . this!' a straining trooper warned.

A battering ram smashed through the door, demolishing what was left of the barricade. Swinging again, the ram destroyed the vestiges of the door and sent debris flying.

The troopers quickly moved away. Save one, caught in the confined space and entangled by wreckage. There was a high-pitched whistle. An arrow flashed through the gaping entranceway and struck him. Two more instantly followed. He went down.

His companions retreated, weapons drawn, and backed along the aisle between the lines of camp beds on either side. Shadowy figures were swarming through the ruined entrance. Ugly, grotesque beasts. Monsters.

The soldiers upended cots and tossed them in their pursuers' path, hoping to slow their progress. A couple of the troopers had shields and deployed them in fear of more arrows. No arrows came, but the repellent creatures kept up their remorseless advance, leaping the obstacles or simply kicking them aside.

Soon the fleeing group came to the barracks' end, an area uncluttered with furnishings, and had no option but to make a stand. They gathered in a knot, backs to the wall, bracing themselves to brave the coming assault as best they could.

There was no let in the creatures' progress. They rushed onward, heedless of the bristling swords intended to keep them at bay.

A frenzy of colliding blades and clashing shields ensued. Soon, screams were added to the cacophony. A trooper collapsed, his skull split by an axe. Another lost an arm to the sweep of a broadsword, then succumbed to multiple stabbing.

The fight grew yet more feverish. Fuelled by desperation, the two remaining defenders battled with ever greater ferocity. In the blizzard of stinging steel one misjudged the tempo of the battering and left open his guard. A sword found his belly; another stroke sliced cleanly through his neck, sending his head bouncing to one side. The headless corpse stood for a second, gushing crimson, before it fell.

Only the captain remained. Bloodstained, panting, her blade near slipping from moist fingers, she readied herself for the final act.

The monsters could have attacked en masse and finished her in an instant. But they held back. Then just one came forward.

It took the captain a moment to realise that the creature was waiting to engage her. She raised her sword. The being mirrored her and they set to.

Silence had fallen again, save for the pealing clatter of their blades. She fenced well, for all she had suffered and witnessed. The beast matched her in skill, though its method relied more on power and a *boldness that was almost reckless. Their duel ranged back and forth across the cramped barracks, but none of the other creatures impeded her or tried to join in. They merely watched.*

The finale came when the captain suffered a deep gash to her sword arm. A swift follow-through saw her take a further wound to the flank. Staggering, she lost her footing and went down.

The creature stood over her. She looked up into its eyes. What she saw was something more than brutishness. The bestial was there, but tempered with what she could only think of as a kind of empathy. And, perhaps, even a hint of nobility.

It was a fantastical notion, and it was the last one she would ever have.

The monster plunged its blade into the captain's chest.

Wrenching her blade from the female's corpse, Coilla said, 'She fought well.'

'They all did,' Stryke agreed.

'For *humans*,' Haskeer sneered.

More than a dozen other orcs were crowded into the barracks with them. All were Wolverines, with the exception of Brelan, a leader of the Acurial resistance. He elbowed through the throng, barely glancing at the human's body. 'Time we were out of here,' he told them.

They streamed from the barracks. There were over a hundred orcs in the compound, the majority resistance members, along with the rest of the Wolverines and the Vixens, the female warband Coilla led. They were busy scavenging weapons and torching the place. The few humans left alive were mortally injured, and they let them be.

As Brelan's order to evacuate spread, the force began to leave, moving out in small groups or singly. They took their own wounded, but by necessity left their dead.

Stryke, Haskeer and Coilla watched them go. Dallog, the Wolverines' eldest member, and one of the newest, joined them.

'We bloodied their nose good'n' proper,' he remarked.

Stryke nodded. 'We did, Corporal.'

Haskeer shot Dallog a hard look and said nothing.

'The tyros are shaping up well,' Coilla offered by way of compensation.

'Seem to be,' Dallog replied. 'I'm heading off with some of them now.'

'Don't let us keep you,' Haskeer muttered.

Dallog stared at him for a second, then turned and left.

'See you back at HQ!' Coilla called after him.

'Go easy on him, Haskeer,' Stryke said. 'I know he's not Alfray but—'

'Yeah, he's not Alfray. More's the pity.'

Stryke would have had something further to say to his sergeant, and in harsher terms, had Brelan not returned.

'Most have gone. You get going too. Hide your weapons, and remember the curfew starts soon, so don't linger.' He jogged away.

Their target had been well chosen. Being comparatively small, the garrison was a mite easier to overcome than some of its better manned counterparts. And its location, just beyond the outskirts of Taress city, meant it was conveniently isolated. Not that they could afford to ignore caution. There were likely to be patrols in the area, and reinforcements could be quickly summoned.

Outside the fort's broken gates, the last of the raiders were scattering. Donning various disguises, they left in wagons, on horses and, mostly, by foot. The majority would head for Taress, taking different routes, and melt into the capital's labyrinthine back streets.

Haskeer grumpily declared that he wanted to make his way back alone. Stryke was happy to let him. 'But mind what Brelan said about the curfew. And stay out of trouble!'

Haskeer grunted and stomped off.

'So, which way for us, Stryke?' Coilla asked.

'Haskeer's going that way, so . . .'

She pointed in the opposite direction.

'Right.'

The course they chose took them through a couple of open meadows and into a wooded area. They moved at a clip, anxious to put some distance behind them. At their backs the fort burned, belching pillars of black, pungent smoke. Ahead, they could just make out Taress' loftier towers, wine-red in the flaxen light of a summer's evening.

Not for the first time it struck Coilla how much Acurial's rustic landscape differed from Maras-Dantia, the ravaged land of their birth; and how it so resembled their adoptive world of Ceragan.

'I'm sorry,' she said.

Stryke was puzzled. 'About what?'

'Losing the star you trusted me with, probably to Jennesta. I feel such a *fool.*'

'Don't beat yourself up about it. I lost the other four to her too, remember. Who's the bigger fool?'

'Maybe we all are. We were betrayed, Stryke. It must have been somebody in the resistance who took the star I had.'

'Could have been. Then again . . .'

'You can't mean somebody in our band.'

'I don't know. Perhaps an outsider took it.'

'You really believe that?'

'Like I said, I don't know. But from now on we keep things close to our chests.'

She sighed. 'Whatever. Fact is we're still stuck here.'

'Not if I can help it.'

'What d'you mean?'

'I aim to get the stars back.'

'From Jennesta? From the whole damn Peczan empire?'

'There'll be a way. Meantime we've got our work cut out riling the humans.'

'Well, we struck a blow today.'

'Yeah, and the orcs of this world are waking up. Some of 'em anyway.'

'Wish I had as much faith in them as you do. The resistance's gaining a few new recruits, true. But enough for an uprising?'

'The more the screw tightens, the more we'll see joining the rebels. We just have to keep goading the humans.'

It was nearly dusk and shadows were lengthening. With the curfew looming they upped their pace some more. The edge of the city was in sight now and lights were coming on. Patrols were a real possibility the nearer they got, and they had to move with stealth. They crossed a stream and began skirting a field of chest-high corn that waved in a clement breeze.

Neither had spoken for some time, until Coilla said, 'Suppose . . . suppose we don't get the stars back. If we're stuck in this world, and whether it has its revolution or not . . . well, what's here for us? What place would we have?'

It was a thought that plagued Stryke too, although he was careful not to voice it to those under his command. His mind turned to what he would lose if they really were trapped in Acurial. He pictured his mate, Thirzarr, and their hatchlings, kept from him by the unbridgeable gulf that separated worlds.

'We'll endure,' he replied. 'Somehow.'

They turned their eyes skyward.

There was a light in the firmament, bigger than any star. It had an ethereal quality, as though it were a burning orb seen through many fathoms of water.

Stryke and Coilla knew it to be an omen. They wondered who it bode ill for.

2

On the other side of the city, beyond its periphery, the terrain was less fitted to growing crops. There were moorlands here, and large stretches of bog, where not much more than scrub and heather grew.

It was a place with a reputation. This was partly due to its poor fertility compared to the verdant land thereabouts. Although *poor* was not quite the right way of describing it. *Perverse* would have been a better word. There was something less than wholesome about the flora that bred here, and the animals that roamed were chiefly carrion eaters. The magical energy that coursed through the world had become corrupted in this spot.

The area also had a bad name because of certain artefacts it housed. These were scattered about the moor in an apparently senseless jumble, though there were those who thought they saw a pattern. The ruins were called monuments, temples, shrines and moot-places, but nobody really knew their true function. Certainly none could guess at the purpose of some of the more perplexing and bizarre structures.

The artefacts were fashioned in stone brought somehow from a distant quarry, and they were immensely ancient. No one knew who built them.

One particular stone formation, by no means the most extraordinary, stood at the bleak heart of the moor. It was an arrangement of columns and lintels, standing stones and ramparts, that made a whole yet seemed strangely at odds with geometry. Not so much in a way that could be seen, as felt. Through design or decay, sections of the edifice were open to the elements; notably a ring of stone pillars the colour of decaying teeth.

Inside the circle, a light burned.

A block of polished stone, chest high and weighing several tons, was set in the centre. It was worn smooth by age, but the smothering of arcane symbols it bore were carved deep enough that they were still visible. And now a copious quantity of blood, seeping from a pair of eviscerated corpses, made the markings even more distinct. The sacrifices, one male, one female, were human, opportunely provided by a summary judgement of felony.

A lone figure stood by the altar. Those who favour the night and the creatures that walk it would have called her beautiful. She had waist-length, jet-black hair framing a face dominated by dark, unpitying eyes. The face was a mite too wide, particularly at the temples, and the chin tapered almost to a point. Her well-formed mouth was marred only by being more than usually broad. But her skin was perhaps the most startling feature. It had a faint silver-green sheen, resembling tiny fish scales. In short, her beauty was confounding, yet undeniable.

As dusk slipped into full night she undertook a profane ritual.

On the altar before her, alongside the gutted bodies, lay the five instrumentalities stolen from the Wolverines, and which the warband coined stars. They were small spheres, each of a different colour: sandy, green, dark blue, grey and red. All sprouted radiating spikes of varying numbers and lengths. For the sandy sphere they numbered seven; the dark blue had four, the green five, the grey two, and the red nine. The instrumentalities were made from an unknown material – unknown to all but a sorcerer élite, that is – and the Wolverines had found them indestructible.

Next to the instrumentalities stood a small, unembellished silver casket, with its lid open. It contained a quantity of material that was, impossibly, both organic and inert. The substance's texture was part waxy, part old leather, part lichen. It was unpleasant to the touch, but had a sweet aroma. In the parlance of wizards it was known as Receptive Matter. Sorcerers using it for benign purposes sometimes called it Friendly. But never Safe.

The sorceress recited invocations of tongue-tying complexity, and performed certain other rites both intricate and dreadful. Beads of sweat stood out on her brow. She briefly wondered if such a spell might be too taxing even for her.

Then, at the ritual's climax, she thought she heard the instrumentalities sing.

She had a moment of fusion with them. There was a kind of symbiotic connection, a melding, and brushed by their energy she glimpsed a fragment of their power. What she felt, and saw, was terrifying. Or would have been to any except those who lived by terror. She found it heady.

The Receptive Matter accepted the transfer. It divided and began transmuting into the required shapes. Not long after, exhausted, she gazed at the fruits of her toil and reckoned herself satisfied.

It was not entirely true to say that she was alone in the stone circle. Several others were present, standing at a respectful distance. But as they were technically dead the question of their presence in the normal sense was debatable. They were her personal guardians and fetch-its, the select few nearest to her, whose loyalty was unflinching because they had no other option.

Outside the circle, far enough away for privacy, stood a ring of more conventional protectors in the form of a detachment of imperial guards. Farther back still there was a road, or more accurately a rough track, on which a fleet of carriages was parked. In one of them, two men conferred in whispered tones.

To the conquered orcs of Acurial, Kapple Hacher was known as Iron Hand. He was Peczan's highest representative in the province. Or had been until the empire sent the female they were waiting for. But for all her hints and threats he remained, at least in name, governor; and commander of the occupying army, with the rank of general.

He was entering his years of later maturity. There were lines on his face and hands, but he was as fit as many a younger man, and had seen action before climbing to his present position. His hair, close-cropped, was silver; and he went against tradition somewhat in being clean-shaven. He was a meticulous individual, ramrod-backed and always clad in a pristine uniform. His rivals – and every official had critics in the mire of imperial politics – saw him as being too much in thrall to bureaucracy.

Where Hacher represented the civil and military authority in the province, his companion embodied the spiritual. Brother Grentor was something like half the general's age. It was a measure of his ability that he had risen to become prominent in the Order of the Helix in so short a time. Unlike the general he sported a beard, albeit close-trimmed, and an ample shock of blond hair. The expression he wore was invariably solemn; and as dictated by his title of Elder, he always dressed in the simple brown robes of his order. Grentor had his own detractors, and they held that he too jealously guarded the Order's secrets and privileges.

The soldier and the holy man personified the twin pillars on which rested the Peczan empire. Inevitably, there were tensions between these factions, and a continuous tussle over power and influence, making Grentor and Hacher's relationship occasionally fraught.

Grentor had a lace kerchief pressed to his nose and mouth. He said something, but the words were muffled.

'For the gods' sake speak clearly, man,' Hacher told him.

The Elder gingerly removed the cloth and made a face. 'I said, how you can stand this vile smell of rotting vegetation?'

'I've known worse.'

'It wouldn't be so bad if we hadn't been forced to endure it for so long.' He glanced towards the stone circle. 'Where *is* she?'

'More to the point; what's she doing?'

Grentor shrugged.

'I would have thought you of all people might have known. She is the head of your Order, after all.'

Grentor gave a short, mirthless laugh. 'M'lady doesn't take me into her confidence. I'm only the Elder, after all.'

'I've never heard you sounding so disrespectful of such an important personage,' Hacher needled gently.

'I give respect where it's due. But in this case . . .'

'I did try to warn you about her.'

'No amount of warnings can prepare you for the reality of Jennesta.'

'I'll concede that. But seriously, what do you think she's up to out here? Between ourselves, of course,' he assured him.

'I don't know. Except that it's something important to her, and obviously involves the Craft.'

'It must be vitally important for her to be spending so much time here when there's rising trouble on the streets.'

'Ah, so you're no longer insisting it's all down to a few hotheads?'

'I still think the number of rebels is comparatively small. But a few can make a lot of trouble.'

'I know. My Order's bearing the brunt of it.'

'Along with the military, Brother,' Hacher replied with a trace of irritability. 'We're all having to deal with it.'

Grentor looked to the stone circle again. 'It could be that whatever she's doing has a bearing on the situation.'

'Some magical solution, you mean? A weapon, perhaps?'

'Who knows?'

'I think it more likely that our lady Jennesta's pursuing some goal of her own. She often seems to put herself before the interests of the empire.'

Grentor didn't take the bait. There was a limit to how far

anyone in his position would dare go in criticising Jennesta. 'You've heard what the creatures here think about what's happening in the sky, no doubt,' he said, steering the subject into somewhat safer waters.

'I know they have a name for it. Grilan-Zeat.'

'Yes, and my Order has undertaken some research on the matter.'

Hacher nodded. He knew that in the sect's vernacular so called research often involved torture. 'And what did you find?'

'It's appeared before, apparently. More than once. And there seems to be a regularity about it.'

'I daresay that's of interest to scholars, but what do the comings and goings of heavenly bodies have to do with us?'

'The populace see it as a portent. Or at least some do.'

'Comets are just one of Nature's oddities,' Hacher responded dismissively.

'Signs in the sky should never be ignored, General.'

'Such matters are in your province. They're of no concern to the military.'

'The important thing is how the populace reacts. If they *believe* it to be an omen—'.

'No doubt the rabble-rousers will exploit the masses' superstition. That doesn't mean we can't handle the disturbances.'

'Which will get worse, given the way Jennesta's clamping down on any hint of dissent. She's stirring things up.'

Hacher stiffened. He didn't want to be drawn into the stormy waters of politics any more than Grentor. 'Please don't involve me in the internal machinations of the Order.'

'I'm not trying to. I'm just saying that her actions affect us all. Don't pretend you think she's not making things worse. I don't believe in leniency any more than you do, but we're holding down an entire nation here, and we're few in number. What sense is there in provoking them?'

'You might as well provoke a flock of sheep.'

'Did you know there was a prophecy attached to the appearance of Grilan-Zeat?'

'No, I hadn't heard that particular piece of flummery.'

'It says that the comet is accompanied by a band of heroes. Liberators.'

Hacher snorted derisively. 'Heroes? The orcs are too spineless.'

'Not all of them, evidently.'

'We're talking about a small group of . . . freaks. Generally these creatures are meek. Why else do you think we occupied this land at so little cost?'

'Our research suggests that might not always have been so. The records are far from complete, but they hint that the orcs had a martial history.'

'And you think their fighting spirit could be revived somehow.'

'It's possible. Again, it turns on what they believe.'

'Omens, prophecies, a lost warlike temperament; you're seeing too much in this, Grentor.'

'Perhaps. But isn't it better to be prepared?'

'Planning for contingencies is good military practice, agreed. But you're petitioning the wrong person. Our lady Jennesta holds all the cards now.'

Grentor tugged at the general's sleeve and nodded to the carriage's window. 'Talking of which . . .'

'At last,' Hacher sighed.

Jennesta was returning. She wasn't alone. Three of her personal bodyguards were with her. They were human. Or had been. Considered challengers to her power, Jennesta's sorcery had consigned them to an undead state and made utterly obedient slaves of them. Their eyes were set and glassy, and lacked any vestige of benevolence. Such skin as could be seen was stretched tight, and was of an unwholesome, parchment-like colour. The zombies were combat dressed, in black leather and steel-toed boots, and they were armed with scimitars. One of them carried a steel-banded chest.

Hacher and Grentor were out of the carriage when the little procession arrived. Close to, the zombies stank, and the Elder had his kerchief out again.

'Were your endeavours successful, ma'am?' the general asked.

Jennesta shot him a look laced with suspicion before replying, 'Yes. The energy is particularly strong here, and of a . . . *flavour* I find gratifying.'

She turned away from them to supervise the loading of the trunk into her carriage. From the way she scolded her minions it obviously contained something significant. Not that Hacher or Grentor would have dared ask what.

For his part, Hacher was glad that whatever she had undertaken seemed to have gone well. He thought it might improve her temperament. It was a hope swiftly crushed.

Satisfied that her precious cargo was safely stowed, Jennesta's attention came back to the pair. 'I'm displeased,' she announced.

'Oh?' Hacher responded. 'I thought—'

'Don't. It doesn't become you. There's been more trouble on the streets. Why?'

'A minority inciting the rabble, ma'am. Nothing more.'

'Then why can't you stamp it out?'

'With respect, we can't be everywhere. The territory the imperial forces have to cover—'

'It's nothing to do with numbers, General, as you said yourself. It's what you do with those you have. These upstarts should be hit hard. I know orcs and their inherent savagery, and I've always found that brutality is the best course in a situation like this.'

'If I may be so bold, my lady,' Grentor ventured hesitantly. 'Isn't it possible that harsher action might further aggravate the insurgents?'

'Not if they're dead,' she replied coldly. 'You seem

particularly dense on this subject, Elder. You both do. The equation's simple: rebellious heads rear up; we cut them off. What's so hard to understand about that?'

Grentor was anxiously fingering his string of beads and summoning the nerve to say something more.

'*Wait*,' Jennesta said, stilling them with a raised hand. She looked up, an expression of concentration on her face, as though she heard something they couldn't.

They stood in silence for what seemed an eternity. Grentor and Hacher began to wonder if this was another of Jennesta's eccentricities. Or, knowing her, the prelude to unpleasantness.

Something swooped out of the darkness. They thought it was a bird. A hawk, perhaps, or a raven. But when it came to rest on Jennesta's outstretched arm they saw it had only the superficial appearance of a bird. In subtle but noticeable ways it was like no bird that ever flew. It had the look of magic about it.

The creature moved along her arm and chirruped gutturally into Jennesta's ear. She listened intently. When it finished she made a gesture, as though brushing a speck of dust from her sleeve. The enchantment was annulled in a soundless explosion, instantly transforming the ersatz bird into a myriad of shimmering, golden sparks. The glowing pinpoints gently faded as they were carried away by the evening breeze. All that lingered was the pungent smell of sulphur.

'I have tidings,' Jennesta told them, her face like flint. 'It seems your minority of troublemakers have wiped out one of our garrisons. If you want a more graphic example of my point, just say so.'

Neither man spoke.

'You two need a little adjustment to your attitudes,' she went on icily. 'Things are going to be different in this land, even if I have to have every orc in it put to the sword. Be assured, change is coming.' She turned and strode towards her carriage.

Hacher and Grentor watched her go. Then, as on every other

night during the past several weeks, their eyes were drawn skyward.

There was a new star in the firmament, larger and brighter than all the rest.

3

'*Keep your eyes on the road!*' Stryke bellowed.

'*All right, all right!*' Haskeer yelled, knuckles white on the reins.

In the back of the open wagon Coilla, Dallog, Brelan and new recruit Wheam hung on grimly.

They took a corner at speed. The wagon's wheels lifted on one side, then crashed down at the turn, jarring all of them. Seconds later, half a dozen mounted troopers rounded the bend in hot pursuit. They were quickly followed by a much larger contingent of riders. Some of them had open tunics flapping in the wind, or were minus jackets and headgear altogether, due to the sudden, unexpected start of the chase. Behind them were several wagons filled with militia, and even a buggy carrying a couple of officers. Farther back still, a mob of troops dashed to keep up on foot.

The Wolverines' wagon was in one of Taress' main thoroughfares now, a wide avenue lined with some of the city's more substantial buildings. It thronged with mid-morning crowds, and startled orcs dived clear of the speeding wagon and the humans chasing it.

Stryke's crew weaved through a sea of merchants' carts, lone riders, occupiers' carriages and strings of mules. There were scrapes and collisions, and much cursing and waving of fists. The wagon clipped a trader's handcart, flipping it. Turnips and

24

apples bounced across the road, getting underfoot of horses and passers-by. Riders and pedestrians went down.

Those at the roadside weren't immune. Some of the pursuing humans took to the walkways, scattering bystanders and ploughing through peddlers' stalls. In the process, several riders struck low-hanging awnings and projecting beams, and were unhorsed.

Despite the chaos a substantial number of humans stayed in the chase. And they were beginning to close in on the fleeing wagon. To press their point, they loosed a stream of arrows at it.

A bolt narrowly missed Coilla's head and zinged on over Haskeer's shoulder. He swore loudly and whipped the foaming horses. Another arrow landed at Wheam's feet, embedding itself in a plank. He froze, staring at it. Dallog pulled him to the floor and held him there. The arrows kept coming, zipping overhead and peppering the tailboard.

'Fuck this,' Coilla growled. She took up her own bow and started returning fire.

Brelan, the only other one on board with a bow, followed her lead. The wagon juddered and shook so much that their first shots were wild. Then Coilla got a bead and sent a shaft into the chest of one of the leading humans. The force of the hit catapulted him from his mount. His falling body collided with the riders behind him, downing several more. But it didn't slow the rest.

It didn't do more than briefly interrupt the flow of arrows either. The only solace was that firing from the saddle spoilt the humans' aim. Bolts flew high, wide and low; a couple veered towards the wayside, narrowly missing onlookers. In the rear of the wagon Coilla and Brelan were bobbing up, firing, then bobbing back down. Their shots weren't much more accurate than the humans', but at least kept them busy. At the wagon's front, Stryke and Haskeer were hunched, trying to offer the volatile bolts as small a target as possible.

'Damn!' Brelan cursed. 'I'm out!'

Coilla loosed her final arrow. It missed. 'Me too,' she said.

They quickly ducked as a small swarm of shafts came back at them.

'Try this,' Dallog said. He passed them a thick coil of rope.

Muscles rippling, Coilla flung it at the pursuers, like someone casting a heavy fishing net. Resembling an ungainly discus, the coil spun in a descending arc. It landed in the path of a rider. His horse came to grief on the obstacle, throwing him down to be trampled by the mounts behind. Pounded by hooves, the coil unravelled, tangling several more horses in lashing rope and adding to the confusion.

Brelan hefted an empty crate and launched it over the tailgate. It smashed when it hit the road, strewing wreckage and claiming more casualties. Meanwhile, Dallog and Wheam were zealously ripping up the planks that served as benches. Passed to Brelan and Coilla, they were hurled at the enemy. One human tried to catch the plank hurtling his way. The force of the impact carried him out of his saddle, slamming him to the ground still clutching his dubious prize.

'How much further, Brelan?' Stryke called out.

'Couple of blocks!' He realised where they were. 'Take the next left! Here! *Here!*'

Haskeer tugged viciously on the reins. The wagon swerved sharply and took the corner half on the sidewalk. It also took out a kerbside stall, striking it square on and ploughing through its display of pottery. There was an explosion of broken bowls, flying platters and terracotta shards.

The road they entered was no less crowded. More so, as this was one of Taress' major junctions. The pedestrians who saw them coming ran for their lives. Once it passed, the crowd closed again in the wagon's wake, only to have the horde of humans tear round the corner at their backs. The cavalry fell to hacking at them with sabres as they battled their way through.

The mêlée put a little distance between the orcs and the humans, but Haskeer didn't slow. At their rear, the humans were already emerging from the scrum and picking up speed again. By this time the street ahead was clearer, those further along having seen what was happening and made for cover.

Wheam was shouting. They all turned to look, and saw another wagon gaining on them. It was harnessed to a team of four horses, as opposed to their two, and carried five or six troopers. Haskeer urged on his team, but the greater horse-power of the humans' wagon had it rapidly closing the gap. In seconds, it drew level. The occupants brandished swords, and a couple had spears. As the two wagons neared each other the orcs took up their own weapons and braced themselves.

The humans side-swiped the orcs with a bone-rattling crash. Swords met and the chatter of whetted steel commenced. There was little finesse. Hacking and slashing outbid grace, and the spur was frenzy.

Brelan spilt blood first. More by luck than judgement, one of his swings bit deep into a human's arm, nearly severing it. The man screamed and fell back, showering his comrades with blood. Coilla was next in, driving forward and piercing some-body's lung. She withdrew quickly, narrowly avoiding the thrusts of blades and spears.

Emboldened, Wheam got to his feet and began hacking at the humans too. His efforts were spirited but feeble, his swipes erratic and wide of the mark. Then he overreached himself. Leaning half out of the wagon, stretching to get to a target, his jerkin was grabbed by one of the humans. The man tugged mightily, doing his best to pull the tyro out. Struggling, Wheam let go of his sword. It clattered on the road and was lost. Another human joined in. Wheam started yelling. Coilla and Brelan got hold of him and tried hauling him back. A tug of war developed, with Wheam as the squealing rope.

Dallog joined in, slashing at the pullers. He caught a blade for his trouble. It raked his forearm, forcing him back.

'You all right?' Coilla said.

'Yes!' he shouted, winding a cloth around the wound to staunch the blood flow. 'Look to Wheam!'

'Right,' she replied grittily, and commenced yanking with more determination. Wheam carried on howling.

Up front, Stryke was crossing swords with his human counterpart opposite. The wagons were parting, then bumping and scraping together again, making their duel a strangely disjointed affair. When the gap widened, stretching Wheam and raising his yelping, Stryke and his foe could do no more than exchange scowls. When it closed, they resumed their hacking with renewed zeal.

In the back, they finally freed Wheam. Dragging him into the wagon, Coilla shoved him to the floor and barked, 'Now stay down!'

'Watch out!' Brelan yelled.

Ahead, a driver had abandoned his hay wagon and made off in panic. It was side-on, blocking two-thirds of the highway, its pair of dray horses still hitched.

Haskeer had already seen it. He gave the reins an almighty heave, causing his frothing team to swerve sharply. They avoided the deserted wagon with a hair's breadth to spare. Passing so close spooked the already nervous drays. They lumbered forward a few paces into the gap the orcs had just shot through, blocking more of the road.

The driver of the wagonload of humans, a heartbeat behind, saw the obstruction too late. He tried the same manoeuvre Haskeer had pulled off, tugging desperately on his reins in a bid to steer clear. But the turn was too sharp. The wagon tilted at a crazy angle. Then it jack-knifed and went over, flinging its occupants out and crushing several. As it flipped, the shaft snapped, freeing its team. The quartet of horses bolted, dragging the shaft and striking sparks off the cobblestones.

'That's them fucked,' Haskeer remarked.

'It's not over yet,' Stryke told him, looking over his shoulder.

Their pursuers had reached the wreckage and were bodily shifting it. Those on horseback weaved around.

The orcs' wagon picked up speed again.

'One more turn!' Brelan shouted, indicating a road coming up on their left.

They took the bend at a clip, and found themselves in a narrower, much less crowded street. The humans were still at their backs.

As they progressed, Stryke and the others gave no sign of noticing the shadowy figures positioned in alleyways, in upper windows and on rooftops. They did drop speed, allowing the depleted pack of humans to catch up, but adopted a meandering course to hamper them overtaking.

Once the humans were bunched and slowed, the trap was sprung.

From their hideaways and high places, the resistance loosed a torrent of arrows on their cluster of targets. The cascade of bolts instantly struck down over a score of men. As many were wounded. Some took shelter behind their halted wagons, or used shields to deflect the shafts. Those who tried retreating found their escape route blocked; resistance confederates had rolled hijacked carts across the entrance to the street. Archers were stationed there too, adding to the storm.

Pounded from all sides, the militia lost interest in their quarry.

'Get us out of here,' Stryke said.

Haskeer lashed the horses and they made off at a trot.

Under Brelan's direction, they weaved through Taress' back-streets, keeping to a pace and demeanour they hoped wouldn't attract attention. After a number of twists and turns, taken partly to throw off anyone who might be following them, they arrived in a particularly ill-lit and dilapidated blind alley. It terminated at an apparently solid wooden wall, which to even a close observer passed for the rear of a building whose frontage presumably stood in an adjoining street. It was an illusion. The wall held cunningly concealed doors large enough to admit the wagon. It rolled in, and the doors were hastily secured behind it.

They got out of the wagon in an area the size of a barn. A couple of dozen resistance members were milling around, and several moved in to tend to the sweating horses. Somebody brought Dallog a flask of brandy and dressing for his wound.

Brelan went off to report to his comrades.

Stryke jabbed a thumb doorward. 'That gave 'em something to ponder.'

Coilla stretched her back, fists balled. 'Yeah. Went well.'

''cept for him,' Haskeer complained, glaring at Wheam.

The tyro quaked and started babbling excuses.

'Ah, shut it,' Haskeer growled.

'I was only trying to explain.'

'Dribbling bullshit's what you're doing. As usual.'

'Give the kid a break,' Dallog said. 'He's a tyro.'

'And you're not?'

'I'm saying he's young. We should—'

'We? Not with us long enough to wipe your arse and you're telling me what's what.' He was beginning to seethe.

'No,' Dallog replied evenly, 'I'm just telling you he needs to find his feet.'

'He needs a backbone! He could've fucked the mission!'

'But he didn't.'

'No, I didn't,' Wheam echoed.

'I've had it with you two,' Haskeer said menacingly. He took a step in Dallog's and Wheam's direction.

Stryke put himself in his path. 'You running this band now?'

Haskeer took in his captain's expression. He said nothing and looked away.

'I've had enough of this shit,' Stryke went on. 'So cut the sniping.' With a tilt of his head he indicated the resistance members busy at the far end of the room. 'If any of these local orcs get wind of where we're really from—'.

'Yeah, yeah,' Haskeer muttered.

'I *mean* it, Haskeer. I won't let this thing get screwed by you or anybody else in the band. Got it?'

'Why we doing this?'

'*What?*'

'Why're we fooling around with these rebels when we should be trying to get the stars back?'

It was quite a speech for Haskeer, and for a second, Stryke was stymied. In part, his hesitancy was due to the fact that he held himself responsible for the instrumentalities' loss. 'We help the resistance 'cos it's right,' he said at last. 'As for the stars . . . I'm gonna find 'em.'

'Well, I wish you'd get on with it.'

Haskeer held Stryke's gaze this time, and neither looked likely to back off.

'Lighten up,' Coilla told them. 'We've been in spots tight as this before.'

'Have we?' Haskeer said.

Then he turned and walked away.

4

There was turbulence throughout Acurial, and particularly in its most densely inhabited sector, the capital city of Taress. Responding to civil unrest with a heavy hand, the human occupiers had further increased their repression. Known or suspected dissident haunts were torched. Public gatherings of any size were brutally dispersed. Wayward opinions were silenced. Arrests were arbitrary, torture routine, executions commonplace.

It was what the resistance wanted. Their attacks on the invaders were designed to bring about retribution, in hopes this would goad the citizens out of their passivity and reawaken their slumbering martial spirit. Fed by whispering campaigns, clandestine meetings and daubed slogans, sedition spread. And now the comet Grilan-Zeat hung in the sky for all to see, promising hope for those who believed.

Events balanced on a knife edge, with revolution possible but by no means inevitable. To speed it on, the rebels determined to continue throwing oil on the smouldering embers. To this end the Wolverines had pledged their support.

Early morning saw the warband gathered in one of the resistance's growing number of safe houses. Though under the circumstances 'safe' was a word they used loosely.

The humans Standeven and Pepperdyne were there, as were Brelan and his twin sister, Chillder. Because of the latter – and in some minds the former – the warband were cagey while they were present. But once the twins left, tongues were loosened.

'I'm worried about what she's thinking,' Jup said.

'Who?' Stryke wanted to know.

'Chillder. Her attitude's been different to me ever since she saw me using the farsight. Haven't you noticed?'

'No.'

'Well, you haven't been stuck in these hideouts with the rebels as much as Spurral and me.' There was more than a hint of resentment in the dwarf's tone.

'We told her you just had a hunch.'

'But did she buy it?'

'Your warning stopped us walking into a trap. I reckon that made Chillder grateful enough not to question how you came up with it.'

'I'm not so sure. Like I say, she's been cooler towards me ever since.'

'She's a lot on her mind.'

'Shit, Stryke,' Jup flared, 'it's bad enough that me and Spurral stand out so much as it is without them thinking I'm . . . odd.'

'You are fucking odd,' Haskeer muttered.

'There's no call for you to chip in on this,' Spurral said, fixing him with a look of flint.

'Gods forbid I should take the piss out of somebody called Pinchpot,' Haskeer mocked.

'Lay off,' Jup warned, 'I'm not in the mood.'

'Fuck you.'

'In your dreams.'

Seeing the heat building, Stryke stepped in. '*You*,' he said, pointing at Haskeer, 'rest that jaw or I'll break it.' He turned to Jup. 'And *you* stop taking the bait. Any more bullshit and I'll be cracking skulls. *Got it?*'

They nodded, sullenly.

'All of us are wound up,' Stryke continued, his tone mollified. 'But there's a rebellion coming and we've gotta be united.' The band's grunts, lounging at a distance, were listening attentively. He looked at Jup. 'Way things are going, you'll be out in the thick of it soon enough.'

'You keep telling me that.'

'It'll happen. That thing in the sky, the prophecy, the rallying call Sylandya's going to make; it'll all rouse the orcs in these parts. We've got to get behind 'em. That's the main thing for us.'

'Is it?' Coilla ventured.

'What do you mean?'

'I have to say it, Stryke. Doesn't getting the stars back come first?'

He sighed. 'I admit I fouled up over that, but—'

She raised a hand to still him. 'I'm not knocking you. I was as much to blame over the one you trusted me with. 'Course we're pledged to helping the rebels. But knowing we can get home's more important, isn't it?'

'On my oath, we'll have the stars back.'

Silence descended. It was the younger of the two humans, Jode Pepperdyne, who broke it. 'What can we—' He glanced at his companion, Micalor Standeven. 'What can I do to help?'

Stryke's reply was a cautious, drawn out, 'Well . . .'

'We're stuck here too, you know,' Standeven protested.

'We have to keep plans close to our chests,' Stryke explained. 'For security.'

'You mean you don't trust us,' Pepperdyne said.

'Nobody's saying that,' Coilla assured him.

He scanned the room, taking in their wary eyes. 'What folk say and what they think aren't always the same.'

'Not with me,' Haskeer told him. 'I don't mind saying I reckon too many outsiders know about this band's business.'

Coilla glared at him. '*Haskeer*,' she hissed through clenched teeth.

'And when too many know,' he ploughed on regardless, 'we get treachery.'

'I don't have to take these . . . *insinuations*,' Standeven announced, puffing up his fleshy chest.

'Whatever *they* are,' Haskeer said.

'You're questioning my honour.'

'Well ain't that a shame. If you don't like it, you can fuck off.'

'That's enough,' Stryke warned.

'I know when I'm not wanted!' Standeven responded, summoning up what passed for his dignity. He gestured at Pepperdyne, as though signalling to an obedient cur. 'We're leaving!'

Pepperdyne hesitated, catching Coilla's eye for a moment, then followed his departing master.

'Jode!' she called out.

They slammed the door behind them.

Coilla turned on Haskeer. 'You fucking . . . *moron*! You oaf! We're beholden to Jode. *I* owe him my life.'

'Yeah, *him*,' Haskeer replied. 'What about the other one?'

'I . . . I don't know about Standeven.'

'We can't trust either of 'em; they're humans. And you're getting too chummy with the younger one.'

Before Coilla could hit back, Stryke took a hand. 'Seems we're forgetting something.' His expression grew dark. 'This is supposed to be a disciplined band,' he told them all. 'Only some of you are acting like it's not. But there's just one way we're gonna get through this, and that's in good order. That means respecting the chain of command, and obeying orders without bellyaching. *And it means an end to this bickering!*'

Wheam, along with a couple of the other tyros, visibly winced.

'We're gonna see more discipline in this band,' Stryke went on, 'and less backbiting. I'm not asking, I'm *telling*. And if anybody here thinks they can do a better job than me, now's the time to say it.' No one broke the hush that had fallen, and few met his eyes. 'Right. So no more bullshit. *Clear?*'

There was a general murmur of agreement.

'What *can* we do about the stars, Captain?' Dallog asked.

'Hold your horses. *Noskaa!*' The grunt sprang to his feet. 'Check that we're not overheard.'

Noskaa went to the door, looked outside and gave a thumbs up. Then he stood watch there.

'Whether any of you like it or not,' Stryke continued, taking a brief look at Coilla, 'there could be a traitor, in the resistance or nearer home. So any plan about Jennesta's best kept to us for now.'

Dallog said, 'This might seem stupid—'

Haskeer cleared his throat, making a noise that implied ridicule but stayed just short of insubordination.

Dallog shot him a glare and tried again. 'It could be a dumb question, Chief, but how do we know Jennesta has all the stars? Including the one Coilla had, I mean.'

'We don't. But it's a good bet she has.'

'You mentioned a plan,' Jup chipped in. 'If it involves getting into the fortress . . . well, that didn't turn out too brilliant last time, did it?'

'There could be another way.'

'Such as?' Coilla wanted to know, her irritability about Pepperdyne still apparent in her tone.

Stryke chose not to pull her up about it. 'Something I heard from the resistance might be useful. Seems Jennesta's been making regular trips to some kind of sacred place on the edge of the city. A stone circle.'

'What for?'

He shrugged. 'Who knows? Something rank, I expect.'

'Anyway, what about it?'

'She goes in a carriage, in convoy. It's one time when she might be exposed.'

'Why not go for her at the circle?'

'Too well guarded there, and the ground's too open.'

'What makes you think she'd have the stars on her?' Haskeer asked.

'Wouldn't you?' Stryke replied. 'After all she's been through to get 'em?'

'Even on the road she'd have a heavy guard,' Coilla reckoned. '*'Specially* on the road.'

' 'Course. But the escort peels off for their barracks just before the fortress. That could be our chance.'

'Sounds tight.'

'I didn't say it'd be easy.'

'Brelan and Chillder aren't going to wear another assassination attempt,' Jup decided.

'I'm not saying we should try killing her. Though if we got the chance . . .'

'Whether we try to kill her or not, Stryke, the resistance won't want to be involved,' Coilla said.

'That's another reason we're keeping this to ourselves. We do it without them knowing.'

'How?'

'We'd need a cover story. And if we do this right it'd only take about half the band.'

'We had a small team last time, and look how that turned out.'

'This is different. It's an ambush. We've done plenty of those in the past.'

'Never against somebody like Jennesta.'

'If you've got a better idea, Coilla . . .'

'No, I haven't. But I still think we should let Pepperdyne in on this.' Haskeer let out a loud groan. Coilla ignored him. 'He's an asset. He could help us.'

'And he'd keep it a secret from Standeven?' Stryke said.

'I don't think that'd be hard for him.'

'I don't trust 'em,' Haskeer stated.

'*So you said*,' Coilla responded ominously.

Stryke shook his head. 'No. We won't need Pepperdyne. Not the way I'm thinking of doing it.'

'What if he and Standeven get wind of it?' Spurral wondered. 'Could happen, with all of us cooped up together.'

'If they do, we'll kill 'em.'

Coilla frowned at that, but said nothing.

'So it's settled,' Stryke said. 'We'll work on a plan. Meantime, we fight with the resistance. Pepperdyne can help with *that*. They'll need all the blades they can get with a rebellion coming.'

'*If* it comes,' Haskeer muttered.

'Have faith.'

'I leave that to the temple priests.' He drew his sword and held it up to catch the light, turning its glistening length fiery. 'I put my faith in this.' He gazed at it almost reverently.

Stryke smiled. ' 'Course you do. You're an orc.'

'We can't be sure a rebellion's going to work,' Coilla reminded them. 'This is such a different world. Most of the orcs here are like sheep, and the humans have *magic*. Not to mention the odds we'd be—'

'It's simple,' Stryke interrupted. 'We fight, they die.'

The grunts gave a ragged cheer at that.

'Hope you're right,' she said. 'But trouble has a habit of popping up in this place.'

He shrugged. 'I reckon we'll be fine as long as humans are all we have to cope with.'

Not too far away, outside the city limits in one of the sparsely populated, less fruitful areas, stood an abandoned, semi-derelict water mill. The wheel itself was broken, and the watercourse that fed it had dwindled to a weed-choked trickle. Even an astute observer would see the place as desolate and forsaken.

Except perhaps for those possessing the skills of sorcery, or the gods-given power of farsight. These rare individuals might have detected the coppery taste and faintly sulphurous odour of magic cloaking the place. If they were particularly gifted they may have sensed a certain prickling in the atmosphere, a galvanic quality that made the hairs on the back of their necks stand up, signifying an enchantment intended to deceive.

The mill *was* nearly a ruin, but it wasn't uninhabited. Behind the magically generated façade a special operations unit of the multi-species Gateway Corps had commandeered it.

The group's leader was another deception, in a way. Pelli Madayar, a youthful female of the elven folk, had a petite frame and looks of such delicacy that she could be mistaken for frail. It was a false impression. Her energy and strength were prodigious, her determination inexhaustible.

She was in consultation with a lieutenant, a short, stocky individual with the sour expression habitual to the race of gnomes. All about them, the rest of the unit busied themselves with various chores. Gremlins, centaurs, goblins and a satyr were present, along with pairs of brownies and harpies. A small band of pixies and several trolls laboured beside entities that might have been considered exotic even in such diverse company, including a chimera and a wendigo; creatures normally preferring solitude. It was testament to the Corps' mission that so various a collection of races had chosen to put aside their natural inclinations, and their differences, to join in a common purpose.

Mid-sentence, Pelli Madayar broke off, closed her eyes and lifted a hand to her brow. Then she excused herself and hurried away. Her subordinate understood, having seen her do the same thing many times before.

She climbed the slats of a rickety staircase to the mill's upper level. In one corner stood a barrel, larger than she could have got her arms around, its metal bands red with rust. It was full of rainwater from a breach in the roof, and there was a rainbow film on its oily surface. The water was filthy and foul smelling, but that didn't concern her; it was still a suitable medium. In any event she had no option if this was the way her leader chose to get through to her.

Hands on the barrel's edge, she gazed down at it. The water

immediately became agitated and began to gently bubble as though coming to the boil. Then it changed its nature. It became something other than simply water; a kaleidoscopic eddy of churning matter suffused with radiance. Shortly it settled and an image came into focus.

She was looking at Karrell Revers, supreme commander of the Gateway Corps, his likeness projected across an infinity of worlds. He was in late middle age, his close-trimmed beard and hair turning silver. But he was still enormously energetic, and acuity lit his eyes. Revers was exceptional among humans in being a possessor of magical abilities.

'Pelli,' he said, 'there's been a development.' His voice had an echoing, ethereal quality.

Even though they were separated by an unimaginable void, she could see he was troubled. 'What is it?' she urged.

'I told you we thought there could be another player in the little drama you have unfolding there, and that there are indications someone other than the orcs has the instrumentalities. Now we've detected a further anomaly, making for a new possibility.'

'Yes?'

'There could be another set.'

'*Another? Here?* How likely is that?'

'The odds are . . . incalculable. But I should sound a note of caution. Because this is unprecedented we could be misinterpreting the signs. Though I have to say it's hard to reach any other conclusion.'

'So now we've got two sets to track down.'

'Yes. Well. . . perhaps.'

'Please, Karrell, help me on this. I can't operate properly if I don't know what—'

'I'm sorry. The thing is, it isn't clear. We're getting different magical signatures from what *might* be two sources. Their characteristics vary in a way we've never seen before.'

'All right. So what do we do?'

'We're working hard on resolving this. But you can see this makes your mission even more vital.'

'Yes, but what's my brief now?'

'Essentially, it remains the same. If you can recover the instrumentalities we know exist, those held by the orcs, or that were held by them, we can eliminate them from our search. The important thing is that you act quickly.'

'I can see that.'

'And I have to say, Pelli, I'm concerned that you haven't acted already.'

'Time spent on reconnaissance is never wasted, you know that. Also we've had to be sure that no innocents get caught up in this. Trouble's brewing here. Relations between the native population and their oppressors look as though they're coming to a head, and—'

'We don't concern ourselves with local affairs. It's one of the Corps' primary rules, as you're fully aware. I just hope it isn't some element of sympathy you feel for the orcs that's staying your hand.'

'It's true I think they've blundered into something they don't understand, and in that sense perhaps they're not to be blamed. That's why I hope to use persuasion to get the instrumentalities back before taking the ultimate step.'

'I've told you before that your compassion is understandable, and it reflects well on you.' His tone came across as a mite petulant. 'But these are *orcs* we're talking about. Some races are beyond the pale, even for the Corps. Your sympathy could well be misplaced. The outcome of your mission is more important than mere individuals You must use *all* means to achieve our objective. Is that understood?'

'Yes, it is.' She mulled things over for a second and added, 'There's something I've been meaning to ask you. You gave me no orders about what would become of the warband once we've taken the instrumentalities from them.'

'Assuming they survive their encounter with you and your superior weaponry.'

'Yes, assuming that. Am I to return them to their home world?'

If she didn't know him better, Pelli would have thought the look Revers gave her was unduly hard. 'You have no such orders,' he told her.

Without further word he broke their connection.

5

Like a chunk of ordure floating in the middle of a cesspit, the great fortress at Taress never failed to draw the eye.

Its baleful walls and haughty towers subjugated the city as surely as the human invaders who had annexed it. Built long ago, by orcs when they were warlike, recent events had turned the pile from defensive to offensive. From a place of sanctuary to a place of dread. It stood as a perpetual reminder of the native population's loss of independence and dignity.

There was a great deal of bustle in its spacious central courtyard. A detachment of uniformed men, and some women, were square-bashing. Others were paired off in mock combat. Weapons were being issued, horses groomed, wagons loaded.

From the balcony of his quarters high above, the stern figure of Kapple Hacher surveyed the activity. His aide, and probably closest professional confidant, the young officer called Frynt, stood beside him.

'Now we're training clerks and medics to patrol the streets,' Hacher said.

'I understand more reinforcements are due for dispatch from Peczan soon, sir,' Frynt informed him.

'I'm not sure there'll ever be enough for Jennesta.'

'Sir?'

'Taress is to be entirely purged of subversive elements, to

quote our mistresses' own words. How many troops do you think that would take?'

'With respect, General, you've often said that the trouble-makers are a minority.'

'I still think that's so. But it's a question of definitions. Who *are* the dissidents?'

'Isn't it our job to weed them out, sir?'

'Good question. But not one that unduly troubles m'lady Jennesta. Her view is that any orcs who arouse suspicion should be rounded up. And eliminated if they resist. In effect, they're *all* revolutionaries to her. So we have this ever-increasing clamp-down.'

'You can't deny that incidents have increased of late, sir.'

'Yes, they have. What do you expect when you prod a hornets' nest? I believe the resistance, the actual core, is quite small, but I've never said they weren't dangerous, and I'm all for coming down on them hard. But I can't help but feel that Jennesta's policy is only making matters worse.'

'Perhaps this comet the orcs are so excited about is what's really stirring them up, sir.'

'And who's putting the idea into their heads of linking it with omens and prophecies? No, we should be using a rapier here, not an axe.'

'Regrettably, sir, your counsel is unlikely to sway the lady Jennesta.'

'You're telling me.' Hacher grew thoughtful. 'Though there is one weapon in our armoury that could be useful in winkling out the real insurrectionists.'

'Your . . . source,' Frynt said knowingly.

The general nodded. 'Although it isn't entirely certain that I can keep that channel open, it might prove invaluable.'

'But surely, sir, all this talk of rebellion is somewhat academic in light of the nature of the orcs we're governing. The majority are passive.'

'Jennesta doesn't think so. She maintains the entire race is capable of something like savagery. Though what experience she might have had with them to reach such a conclusion is open to question.'

'And you, sir? Do you think they have some buried appetite for combat?'

Hacher turned and surveyed the city. 'Perhaps we're about to find out.'

At one of the resistance's safe houses, hidden in the tangle of the troubled capital's back streets, Jode Pepperdyne and Micah Standeven had found a secluded room.

'How often do I have to tell you?' Standeven angrily protested.

'Try me one more time,' Pepperdyne said.

'I had nothing to do with Coilla's star going missing!'

'Why do I find that hard to believe?'

'So why do you bother asking me? You know, back where we come from, your badgering would have been seen as gross disobedience.'

Pepperdyne laughed in his face. 'But we're not there, are we?'

'More's the pity.'

'I don't like being stuck in this world any more than you do. Assuming you *do* mind.'

'What's *that* supposed to mean?'

'If the stars hadn't gone missing we wouldn't be here.'

'*And that had nothing to do with me,*' Standeven repeated.

'So you say. But given we are stranded here, why do you keep needling the band? They're the only allies we've got, and they don't trust us.'

'They never did.'

'Speak for yourself.'

'They're *orcs*. Humans aren't exactly their favourite race, in case you hadn't noticed what they're doing to them here.'

'I think they know when somebody's treating them straight. Most of them, anyway.'

'You're a fool, Pepperdyne. The only reason we're still with them, why we're still *alive*, is because it suits them. Don't go misplacing your trust.'

'What, I should put it in *you*?'

'You could do worse.'

'Only if I'd gone insane.'

Standeven's bile was rising again. 'You might do well,' he uttered vindictively, 'to think about your position if we ever get back home.'

'Your threats don't wash here. Or hasn't that dawned on you yet?'

'I'm just reminding you what our relative positions were, and how they could be that way again. How you behave here's going to have a bearing on how I choose to treat you in future.'

'You don't get it, do you? The way things are going, we might not *have* a future. And if we're into reminding each other about events, remember that you wouldn't be here . . . hell, you wouldn't *be* at all, if it hadn't been for me.'

'One of your obligations is to look after your master's safety. It's your duty!'

Pepperdyne lunged and grabbed him by the scruff. 'If you think you don't owe me your life, maybe I'll take it back.'

'Take your filthy hands off me, you—'

The door opened.

Pepperdyne let go of Standeven.

Coilla came in. 'Jode? Are you— Oh.'

Standeven transferred his red-faced glare from Pepperdyne to her. '*Don't mind me*,' he snarled. Shoving past her, he left.

'Let him go,' Pepperdyne said.

'I wasn't thinking of stopping him,' Coilla replied. She closed the door. 'You were arguing.'

'Very perceptive.'

'If you want to be let alone I can—'

'Sorry.' His tone was conciliatory. 'It's just that he gets under my skin.'

'You're not alone.'

He nodded. 'What was it you wanted, Coilla?'

'Well, first off, I thought you could use some of this.' She handed him a brandy flask.

He accepted it, took a swig and gave it back. 'And second?'

'You two left in such a hurry, I just wanted you to know that not everybody in the band thinks badly of you.'

'What, both of us? Me and . . . him?' He nodded at the door.

'I was thinking of you.'

'Thanks.' He smiled. 'But I reckon you're in a minority of one.'

'Oh, I don't know. I reckon Stryke has some regard for you. Maybe a couple of the others.'

'They've a funny way of showing it.'

'You've got to understand how it is between orcs and humans. And not just in this world. We've got . . . history.'

'Maybe that's something I can understand.'

'Can you?'

'You think orcs were the only downtrodden race on our world?'

'You're a human. Your kind does the treading.'

'There are humans and humans.'

'Isn't it time you came clean about yourself?'

'What's to tell?' he came back stiffly.

'Don't close up on me.'

'Would knowing my past change anything? I mean, haven't I proven myself yet?'

'You have to me. But most of the others . . .'

'I give you my word that I had nothing to do with the theft of the star.'

'And what would your partner say if I asked him about it?'

'Standeven's not my partner,' he returned sharply. 'And he'd give you his word too.'

'What value could I put on that?'

'As much as I do.'

'How much is that?'

'If Standeven says he didn't—'

'Why are you so loyal to him, Jode?'

He sighed. 'Habit, I suppose. And not wanting to believe certain things even of him.'

'What *is* the bond between you two?'

'Complicated.'

'Not enough. Tell me more.'

He had to grin. 'You're persistent, Coilla, I'll give you that.'

'So reward me. Open up a bit. I'd like to know something about the man I owe my life to.'

'How about that flask again?'

She dug it out. He took another draught. Coilla had one too. 'Well?' she said.

'I'm a Trougathian.'

'You're a *what*?'

'A Trougathian. After Trougath, the place we come from.'

'Never heard of it.' There was a chair by her, and she sat.

He followed her lead and perched on a barrel of nails. 'The world you and I come from is much bigger than the part you call Maras-Dantia.'

'And your race renamed Centrasia,' she replied with a trace of bitterness.

'*Some* humans did. My sort didn't get to name places.'

'So what sort are they?'

'A little like you orcs.'

'Yeah?' She couldn't keep the scepticism out of her voice.

'Well, I said a *little* like. But there's a couple of similarities. One is that my race has a martial tradition, too.'

'That explains your skill with a blade. So your race fights as a living, like we do?'

'No. It's not inborn with us; it's learnt. Though over so long a time it practically *is* inborn now. But we're not fighters by inclination, or even choice. It was just practical. Most of my race would prefer untroubled lives.'

48

'If you didn't choose to fight, you must have something to defend.'

'Ourselves. And our land.'

'The first I understand. But dying for land, that seems odd to me. Maybe because orcs never had any.'

'They did here.'

'And your race took it from them.' She raised her hands. 'Sorry. Tell me about your land.'

'Trougath's an island off . . . well, it doesn't really matter where it is. It's large enough for us and the soil's good. So's the fish harvest. We're islanders, we have an understanding with the sea. Most of all, it's our homeland. But it's got one flaw.'

'Its location.'

'You're smart.'

'For an orc, you mean?'

'No, just smart.'

'Stands to reason you'd only have enemies if there's something you've got they want, or if you're in the wrong place.'

'I can see why you're the band's Mistress of Strategy. But you're right; a very wrong place. At least, that's what it became. Trougath stands at a point where it could threaten free passage for its several neighbours, had we wanted to do that, which we didn't. So we sat in the middle of a wheel, each spoke sharpened and pointing at us. All the neighbouring states had a lustful eye on such a favourably placed island. Whoever took it could cow the others. That's why my people embraced warfare, and kept them out.'

'How come, if those nearby states were so strong?'

'My people had been there since long before the rise of the powers that came to surround us. We were numerous and well established. We knew the terrain. And we fought well, as people will when they're protecting all they've got. We were always on alert, and often under actual siege. We did without enough arms, we did without salt. Even water, at times.'

'How long did that last?'

'Generations. Eventually it dawned on them that they couldn't conquer us, so they took to flattering us. So in addition to the skills of combat, we learnt the black art of politics. The game became playing one off against the other. That, and occasional wars, kept us sovereign for a long time.'

'But I'm guessing your luck ran out. Otherwise you'd be there now.'

He nodded. 'Our leaders sided with the wrong tyrant. Not through any liking of him, but by necessity. That caused a schism among my people. Not a civil war exactly, though that came close, but enough of a distraction for us to drop our guard. The very warlord our leaders befriended was the one who took advantage.'

'There's a surprise.'

'It seemed like treachery to us. Hell, that's what it *was*. Those were dark days, and we all did things we weren't especially proud of, in the name of patriotism. None less than me. I won't bore you with the ins and outs. The upshot was that our nation was smashed and what survived of the population scattered. We became drifters, peasants in foreign lands, impoverished merchants, even mercenaries. Some were enslaved.' The latter came out with particular vitriol.

Coilla kept her peace for a moment, then, 'You said there was more than one way your race was like mine.'

'We're both maligned. And once your enemies stigmatise you, they can justify any crime, any indignity they heap on you. Our name was blackened and it sticks. Even false ignominy carries on, like a rock cast down a hill.'

She could relate to that. 'The storytellers, the scholars with their books; they're from the winning side, more often than not. You wouldn't believe the shit they spew about orcs. They say we favour human flesh, or even that we eat each other. They put it about that we sprang from *elves*, for the gods' sake. All lies!'

'They said we conjured demons and sodomised goats.'

Coilla burst out laughing. Pepperdyne looked stern for a moment, then joined her.

'So,' she said when that was subsiding, 'how does Standeven come into all this?'

Amusement died in his face instantly, like a snuffed candle.

'Is he a . . . Trougathian too?' she asked.

'No, he's a bastard.'

'But one with some kind of charge on you.'

'Let's say I'm working a debt off with him.'

'Even while you're in this world? Doesn't that change anything?'

'Only here. Back home . . .'

'We might never see our homes again, Jode!' She checked herself. 'Shit. That's not good for morale, is it? Stryke'd hate hearing me say that.'

'It's no secret, Coilla. I reckon we all think that staying here's the most likely thing.'

'Well, it'd be no different to what's happened in the past.'

'What do you mean?'

'Something we were told before we left Maras-Dantia the first time. Do you know why the elder races came to be there?'

'*Why?* They . . . you . . . were just . . . always there. Weren't you?'

'No. I don't say I understand it, but out there—' she waved a limp hand in the general direction of away '—out there, there are whole worlds of elves and centaurs, and pixies and gnomes, and all the rest. And orcs,' she added hastily. 'Crowds of the races . . . I don't know . . . *fell through* to Maras-Dantia. Scooped up like fish in a net by a powerful sorceress.'

'Humans too?'

'We were told you were our world's true race.'

'Ironic.'

'We didn't think so.' There was a flash of steel in her eyes.

'So all orcs would have originally come from Ceragan.'

She frowned. 'I don't know. The world we've been living in

51

has only orcs too. But a damned sight more spirited than the ones here.'

'So humans might not have started off on Maras-Dantia. Who's to say where orcs, humans or any other race could have originated? Or how far they've spread. Doesn't that intrigue you?'

'No, it makes my head hurt. I see things simpler. Like, maybe we should look at this as being just like moving from one camp to another. Your people are drifters; you must understand that.'

'It's a hell of a trek, Coilla. Sure you're not just making the best of it?'

' 'Course that's what I'm doing. It's the orc way. We never say die.'

'That could have been Trougath's motto.' He grew sombre. 'But lately I feel almost like—'

He broke off at the sound of approaching footsteps. They were loud and hurried, and could mean trouble. Pepperdyne and Coilla got up, hands on sword hilts.

Chillder burst into the room. She was breathing heavily.

'We've got a situation,' she announced, 'and we need all the swords we can muster.'

6

A crowd had gathered in one of Taress' largest squares. The mob was several hundred strong, and tempers were fraying. What began as a series of protests – against taxes, restricted access to holy places, the razing of certain venerated buildings, food rationing, curfews, heavy-handed policing and any number of other grievances – had distilled into a general outpouring of bitterness at the occupation. The situation was near flashpoint. But it wasn't an incipient riot that drew the resistance. Their aim was to use it as cover.

A number of the rebels were present, along with most of the Wolverines, and the Vixens, the all-female unit Coilla had formed. Scattered around the square, they were dressed soberly, with weapons well concealed.

'Not that long ago these orcs wouldn't have been this restive,' Stryke whispered in Brelan's ear.

'They wouldn't even have come onto the streets.'

The pair were standing together at the edge of the milling crowd. There was a knot of human militia nearby, disquiet on their hard faces.

Stryke could see Haskeer not far off, and a little way on, Dallog with a team of grunts. Further afield, Chillder stood alongside several Vixens. But there was no sign yet of the comrades they were waiting for.

'Sure everybody knows what they have to do?' Brelan asked softly.

Stryke replied pointedly, 'My band does. I hope *your* facts are right.'

'There's no doubt. What we want is there.' He flicked a glance at a building on one side of the square. It stood apart from its neighbours on either side, and looked recently constructed. A squat, one-storey structure, its facing was white, with barred windows. Weapons drawn and watchful, a group of nervous militiamen stood guard outside its heavy door.

Stryke was careful not to be seen staring at the place. 'So what happened?'

'Seven of our comrades were in the area checking out a target. They got unlucky. The troopers took them without blood being spilt.'

Stryke raised an eyebrow at that.

'We don't know how they came to be caught, except they were outnumbered.'

'How come they're in this guards' station?'

'They couldn't be taken to a proper prison for fear of the crowd. We reckon they'll be kept in there until this blows over. Or until an escort arrives.'

'Plenty of soldiers around as it is,' Stryke said, scanning the scene.

'They'll have other things to think about soon.' He chanced another quick peek at the guardhouse. 'If we don't get them out they'll be at the mercy of Iron Hand's torturers. They're good patriots, and loyal, but they'll talk. And that could be a real blow for us.'

Stryke nodded, then gave Brelan a nudge. Robed members of the Order of the Helix were weaving through the crowd. 'Looks like we'll have more than military to deal with.'

'Where's that human of yours?' Brelan wondered irritably.

'He's not *mine*. And he's— Hang on. There he is.'

Pepperdyne came into sight. He was wearing the stolen officer's uniform that had served them well on previous missions. Coilla and two members of the Vixens were with him, walking a couple of paces behind, as though being led.

'The females should be shackled,' Brelan said. 'It'd look more convincing.'

'Even Acurial's tame orcs might find that hard to swallow. Unless you want this crowd tearing him to pieces.'

'Granted. Though I never thought I wouldn't want that to happen to a human. It's time to set things in motion, Stryke.'

Stryke nodded, then raised a cupped hand to his mouth, as though stifling a cough. The other nearby Wolverines, watching for it, began passing the signal on. Brelan did the same with his resistance members. The unspoken order passed through the crowd.

Pepperdyne and his little entourage were making for the guardhouse. They met no open opposition on the way, but there were plenty of hostile stares and the odd shouted comment. That the females were following him with no sign of compulsion seemed to confuse the onlookers, and mollified many of them. In fact, their reflexive passivity, and the sense of obedience to authority that had been drummed into them, meant most of the crowd cleared a path.

Pepperdyne kept his eyes firmly on the target and maintained an unhurried pace. The females in his wake ignored shouts directed at them.

The rebels stationed around the square knew to hold back until Pepperdyne's group had reached the guards' station. Shortly after that, they would act.

Pepperdyne and the others were coming to the crowd's outer edge, which like the rest of the perimeter ended at a thin line of soldiers. Behind them was an empty space in front of the guardhouse, perhaps thirty paces in depth.

Coilla moved closer to him and whispered, 'Remember, you're an officer. Act like it.'

'I never would have thought of that,' he hissed sarcastically. 'Now leave the talking to me.'

She glared at his back.

The soldiers containing the crowd took Pepperdyne at face value. They saluted, and let him and the females through. The party of sentries at the guardhouse door seemed less sure. They were obviously surprised to see this unknown officer and his charges. They looked quizzical. All were noticeably tense.

As Pepperdyne and his retinue approached, one of the guards shouted, '*Halt!*'

The man who spoke stepped forward, and after a second's hesitation offered a perfunctory salute. He was short and wiry, with a pencil-line moustache and features that reminded Pepperdyne of a rodent. The stripes he wore showed his rank as sergeant.

Pepperdyne returned the salute in a languid fashion he hoped was fitting to his supposed status. He was about to speak.

'Can I help you . . . sir?' the sergeant got in first. There was a tinge of scepticism in his manner.

Pepperdyne adopted an authoritative tone. 'I've got three more detainees to join the ones you're holding.'

'I've had no orders to that effect.'

'I'm ordering you now.'

'On what authority?'

'By the authority of my rank. And you'd do well to address a superior officer in the proper fashion.'

'Yes, sir,' the sergeant replied, but it was cursory, almost insolent. 'However, my brief's strict. I'm to take no prisoners here without official say-so. That means a direct order from an immediate superior or written authorisation from—'

Pepperdyne pointed at the crowd. 'We have a situation here, Sergeant,' he blustered, 'in case you hadn't noticed. Sticking to the rules does you credit, but things are moving fast on these streets. These captives are linked to the rebels and they need locking up.'

'So why aren't they restrained, sir?'

'Are you implying that I can't control a few females, Sergeant?'

'I wouldn't know about that, sir.'

'I'm getting tired of this. Are you going to obey my order and take these prisoners?'

'If I have the proper authority.'

'*Which I'm giving you.*'

'Your name and division. Sir.'

Pepperdyne stared at the unsmiling pedant. 'What?'

'To check your credentials. I'll have to send a runner to HQ and—'

'You should know that I act under the direct mandate of General Hacher himself. I don't envy your position when he hears about this.'

'That may be so, sir. But we've had reports of bogus officials. It's my duty to verify the credentials of any . . . *officer* presenting themselves at this station.' He was maddeningly cool.

'Are you questioning my patriotism?'

'That's not my place, sir.'

'Don't you care that apart from your insubordination, your worship of the rulebook's stopping me from carrying out my duties? That's a serious step for somebody in your position, Sergeant.'

'My commanding officers would be the best judge of that, sir.'

'Of which I'm one!'

'Perhaps it would help if I went through it again, sir. Once you give me your name and—'

Pepperdyne capped his rising tension by maintaining a stern face. He saw that the other soldiers were eyeing him with something close to hostility. He was aware of Coilla shifting uncomfortably behind him.

From their vantage point, Stryke and Brelan were growing restive too.

'What the hell's going on?' Brelan muttered. 'He should have got them to open that door by now.'

'Maybe we've pulled this trick once too often.'

'What do we do?'

'Stick to plan. Be ready to give the signal.'

Pepperdyne made a show of listening as the sergeant spouted regulations, but his mind was on contingencies. And his hand was drifting towards his scabbard.

'So if you'd care to give me those details, sir,' the sergeant concluded, 'we can clear this up.'

'Eh?'

'Your *details*, sir. As I explained.'

'Look, if you're going to persist in—'

'*Oh for fuck's sake.*' Coilla came out from behind Pepperdyne and thrust a dagger into the sergeant's midriff.

He looked down at it dumbly, swayed, then fell.

'*Shit!*' Pepperdyne said. 'What the *hell*, Coilla?'

'Just moving things along.' She swiftly drew her hidden sword. The pair of Vixens did the same, and so did Pepperdyne.

The other guards, stunned into immobility for a second, now raised their own weapons and closed in.

'That did it!' Brelan exclaimed from his place at the crowd's edge.

'Signal!' Stryke bellowed.

Any thought of concealment gone, they began frantically gesticulating at their confederates. As the order rapidly spread, Stryke and Brelan started forcibly elbowing their way towards the guardhouse.

Pepperdyne and the females fell into a defensive semi-circle, their blades jutting like a predator's fangs. They gambled that their backs were safe. The nearest in the crowd, who had seen what happened, were reacting. So had some of the guards keeping them in check, but they were torn between joining in and holding the line.

The dead sergeant's comrades advanced, spitting rage. Pepperdyne, Coilla and the Vixens braced themselves.

A great roar went up from the crowd.

There were whirlpools of violence in that churning mass. Attacked by well placed rebels and Wolverines, the scattered groups of militia were already beleaguered. And here and there, ordinary orcs, civilians, were taking part. Hastily improvised weapons appeared. Some used their bare hands. The points where the fighting started were like raindrop impacts on the surface of a lake. They sent out ripples of agitation that built to waves.

The soldiers defending the guardhouse froze at the uproar. Pepperdyne didn't. He tore into the nearest trooper. They battered away at each other, blades pealing, and Pepperdyne instantly proved himself the better swordsman. The man's defence crumbled under the onslaught. He took a hit to the groin, and while he was busy with that, Pepperdyne followed through with a chest thrust. Another guard slid into the fallen one's place and the fight carried on seamlessly.

Coilla had already downed her first opponent and was hacking at two more simultaneously. Her speed and agility vexed them, and they struggled to land a blow. She inflicted a wound on one man, putting him on the back foot with a streaming shoulder, then improved the odds by dropping his companion. The next to step in was more seasoned, or at least cannier, and she found herself fencing rather than hacking.

Battling shoulder to shoulder, the duo of Vixens gave a good account of themselves, despite their relative inexperience. They fought with a zeal not far short of savagery, and a sense of ruthlessness that had their foes wary of engaging them at too close quarters. Glancing from his own labours, Pepperdyne was in awe of the females' aggressiveness. But with at least ten guardsmen still on their feet, and who knew how many more zeroing in, fervour might not be enough.

The crowd was boiling now, with brawls all across the square. Wolverines and rebels were at the centre of nigh on every storm, and the Vixens were fighting with particular resolve. Dead and wounded soldiers were underfoot. To a lesser degree, so were orcs, resistance and civilians alike. But far from sobering the horde, the casualties fuelled its anger.

Haskeer was in the thick of things, cutting a swathe for the bunch of privates in his wake. He favoured an axe, which he swung with abandon, cleaving heads and severing limbs. In another part of the crowd Chillder and a gaggle of Vixens were beating in the brains of several hapless troopers. Not far off, Dallog led a contingent of the Ceragan inductees. Wheam wasn't among them. It was thought better to confine him to lookout duties beyond the fighting.

Joined by hand-picked rebels and Wolverines, as planned, Stryke and Brelan were a spit away from the guardhouse. By the time they arrived the crowd had become a mob. But the sentries holding the line against it weren't a problem. There was no line. The whole area was one seething mass of fighting orcs and humans, and they gave off a deafening roar.

The arrival of Stryke's crew was timely. Pepperdyne and the three females were holding their own, although several sentries from the broken line had attached themselves to the guardhouse defence, upping their numbers. Pepperdyne was dragging his blade from a guard's guts. The toll was starting to show. His movements were growing leaden and his sword arm was cramping. One of the Vixens nursed a wound, but kept fighting. Coilla was covered in foes' blood. She was smiling.

Stryke, Brelan and their back-up came in like steel surf. The balance was tipped, and after a brief flurry of bloody confrontation the remaining guardsmen were overcome.

'Took your time,' Coilla said.

'We were picking wild flowers,' Stryke told her, deadpan.

'Come *on*,' Brelan urged. 'Time's running low.'

They searched the dead sergeant's pockets and found a bunch of keys. While most of the group kept watch, Brelan made for the door and began trying them. On the third attempt the locked turned.

Brelan gave the door a shove. 'It's not the way we thought it'd go,' Brelan said, shooting a glance at Pepperdyne, 'but—'

'*Look out!*' Coilla yelled, pushing him aside.

An arrow flew out of the open door, barely missing him. It zinged into the crowd and struck a gesticulating protestor, piercing his raised arm.

Stryke rushed through the door, with Coilla, Brelan and Pepperdyne close behind. Inside, a sentry was groping in his scabbard for another arrow. Stryke got to the man first and thrust a blade into his chest.

'*To your left!*' Pepperdyne shouted.

Stryke spun just fast enough to block a sword swipe. Its wielder had come from the only blind corner, and he attacked with an ardour born of desperation. His frantic state suited Stryke. A panic-stricken opponent rarely had sound judgement; and so it quickly proved. After a couple more of his blows were deflected, the human looked spent, and his defence was sloppy. Stryke reaped the benefit by puncturing his heart.

There were no other humans in the building. At its far end were two cells, essentially cages, and the seven resistance members were crammed in one of them. None of the sergeant's keys undid the cell's robust lock, and it didn't succumb to a battering. But a hasty search turned up another ring and they got the door open. The prisoners had obviously been mal-treated. They had black eyes, cuts and bruises, but no worse injuries. Their rescuers gave them weapons, some brought, some taken from the dead guards.

If anything, the riot outside had stepped up.

'That was sweet,' Brelan said, leading his freed comrades.

'We're not out of here yet,' Stryke reminded him. He turned to Pepperdyne. 'Ready?'

'This bit I don't like,' the human told him.

'You can't just walk away with us,' Coilla said. 'This mob would go wild. Wilder.'

'They'd kill you,' Stryke summarised. 'But if they think you're our prisoner—'

'Right, right. I get it.' He looked unhappy.

They surrounded Pepperdyne as though escorting him, and started off. Their route would keep them close to the frontage of the square's buildings, skirting the edge of the crowd, until they came to a side street and waiting transport. The rioters who noticed the human officer in the group's midst assumed he was being taken hostage. Some cheered.

Stryke and the others had hardly set out when there was a series of brilliant flashes. They erupted in the heart of the crowd; scintillating bursts of red, green and violet that scarred the eye.

'The Helix!' Brelan exclaimed.

'The more reason not to linger,' Stryke said. 'Keep moving.'

There was another vivid flash in the crowd. A rioter collapsed with a smouldering hole in his chest. The odour of charred flesh permeated the air as those around backed off in dread. Robed men were discharging the magical beams almost wantonly, targeting anyone in their way.

Close by, Haskeer was tangling with a trooper. The man was armed with sword and shield, and had proved stubborn in preventing the orc from killing him. Haskeer relished the challenge. He rained the trooper with boneshaker blows, forcing him into a purely defensive mode. The man was flagging when a particularly intense bolt of magical energy went off near to hand. Dazzled by the light, Haskeer and the trooper stilled, blinking.

Haskeer snapped out of it first and resumed his assault. The militiaman, still in a daze, managed only a confused resistance. Several hefty jolts from Haskeer's axe was enough to throw him completely. A meaty strike to his head had him first on his knees, then keeling over.

There was another flash, as brilliant as the last, and a further victim succumbed to a fiery bolt. As Haskeer's vision seeped back he could just make out the figure of a Helix member no more than twenty paces away. He had seen Haskeer and was raising his power wand. Haskeer dived. A searing beam swept over him, close enough for its heat to be felt. Scrabbling on hands and knees, he made for the fallen trooper as the Helix initiate took aim again. Reaching the corpse, he wrestled the shield from the human's death grip. Then, still kneeling, he flung it with might at the Helix. It skimmed like a discus and struck him squarely in the neck, nearly decapitating him.

Onlookers got the message. Fearsome as their trident weapons might be, the Helix weren't invulnerable. In seconds they were under siege. Haskeer and his troop melted into the throng.

Stryke and the rebel party stayed out of such clashes. They moved as swiftly as they could towards the turning that led out of the square. But when they were almost at the corner, they halted.

'Oh, great,' Coilla grumbled. 'More shit.'

Two wagonloads of troops came along the street they were heading for. When the wagons reached the square they stopped, blocking the road. The troops began getting out.

'Time for these,' Brelan said, digging into the canvas bag hanging from his shoulder. He produced a number of earthen cylinders, similar to water bottles, and handed them out.

Coilla grabbed one gleefully. 'I *love* these things.'

'What is it?' Pepperdyne asked.

'Acurialian fire,' Brelan told him. The human looked blank. Brelan mimed throwing one, then mouthed '*Boom*.'

'I've seen similar,' Pepperdyne realised.

'*Use 'em*,' Stryke grated.

They struck sparks against the oil-soaked wads of fabric stuffed into the containers' necks. When the cloth fuses were well alight they started lobbing. The cylinders soared in the direction of the wagons and disembarking soldiers. They shattered on impact, exploding in plumes of orange fire. The burning oil had been mixed with certain compounds that made it viscous. It stuck fast to whatever it touched, igniting the wagons, the walkway and any troopers unlucky enough to be in range. Converted to fireballs, they stumbled aimlessly, yelling and beating at their clothes. The wagons were blazing.

The few soldiers untouched by fire were either making futile efforts to put out the flames or loosing sporadic arrows in the direction of Stryke's group. But panic made their aim wild. And now they had another problem: the crowd was turning on them. Chunks of paving stone rained down on a scene already engulfed by fiery chaos.

'Should keep 'em busy,' Coilla remarked with satisfaction.

'Let's go,' Stryke said.

With Pepperdyne back in the middle of the scrum, they bypassed the mayhem and charred bodies without challenge. All over the square the other Wolverines, rebels and Vixens were slipping away too. Singly or in small groups they would make for hideouts or the cover of false identities.

Off from the square, in near empty streets bled clean by the riot, Stryke, Coilla and the rest met up with their transport.

Bumping along in a covered wagon, moving slowly to avoid attention, they allowed themselves to relax a little.

'Looks like the uniform trick's stopped working,' Coilla said.

Pepperdyne nodded. 'They were bound to catch on eventually. Your Vixens fought like she-devils, by the way. I've not seen them that ferocious before.'

'Then you haven't been moon-gazing lately,' Coilla told him.

'Moon-gazing?'

'Not well up on the ways of females, are you, Jode.'

Comprehension dawned. 'Oh. You mean—'

'The time of the moon's cycle when my sex can get a little . . . cranky.'

'From what I just saw I'd have used a slightly stronger word. Like murderous. But how come you *all*—'

'You *really* don't know much about females, do you? When

any number of us spend time together in the same place it's not unusual for our cycles to tally. That's what happened today.'

Pepperdyne grinned. 'A whole squad of moon-crazed she-orcs. Gods help the enemy.'

'Gods *damn* 'em,' Brelan said. 'But the citizens acted well too. I'm proud of them.'

'They do seem to be finding their orcish natures a bit more,' Stryke agreed. 'But are they ready for a full-scale uprising?'

'The tipping point's near. Very soon my mother, as Principal, will come out of hiding and make her rallying call. After that, what happened today's going to look like a picnic.'

'Let's hope,' Coilla remarked cautiously.

The wagon was arriving at its destination. It pulled through high gates and into the courtyard of an abandoned villa the resistance had occupied. It looked as though none of the other rebels had got back yet.

As they were climbing out, Wheam said, 'Today was a great success, wasn't it, Brelan?'

'It was a success. Not sure about great.'

'But the sort of thing orcs will be telling tales about for generations. A tipping point, you said.'

'If it helps bring about the revolution,' Brelan conceded, 'it could be remembered as a key day.'

'And the wordsmiths will tell tales about it, and the balladeers will sing songs.'

Coilla groaned. 'I can see where this is going.'

'As it happens,' Wheam sailed on, 'I've already begun composing an epic ballad about this great day.' He pointed at his brow. 'Here. In my head.'

'I'm surprised there's room for it,' Coilla observed.

'I don't have my lute with me, of course . . .'

'Oh, good,' Pepperdyne said.

'. . . but I'm sure I could give you a recital without it.'

'Yes, well—' Stryke began.

'But bear in mind that it's a work in progress.'

'Aren't they all,' Coilla muttered.

They were walking towards the safe house's doors. As Wheam spoke, everyone increased their pace.

'I call it The Battle of the Square,' he intoned grandly, and cleared his throat.

> ''Twas upon that fateful day we beat the foe to their dismay
> With blade and axe we thrashed them sound
> All round the square and into the ground
> And all who were there, you could hear them say
> That was the day we made the humans go away

'That bit needs some work. It goes on . . .

> 'Oh let the humans wail, oh let them grieve
> Oh let their hearts bleed, oh let—'

'Oh, let *up!*' Coilla snapped.

'Wouldn't you like to hear the bit about how—'

'Moon!' she barked threateningly, jabbing a finger at her chest.

Wheam flinched and fell silent, crestfallen.

As they approached the doors they were thrown open. A couple of resistance members came out, and Jup and Spurral were close behind them. Their expressions were grim.

'What's happened?' Stryke said as he pushed his way in.

'We've had an . . . incident,' Jup replied.

'What?' Brelan demanded.

The dwarfs exchanged glances. 'Best to show you,' Spurral said.

The place was in turmoil as they led them through the house and down steps to the extensive cellars.

Passing through an arch and into one of the smaller rooms, Jup pointed. 'There.'

The others crowded in. On the rough flagstones the corpse of an unknown orc lay in a pool of blood. On the other side of the chamber Standeven was held fast by a pair of rebels.

'What the hell have you done?' Pepperdyne said.

7

'Somebody better tell me what happened here,' Brelan demanded.

'This is how we found it,' one of the rebels holding Standeven said. 'With him standing over the corpse. And he had this.' He held up a bloody knife.

'Who is he?' Stryke asked, nodding at the dead body.

They all shook their heads.

'He's a stranger to me,' Brelan confirmed. He turned to Standeven. 'Did you do this?'

'Yes.' He was pale, and he was shaking. There were beads of sweat on his pallid brow.

'Have you gone *insane*?' Pepperdyne exclaimed.

'Let him speak,' Stryke said.

'It was self-defence,' Standeven claimed. 'I'd no choice.' He was growing agitated. 'I'm not the villain here! You should thank me for—'

'*Calm down*,' Stryke told him firmly. 'Get a grip and tell us what happened. From the start.'

The human swallowed. 'I was told this was going to be a storage area, and I was moving boxes of rations in.'

'Seeing as you're no good for anything else,' Coilla muttered.

'Button it,' Stryke grated. 'You were moving stuff.'

Standeven nodded. 'When I came in, he was here.' He indicated the body, but avoided looking directly at it.

'Seen him before?'

'No.'

'What happened?'

'He attacked me.'

'Just like that? He didn't speak?'

'Not a word.'

'But you had a knife.'

'Er . . . no. That was his.'

'You took it off him?' There was scepticism in Stryke's voice.

'I. . . Yes.'

'You're no fighter,' Pepperdyne sneered.

'I expect you to back me!' Standeven flared. 'You know I'm not the sort to—'

'I know you'd rather run than fight.'

'I couldn't! I was *attacked*!'

'And you, no fighter, disarmed a knife carrier and killed him. You expect us to believe that?'

'You find . . . reserves when your life's at stake. He pulled the knife and we struggled. It was more luck than anything else that he ended up with the blade in him.'

'Then what?' Stryke asked.

'What do you mean?'

'What did you do after you'd stabbed him?'

'I called for help.'

'Not until then? Not when you were actually fighting him?'

'It all happened so quickly, I—'

'Right. What was he doing when you came in?'

'Doing? Nothing that I could see.'

'What do you *think* he might have been doing?'

'How the hell should I know? He was an intruder; maybe a spy for all I know. I would have thought I'd be congratulated for stopping him.'

'Is there anything to identify him?' Brelan wanted to know.

'No, we looked,' one of the rebels confirmed.

'How did he get in?' Coilla wondered.

'That wouldn't have been too hard,' Brelan admitted.

'*What?*'

'We're fighting *humans*, not fellow orcs. You must have noticed we have all sorts through here; citizens who might not be actual resistance members but secretly support us. Offering information, donating supplies, bringing messages . . .'

'Could that be what he was? A messenger?'

'We tend to know them by sight.'

'So by and large,' Stryke summed up, 'you let anybody in except humans. Which is fine if you think all orcs support your cause, and can keep their mouths shut.'

'We're not that sloppy,' Brelan protested. 'We take measures. And yes, I do believe the orcs of Acurial support us, at heart.'

'Hope you're right. But you need to beef up security.'

'We're off the point,' Brelan came back defensively. 'All I know is that a human's killed an orc, right here in a safe house. And if there wasn't doubt about why—' he jabbed a finger at Standeven '—*he'd* be dead now.'

'Why don't you make sure the intruder wasn't known to anybody here?' Stryke suggested.

'You bet I will. What do we do with him?' He glared at Standeven again.

'I want to talk to him. Privately.'

There was a hint of suspicion in Brelan's eyes. 'Why?'

'He's attached to my band. It's my charge. Just like you discipline your group. You've my word that if there's more to come out about this, you'll know.'

'And if it turns out to be murder, plain and simple?'

'Why should I?' Standeven protested heatedly. 'What could I possibly gain by—'

'*Shut it,*' Stryke ordered. 'If that's what happened, Brelan, he'll pay for it. Dearly.'

'He'd better.' He gestured at the rebels holding Standeven to let him go. 'We'll take the body out when you've finished here.' Then, grim faced, he led his comrades from the room. The door slammed behind them.

Stryke turned to Dallog and Wheam. 'You, too. Out.'

'Aaaahh,' Wheam complained, disappointed.

A look from Stryke silenced him. 'But stay close, Dallog. I might be needing you.'

They went out, leaving Stryke, Coilla and Pepperdyne with Standeven.

'Right,' Stryke said, confronting him, 'what really happened here?'

'I told you. But—'

Stryke grabbed him by the scruff and wrenched him close. 'You're saying that was the whole story?'

'I'm trying to explain! There was . . . something I didn't mention.'

'I knew it!' Pepperdyne snarled.

'No, wait, wait!' Standeven pleaded. 'I couldn't say it in front of the others.'

'What?'

'Let go, Stryke, and I'll show you.'

Stryke hung on to him for a moment, eyes locked on his. Then he let go and pushed him away. 'This better be good.'

'It is,' Standeven said. 'Least I reckon you'll think so.'

'*Get on with it.*'

'After *that* happened—' he waved a hand at the dead orc '—I didn't call for help right away. I searched the body.'

'Why?'

'I like to know who's trying to kill me. I was just curious.'

'Looking for valuables, more like,' Pepperdyne remarked.

'Oh, I found something valuable all right.' Standeven thrust a hand into his pocket. What he brought out filled the palm of his hand. It was a green sphere with five projecting spikes of varying length, made of a material no one had been able to identify.

'*The star*,' Coilla gasped.

Stryke snatched it and began scrutinising it. 'It's the one stolen from you, Coilla,' he decided at last. He looked to Standeven. 'And this was on the body?'

The human nodded. He was still flushed and had a lustre of perspiration.

'You *say* you found it on the corpse,' Pepperdyne speculated, 'but how do we know that's true?'

'Where else would I have got it? And if I had anything to hide, why would I give it to you?'

'To save your skin?' Coilla put in. 'It's a good bet we might go easier on you after getting a prize like this.'

'For all we know you could have been walking around with it ever since it disappeared,' Pepperdyne added.

'Why would I do *that*?' Standeven asked. 'I know you all think I stole it. But if I had, how come I've still got it? Wouldn't I have sold it or—'

'Or given it to Jennesta,' Coilla said.

Standeven made no comment.

Stryke sighed. It was part exasperation, part bafflement. 'Let's get this straight. You're set upon by an orc you've not seen before. You kill him.' He hefted the instrumentality, 'And you find this on his body.'

'Yes.'

Coilla spoke for all of them. 'It makes no sense.'

Stryke put the star into his belt pouch. 'Sense or not, least we've got it back.'

'But it doesn't add up, Stryke. Who was he?' She pointed at the body. 'What was he doing here? Why did he have—'

'Yeah, I know. But unless you two have any bright ideas, I can't figure it.'

'Assuming what we've been told is true,' Pepperdyne said, staring pointedly at Standeven.

'I meant what I said to Brelan. If something deeper's going on here, there'll be a price to pay. Otherwise . . .'

'We accept his story,' Coilla finished, eyeing Standeven.

'Could be out of our hands.'

'Meaning?'

'We're strangers here. If it turns out this dead one *was*

connected to the resistance, or they decide they don't believe what happened, it'll be their call.'

'So where does that leave me?' Standeven asked.

'You're not a member of my band.'

'Thank the gods,' Coilla mumbled.

'You're not in the band,' Stryke repeated, 'but we brought you here, and we stand together. So whatever I feel about you, which ain't good, I'm still responsible for you. Call it Wolverine pride.'

'I understand,' Standeven said, 'and I really—'

'I'm not finished. But if it turns out you've been lying about all this, you're alone. And I'll kill you myself. Understand *that*?'

He nodded.

'Keep yourself to yourself. Avoid the rebels' company, if you can, and stick near band members. Maybe this'll blow over.'

'Think it will?' Pepperdyne wondered.

Stryke shrugged, then went to the door and called Dallog in. 'Escort Standeven to our billet. Make sure the band keeps an eye on him for at least a couple of days.'

'How much do I tell 'em about all this?'

'They've a right to know. But I'll take care of it. Now get him out of my sight.'

Dallog took Standeven by the arm and hustled him out.

Stryke looked to Pepperdyne and Coilla. 'What do you think?'

'It stinks,' Coilla offered. 'Only I can't see where the smell's coming from.'

'Pepperdyne? You know him best.'

'He's a lying, two-faced bastard. But I never saw him as a killer. Not because he isn't ruthless, mind you, but because he's a coward.'

'Lots of murderers are cowards.'

'I suppose I'm saying . . . I don't know what to think, Stryke. He's twisted enough to kill if it furthers his ends, or at least not to fret if somebody loses their life over him. But he's got no guts. Fuck him. He *always* screws things up.'

'He's not doing that to us.'

'We're going to have to baby-sit him now,' Coilla said, 'That's not what I signed up for.'

'Me neither,' Stryke agreed. 'But I'm more worried about our bond with the resistance. We've worked hard for their trust. This could break it.'

'Ever get the feeling we aren't in control? Not just over this, but what's going on here in Acurial?'

'It's what troubles me most; not having control over our own fate.'

'Well, we fought hard enough for it in Maras-Dantia, and once a race gets a taste for freedom they cling to it.'

'I'll second that,' Pepperdyne contributed.

Stryke gave him a quizzical look, then glanced at Coilla.

'Jode's a Trougathian,' she told him.

'A *what*?'

'Long story. Maybe he'll tell you sometime.'

Pepperdyne didn't offer to explain.

'But you're right about control,' she went on. 'We've got no easy way out. Not as long as we've only got the one star.'

'We're going to go for the others.'

'When?'

'We need to make a plan, scout Jennesta's route, think of a cover story for Brelan and Chillder—'

'*When*, Stryke?'

'Tomorrow.'

74

8

Stryke kept the team small. He decided on Coilla, Haskeer and Dallog, the latter the only new recruit; along with eight privates, none of them tyros.

It was late the following day, and the shades of night were falling. Stryke's group had established that Jennesta was at the stone circle on the outskirts of Taress, and the route she usually took back to the fortress was confirmed. Now they waited in hiding by a road leading to the redoubt.

'I'm surprised the resistance let us out of their sight,' Coilla said. 'What did you tell them?'

'Brelan and Chillder think we're freelancing,' Stryke told her, 'helping to keep the pot boiling. Reckon they were glad to have us out of their way after what happened with Standeven.'

'How's that going? I've been here all day, remember.'

'The rest of the band's looking out for him. Pepperdyne's closer than his shadow. The rebels are as cold as a dead witch's arse to him. But it turned out the orc he killed isn't known to them, which might make it easier.'

'I still don't see how we're going to keep this mission from them. They're bound to hear about it.'

'The humans won't boast about a defeat.'

'And if they do?'

'They're not going to say anything about the stars.'

'That's not what I meant. My worry's about what Brelan and

Chillder are going to do when they know we went after Jennesta again behind their backs.'

'What *can* they do about it?'

'Shut us out?'

'We can still help bring about an uprising. That's what we came here for.'

'It'll be harder if we make enemies of the resistance.'

'We thrive on enemies, Coilla. But you're right; we don't need the rebels on our necks.'

'So how do we avoid it?'

'Like I said, Jennesta wouldn't boast of a defeat, so the resistance won't hear about it. But she would crow if it goes wrong.'

'You mean we can't screw this up.'

'Right.'

'What I wanna know,' Haskeer said, 'is do we kill her if we get the chance?'

'Not if it gets in the way of snatching the stars,' Stryke decreed. 'Otherwise . . .'

'The rebels would hear about *that*,' Coilla remarked.

'And wouldn't bellyache if we pulled it off. Killing the Peczan envoy'd be a big boost for them.'

They fell silent and returned to watching.

Their hiding place was just beyond a fork in the road. The turnoff led to the main barracks, which were out of sight, where the majority of the fortress's garrison was billeted. The road Stryke, Coilla and Haskeer overlooked went to the fortress itself.

Despite being near the city's heart, the area was almost semi-bucolic due to the acres of land belonging to the fortress. Land once used for leisure and hunting by long-dead rulers, and now employed for drill by the citadel's battalion. Graced with more trees than anywhere else in Taress, it was quiet compared to the rest of the metropolis, with little traffic and few passers-by. The reputation of the place was such that citizens preferred to avoid it. But there were patrols of troops to be wary of.

'How much longer we got to wait?' Haskeer grumbled.

'Most times she's back around now,' Stryke said.

'Waiting's the bit I hate.'

'It's part of the job. Take it easy.'

'Count your toes,' Coilla suggested.

Haskeer scowled at her.

They waited until it was nearly dark, and were passed only by the odd rider or wagon, usually travelling at speed to get through the district as quickly as possible. Haskeer grew more restless, and Stryke was beginning to think the mission would have to be scrubbed.

It was Coilla who snapped them out of it. 'There,' she said, pointing up the highway.

A convoy was coming along the main road and approaching the fork. It was headed by a group of mounted cavalry, followed by two coaches, each with a trooper sitting alongside the driver. Another contingent of cavalry brought up the rear. The procession moved at a clip, but short of breakneck speed.

'Hope the others are watching this,' Coilla added.

'If they're awake,' Haskeer muttered.

Stryke shot him a frown.

'Well, Dallog's with 'em.'

'He's a pro,' Stryke told him, 'and so are the grunts with him. So quit sniping.'

Haskeer grunted in a noncommittal kind of way.

The convoy had reached the fork. The cavalry in the lead peeled off and headed for their barracks, as did the contingent bringing up the rear. The unescorted pair of carriages picked up speed for the home run.

Coilla gazed into the trees on the other side of the road. She couldn't see anything. Not that she expected to. 'They're cutting it fine.'

'The timing has to be spot on,' Stryke reminded her. 'Relax.'

She smiled at the thought of relaxation as she reached for her bow.

The convoy was almost on them. Coilla and Haskeer nocked their arrows.

'Make those shots count,' Stryke told them. 'You might not get a second chance.'

'I know, I know,' Haskeer came back irritably.

The convoy was almost level with their position when a loud crack rang out. Ahead of the first carriage a mature tree crashed down in a flurry of leaves, blocking the road. The carriages skidded to a halt. Another substantial tree fell behind the second carriage, boxing them both in.

'*Now!*' Stryke yelled.

Coilla and Haskeer loosed their arrows. Coilla's struck the trooper next to the driver on the lead carriage. It was a righteous hit, pitching the man from his seat. Haskeer's arrow missed. Stryke and Coilla glared at him.

Cursing, he fumbled for another bolt. Coilla reloaded first, took aim and brought down the trooper on the second carriage. Haskeer's next shot was true. It killed the first carriage's driver. By that time the driver of the second had scrambled down on the far side and disappeared into the tree-line.

'Remember,' Stryke warned, 'Jennesta's magic can be lethal. She should be in the first carriage, so leave that to me. Now *move!*'

They came out of hiding and charged toward the road. Before they were halfway the rest of the raiding party, with Dallog to the fore, emerged from the foliage. Several of them still clutched the axes they used to fell the trees. Two grunts ran to stand lookout at each end of the halted convoy. The rest made for the carriages.

An arrow shot out of the open window of the second coach. It was aimed at Coilla, and came near to claiming her. She dropped and hugged the ground. Stryke and Haskeer did the same. Coilla got off an arrow of her own. It smacked into the carriage door. Whoever was inside returned fire, but the bolt flew over their heads. Haskeer unleashed an arrow, sending it through the window. Somebody in the dark interior shrieked.

The sound of battering came from the far side of the carriage. Dallog's crew were laying siege to it. Stryke, Coilla and Haskeer got up and raced for their goal. As they approached, the door of the second carriage burst open and four troopers spilled out.

'You go ahead!' Coilla shouted to Stryke.

He sprinted off.

Swords drawn, the troops came at Haskeer and Coilla, who rushed forward to meet them. The chime of steel on steel echoed through the twilight. Almost immediately, Dallog and the others poured around the carriages and joined in. Jennesta's guards fought with spirit, but had no hope of not being overwhelmed.

Stryke reached the first coach. He hesitated for a fraction of a second at its door, then wrenched it open.

A bulky, shadow-swathed figure filled the doorway. It half fell, half leapt on Stryke, pinning him to the ground and knocking the wind out of him. His sword was dashed from his hand.

Stryke immediately knew his foe as one of Jennesta's zombie bodyguards, if only from the foul odour it gave off. Struggling under the creature's oppressive weight, he was aware of its skin, dried out and wrinkled like ancient parchment. He saw the black chasm of its dead eyes.

The zombie encircled him with its fetid arms. Fists balled, Stryke pummelled the once-human, landing hefty blows to its head. But he couldn't break its iron grip. The zombie's abnormal strength began to crush the life out of him. Stryke writhed and kicked, but the bear-hug held.

Then his flailing hand touched metal and he grasped the hilt of his dropped sword. He brought it up and round in an arc, striking the zombie's side. The blade cut deep, but brought only a puff of grey dust from what should have been a wound. It hardly troubled the zombie. Gasping for breath now, Stryke tried another tack. He hacked frenziedly at the creature's arm. After three blows it severed, exuding more rank dust. The arm fell away. Half free, Stryke exerted pressure and rolled the thrashing zombie far enough for him to scramble clear. Quickly, he found his feet.

The creature rose too. It looked about itself, lifeless eyes unblinking, and saw its amputated arm. Reaching down, he grabbed it, hefted it as though it were a club, and lumbered in Stryke's direction. Stryke charged and plunged his blade into the thing's chest. It met little obstruction. Its tip exploded from the zombie's back, liberating yet more dust. Stryke yanked the sword out and withdrew a couple of paces. The zombie kept coming, apparently unharmed. Stryke made to attack again.

Haskeer appeared and darted between them. 'It's mine,' he growled, facing the creature. 'You *go!*' Ducking to avoid its fleshy club, he commenced chopping and slashing at the zombie.

Stryke ran for the open carriage door, leapt up and jumped in.

Jennesta sat alone. She wore an expression that could have been called serene.

He seized his chance and thrust his sword at her heart.

It felt like the blade had struck an anvil. The impact sent a shockwave up his arm that instantly suffused his entire body. It was a pain unlike any he had ever known. He imagined that being stung by a dozen venomous serpents would be like this. An energy ran through him, a malevolent force, bringing agony to every fibre.

He was flung backwards, landing on the floor, his back to the opposite seat. The pain immediately began to fade.

Jennesta was swathed in a semi-transparent aura that looked like air rippling on a hot day. It was shot through with a brilliant violet patina that shifted, melted and reformed itself. Stryke knew a mere sword was no match for such sorcery.

'Did you think to find me unprotected?' she said.

'It was worth a try,' Stryke grated. He was fighting against his inbred deference for her, and his wariness of her powers.

She laughed. It was a disturbing sound. 'Your race may be unparalleled fighters, but you hardly excel when it comes to thinking.'

'If brainwork means something like you,' he replied defiantly, 'I'll stay dumb.'

'Insolent cur!' She made a movement with her hand, as though lobbing an invisible ball.

Stryke was hit by a jolt as powerful as the shock he'd just recovered from. He bit his lip to stop himself crying out.

'So you came here to kill me?' she added. Her tone made it sound conversational.

He said nothing.

'Or perhaps you hoped for a different prize,' Jennesta went on. For a fraction of a second, and apparently involuntarily, her eyes flicked to a bulky silk pouch on the seat beside her.

Stryke hadn't noticed it before, and now he willed himself not to look at it. 'Your death's the best prize I can think of.'

'Then you really do lack imagination, dullard.' She made the hand gesture again.

He took another punch of psychic force. The hurt inundated every cell in his body. He felt it in his bones, his teeth. And he knew he couldn't take much more; assuming she didn't simply kill him outright.

'Your view of the universe is so depressingly limited,' she said. 'You grasp no more than a sliver of the truth. If only you had the intellect to see how much *more* there is to reality.'

Stryke thought that was an odd thing for her to say. But then, most of what she said had always struck him as bizarre. He held his silence.

'Why am I bothering?' Jennesta asked. 'You and your kind have the acumen of worms. And to think I once believed that you, Captain Stryke, had the wit to rise above your animal state.'

'You never showed it.'

'You never earned my trust.'

It was Stryke's turn to laugh, even if it risked a further jolt. 'You talk as though your trust's a gem, and not a sham of paste and glass.'

'What a poetic turn of phrase. For an animal. You could have been great, Stryke.'

'I'm flattered.'

'Low sarcasm. I shouldn't expect more. But what you're too dim to understand is that by your treachery you've traded my patronage for a life of struggle and hardship.'

'We call it freedom.'

'It's overrated,' she sneered.

The carriage door was still open. Outside, the sound of fighting continued, but it was strangely faint, as if heard from a distance.

Stryke said the first thing that came into his head, purely to keep her engaged. 'You might have the upper hand now, but—'

'Oh *really*. Foolishly, I expected more of you than empty threats and petty chatter. Let's not beat about the bush. Neither of us are mentioning the enormous basilisk in the room. The *instrumentalities*, dolt.' She fleetingly glanced at the pouch again. He took that as confirming his hunch and tensed himself.

'What about them?'

She rolled her eyes.' "*What about them*," he asks. So you're happy that you no longer possess them, is that it? No answer? Perhaps a little encouragement's in order.' She raised her hand.

Stryke sprang forward, snatched the pouch and dived out of the carriage. Thinking he'd be struck down at any instant, he ran towards Haskeer.

His sergeant had decapitated the zombie and was staring down at it. Even headless, the creature still showed signs of life, writhing and twitching in the dirt.

'*Move it!*' Stryke yelled. '*Run!*'

Haskeer fell in behind him.

Stryke looked back. He expected to see Jennesta coming out

of the coach, but there was no sign of her. Up ahead, Coilla, Dallog and the others were surveying the corpses of the troopers littering the road.

Loosening the drawstrings on the pouch, Stryke checked its contents. The instrumentalities were inside. Triumphant, he stuffed the pouch into his jerkin.

'Got them?' Coilla asked as he approached.

He gave her a thumbs up.

'*Company!*' Dallog shouted, pointing with his sword.

A detachment of cavalry was heading their way from the direction of the barracks, and they were moving fast.

Stryke ordered a retreat. They ran into the trees and mounted hidden horses. In her carriage, Jennesta smiled.

They split into four groups to avoid attention, with Stryke, Coilla and Haskeer staying together. As a precaution, the safe house had been changed following the incident with Standeven, and they rode hard for it to beat the curfew. But they slowed their pace when they got into the inner city's narrow, winding streets, where many others were hastening home before full dark. Finally, finding the lanes too crowded to ride, they had to dismount and lead their horses.

'Now we've got the stars back,' Haskeer said, 'we can leave anytime we want.'

'Not until things are settled here,' Stryke replied sternly.

'Didn't say we should. It's just good to have the option.'

'I'll drink to that.'

'Now you're talking.' Haskeer spat plentifully, narrowly missing the feet of an irate passing citizen. 'My throat's as dusty as a troll's crotch.'

'Is it just me,' Coilla wondered, 'or did this mission seem just a little too easy?'

'You wouldn't say that if you'd been in there with Jennesta,' Stryke replied.

'You're still alive, aren't you? And, all right, we met some opposition; but nothing we couldn't handle.'

'We got lucky.'

'Don't you think Jennesta would've taken more precautions? Not just for herself, but the stars?'

'You know what it's like with rulers. They get full of themselves. Too brash. They never think anybody'd dare go against 'em. The important thing is we got these back.' He patted his jerkin.

'Guess so.' She didn't sound entirely convinced.

'We're nearly there,' Stryke said, changing the subject. 'Expect the rebels to be nosey about what we've been up to today, and stick to our story. Remember, we've just been harrying the militia.'

Coilla and Haskeer nodded.

But when they got to the disused grain store the resistance were using they found the place abuzz. No one seemed interested in where they'd been. Eventually, Chillder located them, and she was animated.

'What's happening?' Stryke asked.

'The resistance council's decided the Principal should come out into the open. Isn't it great? Our mother's going to issue her rallying call!'

'When?'

'In the morning.'

'That soon?'

'The time's right, Stryke. Make sure your band's ready; we're heading for the revolution!'

9

Hacher had grown used to Jennesta's nocturnal habits. Or at least accepted them. In the weeks she had been in Taress as the empire's special envoy, he had reason to wonder if she ever slept at all. And if she didn't sleep, those who served her were expected to be awake and on hand, whatever the hour.

So it was that Hacher found himself in her chambers near dawn, having been at her beck and call for most of the night. Jennesta herself was outside on the balcony, watching Grilan-Zeat. The comet was big in the sky, a boiling light to rival the sun that was soon to rise.

Hacher was alone in her apartment. His aide, Frynt, had been dispatched on some errand Jennesta demanded, and Brother Grentor had likewise been dragged from his bed to attend to her whims. Her undead personal guards were nowhere to be seen. Hacher suspected that they were slumbering in some state of coma necessary to revitalise their strength, but preferred not to dwell on the thought.

He was bored as well as exhausted. Though the anxiety Jennesta always managed to generate in everyone gave his fatigue an edge. It was rather like the way he remembered feeling as he prepared to enter a battle when he was a younger man. But this night trepidation had reached new heights, given Jennesta's ambush during the evening. Not that she had done more than mention it, almost in passing, let alone discussed it with him. He wasn't so naïve as to think it would end there, and his concern was when and how she might show her displeasure.

As he pondered, she entered the room. Hacher intuitively stiffened, almost to attention, as he always did when she was around, and doubly so when there was a chance she was going to be wrathful.

Worn out by anticipation, he decided on the risky strategy of pre-empting her by broaching the subject first, greeting her with, 'I owe you an apology, my lady. The assault you were subjected to earlier was inexcusable.'

'Yet you are about to make excuses for it, no doubt.'

'No, ma'am. I merely wish to express the military's regret that you should have been put in harm's way.' He consulted a parchment he'd been reading. 'And I see from the report that you lost a personal possession to the outlaws.'

'The item in question is not your concern, General, and in any event it was unimportant, trifling.'

'I'm pleased to hear it, ma'am.'

'The matter of my personal security, however, is not insignificant. In allowing my convoy to be attacked, those under your command were both incompetent and cowardly.'

'A number of men gave their lives for you, ma'am.'

'But not all, I think.'

'Ma'am?'

'Who survived the raid?'

Hacher scanned the report. 'A coach driver, and one of the troopers accompanying you, though he's severely injured.'

'Execute them.'

'With all due respect, ma'am, I think—'

'Only you don't, do you? Think, that is. The only way you're going to put down this growing rebellion is by being utterly ruthless with your underlings. They need to be toughened to pass that mercilessness on to the scum on the streets.'

'I have complete confidence in our armed forces,' Hacher

protested indignantly. 'Their expertise and bravery are next to none.'

'The rulers of every nation tell their subjects lies. Do you know one of the biggest? That they have the best army in the world. While in actuality armies are a rabble, a dumping pit for felons and cutthroats. Only absolute obedience, born of the rope and the lash, enables them to function.'

'Our forces *are* properly disciplined, ma'am. And as a result, as fighters they're peerless.'

'You don't know the meaning of the word. Nor will you until I fashion a force that's *truly* peerless. Merciless and totally compliant. The executions will go ahead. As to your own behaviour, as the one ultimately answerable, I've issued you with enough warnings about your behaviour. Be sure that this is the last one.'

'Ma'am.' For all his iron reputation, and his position of command, he lowered his eyes from hers.

'Cheer up, General,' Jennesta told him. 'Your forces will have the chance to prove you right very soon.' She looked out at the rising sun, bloody red on the horizon. 'Something tells me it's going to be an interesting day.'

On a periphery of the city, in a location passed on by word of mouth in marketplaces, taverns and cornfields, a crowd was gathering. The area was shabby, with little to tempt visitors, and dawn had barely broken, yet a large number had collected. More were arriving by the minute, on foot, by horseback, in packed wagons.

Up above, the comet was plain, even when rivalled by the climbing sun.

The quarter was one of mean dwellings, stables and depositories, largely derelict. The focus of the crowd was a particular warehouse, some three-storeys tall, that once served as a grain store. There was a gallery, or veranda, projecting from its second floor, onto which sacks were hoisted. It was a perfect point to address the crowd from.

Inside the building the atmosphere was tense. Many rebels were assembled, along with all the Wolverines. The humans, Pepperdyne and Standeven, were not present, and nor were Jup and Spurral. It was thought best to keep them out of sight of the crowd.

Principal Sylandya, Acurial's aged matriarch, was the centre of attention. She sat as though enthroned, on a hastily found, down-at-heel chair, and she wore the scarlet robe that signified the office she had never renounced. A small army of rebels buzzed about her. But her offspring, the twins Brelan and Chillder, stayed closest. A privilege that had been temporarily extended to Stryke and Coilla, though Stryke at least suspected this was because Sylandya found the Wolverines intriguing, and perhaps a bit exotic.

'Do you have your speech prepared, Mother?' Chillder asked.

'No. This is not a time for lectures. I'll speak from the heart, and the words I need will come.'

Brelan smiled. 'A typically wise decision.'

'You always knew how to flatter your old mother,' Sylandya told him. 'But no soft-soap today, I beg you. I need an honest steer from both of you on what we're doing here.'

'You have doubts?' Chillder said, frowning.

'*Of course* I have doubts. I hope I've raised you well enough to know I would. What I'm about to say to that crowd is going to have a price. A price paid in blood. Citizens are going to suffer.'

'They're suffering already, and the way things are it'll never stop. Surely it's better to pay that price to rid ourselves of the occupiers?'

'That's what my head says. My feelings aren't so clear-cut.' She turned to Stryke. 'What do our friends from . . . the north think?'

Stryke didn't miss her slight hesitation, and not for the first time suspected she was more sceptical about his band's story

88

than her children were. 'The orcs here have a choice. They can be cattle fit for slaughter or snow leopards lusting for prey. If they're going to throw off the yoke they need to remember what they are. Your call to arms and that thing in the sky could do it.'

'Snow leopards? That's a class of beast I'm not familiar with in what I know of Acurial. They must be confined to your northern wastes.' She eyed the necklace of leopards' fangs he wore as a trophy about his neck, and gave him a look half quizzical, half amused.

Stryke cursed himself for mentioning something unknown in this world. He said nothing.

'But of course you're right,' she went on. 'Most of this land's orcs have lived too long in a dream. My hope is that we can wake them. Whether Grilan-Zeat and my poor words can bring that about is moot.' She smiled. 'Oh, and the prophecy concerning a band of heroes. Let's not forget that.'

'How much stock do you put in it?' Coilla asked.

'Prophecies and comets? It could all be so much moonfluff. Though I wouldn't tell your Sergeant Haskeer that; he seems rather taken with the romance of it.'

'A big old softie, that's our Haskeer,' Coilla told her with a straight face.

'I've no idea if the legends and omens have any real meaning,' Sylandya repeated, 'and frankly I don't care. I'll use whatever it takes to gain our freedom. Needs must.'

'You've no qualms about telling the citizens a lie?'

'I didn't say it *was* a lie. But even if it is, sometimes a lie in the service of truth is tolerable.'

'Makes sense to me,' Stryke remarked.

Brelan came forward. 'It's time, Mother. Are you ready?'

'Ready as I'll ever be.' She clutched his hand, and reached for his sister's. 'We're about to enter an abyss, in hope of finding the light beyond. You two have to promise me that whatever happens you'll keep faith with our cause.'

'You'll be here to make sure we do,' Chillder replied.

'The fate of the nation doesn't depend on one individual. Things change. *Promise.*'

'I promise.'

'Me, too,' Brelan echoed. 'But I think you're being—'

Sylandya placed her fingers on his lips, stilling him. 'You said it was time.'

The twins nodded. She rose and they moved to either side of her, taking her arms.

A little procession formed, led by the Primary and the siblings. Several members of the resistance council followed, with Stryke and Coilla falling in at the rear. They made their way up a staircase to the floor above, and from there out onto the balcony-like veranda. A number of rebels were already there, as were a handful of Wolverines, including Haskeer.

From their vantage point they could make out the size of the crowd, which had further swollen. More orcs were arriving. When they recognised Sylandya, their roar was like thunder.

'How's she going to make herself heard over this din?' Coilla bellowed into Stryke's ear.

He shrugged.

When Brelan raised his arms, the crowd immediately fell silent. They boomed again when he announced the Principal, then resumed an expectant hush.

Gently refusing her children's support, Sylandya stepped forward. Straight-backed, her face a picture of resolve, she seemed the exact opposite of the frail oldster of a moment before. And when she spoke it was in an impressively strong, loud voice. 'Citizens of Acurial!' They roared once more at that, and even louder when she amended it to, 'Citizens of *free* Acurial!'

When the clamour died down she continued, 'We have suffered greatly in recent times! Our liberty has been stolen and our land defiled! Too long have we stood back and endured the indignities heaped upon us and the assaults on our pride!'

Archers were on the veranda, scanning the crowd. In the

horde itself, rebels, Wolverines and Vixens were watchful for any sign of opposition.

'The time is long overdue for us to throw off the shackles the outsiders have forged for us! And now we have a sign!'

Stryke couldn't say what drew his eye to a figure way over beyond the farthest edge of the crowd. It was true that whoever it was wore a cloak and hood that obscured their features, but many in the crowd were dressed that way, for fear of being identified. And the figure was far enough away to present no threat to the Principal; too far even for an arrow to be unleashed with sufficient strength or accuracy. Yet Stryke still stared.

'We have the blessings of our revered forebears! We have the assurance of a prophecy! There! There in the sky!' She pointed to the heavens. The crowd went wild.

Stryke saw the figure take something from the folds of their cloak. He couldn't make out what it was.

'Peczan has held us in bondage long enough! Now Grilan-Zeat has come, a hammer to break the chains that bind us!'

The figure cast the object into the air. Or rather, released it. Whatever it was soared upward, seemingly of its own volition. Then it levelled out and started moving over the crowd.

'We have a heritage! A heritage of ferocity and battle, of victory over our foes! A heritage we have allowed ourselves to forget! Well, now the time has come to reawaken that slumbering spirit! To set free the hounds of war!'

As it got nearer, Stryke could see that the object had wings. At which point he stopped thinking of it as an object and started thinking of it as a bird. A white bird, not particularly large, flapping unerringly in their direction. He wondered what harm a bird could do.

'Coilla,' he whispered, nudging her. 'See that?' He pointed, but not obviously so.

She squinted. 'A bird? Looks like a dove.'

'Yes, I think it is a dove.' He noticed that the figure who released it had gone.

'What about it?' she asked slightly peevishly, irritated at him talking over Sylandya's speech.

'It's . . . not right.'

'When we raise arms against our oppressors it is in pursuit of a righteous cause! The cause of freedom!'

'What do you mean, not right?' Coilla hissed. 'It's a fucking *bird.*'

'No,' Stryke replied. 'I don't know what it is, but . . .'

The dove was a stone's throw away and heading straight at them.

'No longer will we dwell miserably in the dark! We shall take up our blades and carve our way to the light! No matter how much human flesh stands in our path!'

'Brelan! Chillder!' Stryke yelled. '*Danger!*'

The principal faltered, and looked at him. Everyone else on the veranda did likewise, some open-mouthed, others with angry expressions.

'Something's coming!' Stryke shouted. 'There!' He thrust out an arm to indicate the approaching threat.

As he did so, a change rapidly came over the dove. It became somehow indistinct, and began to alter its shape. But it kept coming. Some in the crowd noticed it and reacted noisily.

Stryke snatched a bow from one of the rebels, drew it and took aim.

The dove transformed into a swirling black cloud, with streaks of gold and silver pulsing at its core.

Everyone on the balcony was in disarray. Stryke loosed his arrow.

A bolt of pure white light, blindingly vivid, erupted from the cloud. It covered the distance to the balcony in an instant, striking Sylandya. She collapsed, a smouldering wound in her chest.

The cloud that had been a bird that wasn't a bird, dissolved.

There was uproar. Brelan and Chillder, ashen with shock, half carried, half dragged their stricken mother inside. Stryke, Coilla and a number of the rebels went with them.

The crowd was in turmoil.

They laid Sylandya on some sacking. Brelan slipped out of his jerkin and folded it as a pillow for her head. He and Chillder seemed distraught to the point of panic. A rebel medic elbowed his way through. One look at the gaping, charred wound told him all he needed to know. He turned to the twins and slowly shook his head.

Sylandya was still conscious. Her lips moved feebly. Brelan and Chillder moved closer.

'Remember,' she whispered, 'remember . . . your . . . promise.'

'We will,' Brelan pledged, squeezing her hand.

Then Sylandya's eyes closed and the last breath went out of her.

The twins surrendered to despair.

Chillder rose. She wore a look of hurt and bewilderment.

Coilla went to her and put her hands on her shoulders. 'Courage,' she said.

'She knew,' Chillder replied, as though separated from the world by a great distance. 'Somehow, she knew.'

The crowd was making a tremendous racket. Stryke went back outside.

Haskeer was still there, surveying the scene below. '*Shit*,' he said. 'And on our watch.'

'We couldn't have foreseen it,' Stryke assured him, though he wasn't entirely sure that was true. 'I'll tell you one thing. I doubt that was Helix magic.'

'Jennesta?'

'Who else? Getting some minion to assassinate the one orc who could rally the populace would be right up her alley.'

'To cow them?' He gazed at the frantic crowd. 'They don't look too put off to me. Just the opposite.'

'No,' Stryke agreed. 'This could be Jennesta's biggest mistake.'

10

Stryke was proved right, and in short order.

Far from intimidating Acurial's population, the murder of Sylandya enraged it. Attacks on the occupiers immediately increased ten-fold. Not just in the city but throughout the country. Many of the assaults were opportunistic, and carried out by individuals or small *ad hoc* groups. One of the resistance's tasks was to coordinate these actions, and to organise the growing number of dissidents into a coherent fighting force. Within days they had the makings of a rebel army.

Brelan and Chillder channelled their grief into these activities, working with demonic energy in their mother's name; and the Wolverines were heavily involved in training the new intake. But the warband drew most satisfaction from doing what they did best: confronting occupiers on the streets of Taress.

In this, Jup and Spurral, and the human, Pepperdyne, were given roles to play. The dwarfs in particular, after being confined for so long, found it a pleasing outlet. Though none of the trio ever ventured out unaccompanied by fellow band members or rebel fighters, lest they be taken for enemies or freaks. For Standeven, little changed. Useless in any kind of combat function, his contribution was centred on manual work at various safe houses, which he undertook grudgingly. But he mostly confined his complaints to the Wolverines. The incident of the dead intruder had been eclipsed by the burgeoning uprising, but not forgotten.

For his part, Stryke kept the instrumentalities with him at all times, even in combat. He was not about to repeat the mistake of entrusting any of them to anyone else, even the most loyal of his comrades. There were mixed feelings about this in the band.

One discovery of the Wolverines, which dismayed them, was that some orcs allied themselves with the occupying humans. They were small in number and didn't dare do it openly, preferring to act as fifth columnists and informers, but the effect on morale was something else to be countered. Chillder and Brelan were especially shocked by this development, having regarded their fellow citizens as patriots, and they dealt with traitors harshly when they were caught. It was an element that added another variable to an already chaotic situation.

The resistance's growing numbers meant the way the occupiers were engaged was changing. There were still plenty of guerrilla raids, but large-scale, more conventional face-offs were starting to replace them. For these, the Wolverines' expertise was invaluable.

So it was that a week after Sylandya's death, which many were already calling her martyrdom, the entire band stood together on one of Taress' main thoroughfares. At their backs was a force of several hundred insurgents, ragtag and ill-armed, but eager for blood. Ahead, a good lance throw away, an equal number of human militia was gathered. They were better ordered and better equipped, but unused to being challenged by creatures with a newfound passion for warfare.

Events were at the sham stage, as the Wolverines knew it, with both sides exchanging catcalls, insults and threatening gestures. A standard practice before a battle.

'How'd you think they'll hold up?' Coilla said, jerking a thumb at the ranks behind them.

'What they lack in know-how they make up for in rage,' Stryke reckoned.

'Still gonna get most of 'em killed,' Haskeer muttered. 'Fucking amateurs.'

'Even a legendary band of heroes can't have a revolution without an army,' Stryke replied.

Jup guffawed.

'What's *your* problem, pisspot?' Haskeer snapped.

'I'm standing next to you.'

'Hang on while I die laughing.'

'Don't mind him, Jup,' Coilla said. 'He's still swollen-headed about a human he killed yesterday.'

'Why? What's so special about that?'

'It wasn't a soldier.'

'What was he?' Pepperdyne asked.

'A tax gatherer.'

Pepperdyne considered that for a moment. 'Well, fair enough.'

They all murmured agreement.

'When's this going to kick off?' Dallog wanted to know as he surveyed the enemy line.

'Yeah,' Wheam piped up. 'When we gonna *fight*?' He swished around the sword he was clutching.

'Careful with that thing!' Haskeer protested. 'You'll have somebody's eye out!'

'It'll start soon enough,' Stryke said. 'Remember the tyros are your charge, Dallog.' He glanced at the new band members, those recruited on Ceragan. They looked tense and ashen. 'Especially him,' he added, nodding at Wheam.

Wheam looked discomfited.

'They'll be fine,' Dallog assured him, though his expression was grim.

'Come on, *come on*,' Spurral muttered, impatiently drumming the cobblestones with her staff.

'Your female's keen for the off, shortarse,' Haskeer observed. It was said not without a trace of admiration.

'Yes, and she'll take it out on you if this thing doesn't hot up soon,' Jup came back.

'Here we go,' Coilla said. 'They're moving.'

The human troops began to advance. Subject to rigid military discipline, they progressed in an orderly fashion.

'*Advance!*' Stryke yelled, raising his blade.

The crowd of orcs was more shambolic as it went forward, but its passion was high. They started to beat their shields and bellow war cries.

As the humans picked up speed and added their own battle cries to the din, they found the orcs had hidden allies. From rooftops and high windows, citizens proceeded to rain objects down on their heads. A volley of tiles, bricks, pots and the occasional arrow fell like lethal hail.

When the opposing forces were near enough to see the expressions of fear, bloodlust, fury and foreboding on each others' faces, both sides broke into a charge.

The two living tides swept together and melded in a brutal frenzy.

The battle, the latest in a series that occurred almost daily, took place in the hub of the city. Central enough, in fact, that although it couldn't quite be seen from the fortress of Taress, it could certainly be heard.

For Jennesta and Hacher, ensconced in her quarters at one of the redoubt's loftiest points, it was a near permanent background noise. Not that they were consciously listening. The events in Jennesta's chambers took precedence over death's raucous clamour.

'Well, I'm waiting,' she repeated, arms folded resolutely.

'I'm at a loss to know what you expect of me, ma'am,' the general replied.

'Yes, and that's the problem, isn't it? Perhaps you could start by telling me what you intend doing about the anarchy out there.' She waved an arm at the window.

'The present situation, with respect, ma'am, has been brought about by the assassination of the female the orcs called their Principal. I could almost believe it was an act designed to stir things up even further, and—'

'Are you questioning my methods?'

'I think I am, my lady. Even before the Principal's death we made certain moves that only worsened the situation in this province. Actions, I have to say, that you drove.'

'*Now* you find the guts! It's a pity you didn't have the resolve you're now showing towards me when you were supposed to be defending Peczan's interests.'

'I've always worked as diligently as I could in service to the empire,' he responded irately.

'No. You might think that, but you haven't. Your actions have undermined everything that should have been done here. And *would* have been done by a competent commander.'

Hacher was allowing himself to grow heated. 'Before your arrival, *my lady*, we had a situation here that was manageable. Your . . . *initiatives* have turned simple law enforcement into a much graver problem.'

'Let me tell you the *real* problem, Hacher.' She counted items off on her bejewelled fingers. 'You failed to anticipate the potential for rebellion these animals harboured, or to recognise their capacity for savagery, despite me telling you so. You led your forces in a shambolic way. You weakened the effectiveness of the imperial presence here because of political infighting with the Helix. Above all, you stubbornly refused to accept that the only thing the natives of this godsforsaken land understand is strength. In short, General, *you* are the problem.'

'Look where an excessive show of strength has got us, ma'am. Look at the streets. See what we've bought with our display of strength and brutality.'

'Too *little* brutality, too *late*! You know, you really do baffle me. Your reputation was of a governor who didn't allow mercy

to cloud his judgement. They call you *Iron Hand*, for the gods'
sake! Yet you shy from taking that hand from its silken glove.'

'Don't mistake my objections for a taste for leniency, my lady.
Mine is not a moral stance. I'd execute the whole population of
Acurial if it furthered our purposes. And I would have ordered
the death of the Principal myself if I thought it would do some
good. It's the strategic line we've taken that I argue with. Your
measures, not least the elimination of Sylandya, have soured the
air and stretched our forces to breaking point.'

'I'm never going to get through to you, am I?'

'I prefer to say that we have an honest disagreement over
policy, ma'am.'

'I don't tolerate disagreement. I tell subordinates where
they've gone wrong and they conform to my will. That's how it
works.' She threw back her head in a gesture of exasperation.
'Oh, why am I wasting my breath on you? And not just you. The
whole system in this place is riddled with far too much free-
thinking, and you're not the only culprit. But that's going to
change. Radically.'

'Ma'am?'

There was a sound at her chamber door. It wasn't so much a
knock as a series of thumps and a coarse scratching. A couple of
seconds later the door opened, and a pair of Jennesta's undead
bodyguards shuffled in carrying something wrapped by a black
winding cloth, not unlike a shroud. They dumped their bundle
at Jennesta's feet and looked up to her as though they were
faithful curs bringing their mistress an outsized bone.

'Ah,' she said, 'the first fruit of my reforms.'

Rather than assign the task to her clumsy servers, she knelt
and began to undo the sheet herself. What she revealed when
she threw it open shocked Hacher to the core.

'Brother . . . Grentor?' he murmured, not entirely sure his
identification was correct.

His uncertainty arose from the state of the cleric's corpse. It
had been horribly mutilated, and to Hacher's disgust some parts

of the body bore signs of having been gnawed upon. A perk allowed Jennesta's zombies, he suspected.

'You appear taken aback, General.'

'Of . . . of course I'm shaken. How did he come to this? Was he a victim of the rebels?' He added the latter in desperate hope that it was the explanation, as opposed to the only other alternative.

'No, he fell victim to me,' she informed him evenly and confirming his fear. 'The leadership of the Order has fallen into as parlous a state as the military. It was time for a change.'

'But this is surely too harsh a way to bring it about?'

'It's the *only* way.' She was talking through gritted teeth. 'I keep *telling* you: a demonstration of ruthlessness is the best remedy for keeping underlings in check. Why should I stand by and watch the Helix squabble and deliberate endlessly before they throw up another Grentor to take this weakling's place? Better that I decide the matter swiftly, with a lesson for them as part of the bargain.'

There was another rap at the door. But this was a proper knock, brisk and crisp.

'Come!' she called.

Hacher's aide, Frynt, entered, giving Jennesta a slight bow of his head as he came in.

The general was confounded to see him. 'Frynt? I thought you were occupied on the west side today.' There was no reply. Hacher's gaze flicked to Grentor's remains. 'I'm afraid the good brother has met a rather unfortunate—'

'Don't bother,' Jennesta said. 'He knows.'

'I . . . I don't understand, my lady.'

'Meet the new Governor of the province of Acurial, and Commander-in-Chief of its army.'

'Am I to understand—'

'You are hereby relieved of all your duties and titles, Hacher. Frynt steps into your clumping boots.'

He turned to his erstwhile aide. 'Frynt? Is this so?'

'Sorry, sir.' He didn't look it. 'But a servant of the empire has a patriotic duty to stand up when called.'

'Or to further their own selfish interests. I thought you were loyal.'

'I am, sir. To the emp—' Jennesta caught his eye. 'To our lady Jennesta and the empire. There is no personal dimension involved.'

'How could you condone this?' Hacher indicated Grentor's body. 'In what warped view can it be considered a positive act?'

'The lady Jennesta has convinced me of the need for change, and for that change to be instigated with a certain . . . vigour.'

'I thought better of you, Frynt. You disappoint me.'

'Then you know how I feel about you,' Jennesta told him. 'There's no point in arguing. Let's save your breath, shall we?'

'Argue I most certainly will, my lady. I'll take this high-handed deed to the ears of the highest in Peczan. If I'm to be sent home in disgrace—'

'Oh no, General; you're not going home. I have a much more useful role for you.'

Her zombie slaves had positioned themselves as the living spoke. Now at her signal they moved in with surprising speed and seized the deposed general. He cried out, protested and cursed, but they held him fast.

Jennesta approached the struggling figure, her hands raised preparatory to casting a glamour. 'As I said,' she intoned, 'let's save your breath.'

Frynt watched, stunned. He didn't know this was going to happen, let alone that he would be obliged to witness the general's fate.

The horror of it gave him an inkling of what it would be like serving his new mistress.

When Hacher started screaming, Frynt closed his eyes.

11

By the end of the third week of the uprising proper, with the ranks of the resistance growing still further, the balance of power started to radically shift. As the Peczan military suffered daily trouncings by armed insurgents, and civil disobedience became widespread, a tipping point was reached. The invaders, until so recently masters of a conquered land, were on the back foot.

Although it was a change the rebels had worked, hoped and died for, even the most optimistic of them were stunned by the speed with which it came about. Ever larger sections of the population shed their former meekness to reveal the inherent fighting spirit that had lain buried for so long. Their pent-up grievance drove a thirst for freedom, and inspired by the radiant presence of Grilan-Zeat, they unleashed a savagery unlike any the humans had faced before.

It was around this time, when fighting was at its most intense, that Wheam took the first small step to redeeming himself.

He had performed competently in the clashes he was allowed to take part in. Or at least he hadn't brought a major disaster down on the warband's heads or got himself killed. Though nor had he managed to slay, wound or greatly inconvenience any of the enemy. Nevertheless it became almost a matter of routine to include him in missions, under the watchful eye of Dallog and other more experienced band members.

The Wolverines had been allotted a role in a raid on a house where army officers were billeted. It didn't go to plan. Due to foresight on the part of the authorities, or possibly because of an informant, a company of soldiers had been concealed nearby. What should have been a clean hit and run attack turned into a pitched battle in one of the few street markets still functioning in the capital. In the process the band was scattered, and Coilla, Haskeer and Wheam found themselves sheltering in a narrow, foul-smelling alley off the main highway.

Haskeer was less than pleased to be stuck with the novice. 'Get in here!' he growled, pulling Wheam back from the alley's mouth. 'You wanna lose your fucking head to an arrow? Not that I should care.'

'Sorry,' the young one replied tremulously.

'Go easy on him,' Coilla said. 'He's still cutting his teeth, remember.'

'Wish he was cutting his damn throat. And what's with *this*?' He slapped at the lute Wheam had strapped to his back. 'What the hell you doing bringing a thing like that to a fight?'

'It's the only way I can be sure not to lose it,' Wheam explained, 'what with us always moving safe houses and—'

'Yeah, yeah. Should have known you'd have some bullshit reason. Just keep it out of my face.'

'Is it clearing out there?' Coilla asked.

Haskeer poked his head round the corner. 'Looks like it.'

'Shall we make a break?'

'Yeah. Our lot are somewhere down on the right.' He turned to Wheam. 'That's *that* way.' He jabbed his thumb rightward. 'Case it's too hard for you to work out.'

'Soon as we're out of here, Wheam, just run,' Coilla told him. 'Fast.'

He nodded.

'Ready?' Haskeer said. 'Right. Three . . . two . . . *go!*'

They came out of the alley at a dash, swerved right and started racing through the debris of the ruined market. There were overturned stalls, and fallen orcs and humans among the trampled fruit and vegetables, broken pottery and strewn clothing.

Coilla looked back. *'We've company!'*

A large gang of soldiers had appeared and were chasing them.

Wheam, at the rear, was struggling to keep up with Coilla and Haskeer.

'Come on!' Coilla urged. 'Move it!'

One trooper, a strong runner, was well ahead of the pack and gaining on Wheam. The tyro himself was flagging, and the soldier got near enough to brush his back with his fingertips. Then he caught hold of the strap holding the lute and wrenched it free. Wheam ran on. The instrument fell clattering to the ground. Two of the strings snapped melodiously. The human, still running hard, kicked the lute out of his path. It sailed across the street and landed with a crash, breaking into pieces.

Wheam stopped, turned and gasped.

Coilla and Haskeer shouted at him. 'Come *on!* Leave it! *Move your arse!'*

The rest of the soldiers were sprinting forward and closing the gap.

'My . . . lute,' Wheam whispered. His eyes moved to the approaching soldier. *'Bastard.'*

An uncharacteristically crazed expression came to Wheam's face. He drew his sword. Seeing this, the running soldier slowed and went for his own.

Wheam charged him, waving his blade and screaming incomprehensibly. He launched himself at the man like a wild thing, thrashing and slashing a storm. Such was the force of his attack that the trooper fell back a pace or two. He had his sword up, but purely defensively.

Coilla and Haskeer had stopped by this time. They watched Wheam laying about the soldier; and beyond, the human's thundering group of comrades, getting nearer.

'We have to go and fetch the little fucker,' Coilla said.

Haskeer made a disturbing noise somewhere deep in his throat and balled his fists. He nodded, curtly.

They unsheathed their weapons and headed back.

Wheam's deranged battering had the trooper retreating at a steady pace. He had no hope of overcoming the pint-sized whirlwind, but could only try to fend him off until his companions arrived.

In the event, it was in vain. Wheam landed a blow on the human's forearm, opening a deep, copious wound. Next he thrust his blade into the man's midriff, setting him staggering. Yelling what sounded like gibberish, though the word *lute* seemed to feature quite a lot, he pummelled his foe mercilessly, shredding flesh and cracking bones.

He was still hacking at the corpse when Coilla and Haskeer got there. Wheam swung round and growled at them, eyes blazing, sword raised.

'*Whoa!*' Coilla shouted. 'It's us!'

Wheam blinked and focused. A little of the bloodlust drained away. He looked at the sword in his hand, then down at his victim.

'Nice one,' Haskeer complimented.

'Don't believe it,' Coilla said. 'A good word for Wheam.'

'Don't sweat it,' Haskeer grated. 'I'm not giving him a fucking medal.'

'Er . . . the soldiers,' Wheam interrupted, pointing along the street with his blade.

They were almost upon them.

'No time to run now,' Coilla decided.

'We stand,' Haskeer agreed.

The three of them stretched out in a line across the road and braced themselves. Near enough that their features could be plainly seen, the soldiers began whooping and waving their swords.

An open wagon careered round the corner from a side street and came to an abrupt halt between the two sides. A couple more followed, loaded with rebels who hastily leapt out to take on the mob of soldiers.

Stryke was in the back of the first wagon, alongside Brelan. He gestured for Haskeer, Coilla and Wheam to jump on. They quickly clambered aboard and the wagon moved off at speed.

Coilla expelled the breath she'd been holding. 'Good timing.'

'Glad you could make it,' Stryke replied. 'How'd you get on?'

'Killed our share,' Haskeer informed him bluntly.

'Wheam gets the gold feather,' Coilla said. 'Claimed his first kill.'

Stryke looked impressed. 'Well done. You'll find it'll come naturally now.'

Wheam mumbled something that included the words *lute* and *bastard*.

'What?'

'Broke my lute,' Wheam grumbled. 'Swine.'

Stryke gave Coilla a quizzical look.

'Human broke his thingamabob,' she explained. 'Lit Wheam's fire.'

'We'll find you another one,' Stryke promised.

'No we fucking won't,' Haskeer exclaimed, alarmed. He saw Stryke's face and shut up.

'Where we going?' Coilla asked.

Brelan spoke for the first time. 'Not far. A place we commandeered near the centre. There's something you Wolverines need to know.'

He wouldn't be drawn on what, and the rest of the journey was spent in silence through streets much emptier than they had been before the uprising took hold.

Soon they came to a large civic hall, complete with columns and surrounded by ornate iron fences. It was an old building, originating in the orcs' distant, more glorious past. Latterly it had been taken over by the occupiers. It was testament to the progress the rebels had made that they had taken it back.

Brelan suggested that Coilla, Wheam and Haskeer clean up and feed themselves while he talked with Stryke. Reluctantly, they obeyed.

Stryke was taken along crowded corridors and past faded embellishments to a room empty but for Chillder.

'We have news,' Brelan stated without preamble.

'So spit it out,' Stryke suggested.

'We thought we'd made things bad for the humans. Now we know it. We've heard that Jennesta's getting ready to flee the city.'

'How do you know this?'

'Oh, the word's reliable. We've an army of informers, some in high places. They say she's got together a bunch of military loyal to her and they're about to make for the south coast, probably to a waiting ship. She might have left already.'

'You can't let her get away.'

'Unfortunately, we can.'

'But—'

Brelan stilled him with a raised hand. 'We can't spare the forces. And when it comes down to it, she's just one individual. It's all the same to us if she's gone or dead. She'll still be out of our way.'

'Brelan, you can't—'

'*But* you and your band are free agents. And we know you have some kind of personal grudge against Jennesta, so—'

'A grudge?'

'We're not stupid. You know, our mother never quite believed your story, and we've always had doubts about where you were from and what you were doing here.'

'There's no need to say anything, Stryke,' Chillder assured him. 'We're grateful enough to you and your band that anything that's gone before isn't important.'

'Will you do it?' Brelan wanted to know. 'We've fresh horses for you, and supplies. What we can't let you have is any of our fighters.'

'Wouldn't want 'em. Though a guide would help.'

'We've maps.'

'Good enough. But I need to talk this over with my band.'

'They're gathered downstairs. Don't be long. Jennesta might already have a head start.'

Stryke was taken to a large chamber that looked as though it had served as a grand feasting room in olden days. All the Wolverines were there, as were Pepperdyne and Standeven. Jugs of water and of wine had been put out for them. Haskeer was sampling the wine. Wheam was being made a fuss over by his fellow tyros, and not a few Wolverines.

'We've got to make this quick,' Stryke informed them briskly. 'You been told what's going on?' Just about everybody shook their heads. 'Story is Jennesta's about to run for the coast. Might have started by now.'

'What are the rebels doing about it?' Coilla wanted to know.

'It's down to us. If we want the mission.'

'Do we fuck,' Haskeer thundered. 'Let's go after the bitch.'

There was a general murmur of agreement.

'Anybody see why we shouldn't?' Stryke said.

No one did.

'So what's the plan?' Pepperdyne asked.

'Wait a minute,' Haskeer objected. 'Who said you were coming along?'

'I'm not wasting time arguing about these two,' Stryke declared, waving a hand at Pepperdyne and Standeven. 'Choice is between leaving them here or taking them with us. I reckon it's better to take 'em.'

'Why?'

'They have a grievance against Jennesta too,' Coilla reminded him. 'Don't you, Jode?'

'Er . . . yes.' He knew this was no time to deviate from the cover story he and Standeven had concocted.

'And we know Jode's more than handy in a scrap,' Coilla added.

'Maybe,' Haskeer granted. 'But why do we need this other one? He's no use in a fight.'

'Talk about me like I'm not here, why don't you,' Standeven protested.

'Yeah, we will,' Stryke assured him. 'I reckon I'd rather have you where I can see you, 'specially given how the rebels feel about that thing with the intruder. Or whatever he was.'

'How many more times,' Standeven responded, 'do I have to explain—'

'We're not going through it again. You two are coming. And like I said, we're not debating this. All of you; get yourselves ready, on the double. We leave as soon as I've seen Brelan and Chillder.'

'I'll come with you,' Coilla decided.

They left the band collecting their gear.

The first thing Chillder said when they found her was, 'You're going?'

Stryke nodded.

'I have a feeling we won't be seeing you again.'

'Who knows?' Strangely, he had a similar feeling.

'I hope we will,' Brelan offered.

'Way things are going,' Coilla reckoned, 'you two are probably going to be too busy running the country.'

'Thanks in part to you. And we're grateful.'

'Yeah, well,' Stryke told them, 'let's not get sloppy. We could lose Jennesta and be back tomorrow.'

'Perhaps.'

'I'd like to have a minute with the Vixens,' Coilla requested.

'Most of them are outside,' Brelan said.

'That all right, Stryke? I'll be quick.'

'Go.'

She wished the twins good luck and went out.

Chillder smiled. 'Whatever your true goal is, Stryke, we hope you reach it.' As he was leaving she added, 'That bit in the prophecy about a legendary band.'

'What of it?'

'Maybe it was true.'

12

There was only one main road leading to the southern coast. Or more accurately only one that was likely to be suitable for the small army accompanying Jennesta. The Wolverines took it.

Before they left, they learned a little more from the rebels' spies. General Hacher, it seemed, had mysteriously disappeared. Having promoted some aide or other to fill the gap, Jennesta had promptly abandoned the successor to his fate. Of more interest to the band was that she had insisted on being transported from the city by carriage, and that supply wagons had been taken along. The Wolverines, on the other hand, travelled light.

After a quarter day's hard riding they got a first glimpse of the sea. Their approach was on high ground, and they could look down on the bay and its tiny harbour.

'No ship,' Coilla said.

'And no Jennesta,' Stryke replied.

'Could she have got away?'

'Doubt it. There's not been time. You'd at least expect to see a sail on the horizon. I reckon the ship she's summoned hasn't got here yet.'

'So where is she?'

'Dunno. Send out scouts.' He had an idea. 'No, wait. *Jup! Over here!*'

The dwarf galloped to him. 'Chief?'

'There's no sign of her.'

'So I see.'

'Think your farsight could help? Might be quicker than searching.'

'I'll give it a try.'

He climbed down from his horse, not without difficulty given his size, watched by an amused Haskeer. Jup flashed him an offensive gesture. Then he walked a little way from the others, knelt down and began worming his fingers into the sandy earth. The tyros and the two humans, unused to Jup's gift, watched with interest.

'What if she *has* gone, Stryke?' Coilla said. 'Maybe she did catch a ship. What then?'

He sighed and gave it some thought. 'Maybe the rebels could help us find out where she's gone, and maybe we could—'

'Follow her to this Peczan empire? A fucking *empire*, Stryke. Want to fight one of those?'

'Or we could go back and carry on with the resistance.'

'We've done about as much for them as we can, and you know it. And what do we do when the revolution's over? Go home, knowing we only coped with half the mission?'

'If she's really got away, we might have to.'

'Shit on that,' Coilla hissed.

Jup shouted and beckoned them over. Stryke gave the order to dismount, and the band went to him.

'Any luck?' Coilla wondered.

Jup nodded. He still had his hand half buried in the ground.

'Where?' Stryke said.

'A little inland and to the west.'

'Sure it's them?'

'Well, farsight isn't like seeing a picture somebody's painted or a page from a book. It. . . it's hard to explain. Just say that what I'm getting is like a spread of gems on a black cloth. There's lots of 'em. That means a sizeable number of living things. Not animals either; they flare differently. And right in the middle of all that there's a big, blood-red diamond, pulsing like . . . well, I don't want to think like what.'

'That's Jennesta?'

'I'd bet a year's pay on it. If we got paid. It has to be them, Stryke. But . . .' He looked troubled.

'What?'

'There's something else. Back the way we came, and further off, but even stronger despite the distance.'

Heads turned in the direction he'd indicated.

'What you saying? Another force?'

'Maybe. I've never seen anything like it before.'

'Could *that* be Jennesta,' Coilla asked, 'and the bunch westward somebody else?'

'No. They have a totally different . . . *flavour*. Jennesta's a murky diamond. Whatever this is, it's . . . a whole string of them, only shining white. If I was using my eyes for this I'd be blinded.'

'Could it be natural?' Stryke said.

'Possibly. Sometimes you get a particularly strong impression from something like a large, fast-flowing river, or certain rich mineral seams. And of course we don't really know Acurial very well; there could be any number of things that affect farsight. Still damn strange though.' He pulled his hand from the earth. 'Like a second opinion from Spurral? Her gift's at least as strong as mine.'

Stryke pondered the offer. 'That won't tell us any more than we know, will it?'

'Unlikely.'

'Then we'll hope it's natural, and harmless. Forget it. It's Jennesta we're concerned about. Let's head west.'

As Jup said the distance wasn't too great, Stryke ordered the band to lead their horses, the better to approach with stealth.

In the event their march took them into the lengthening shadows of evening. Until at last a pathfinder returned noiselessly to tell them the encampment was ahead.

It lay in a grassy hollow at the foot of a chalk cliff. There were guards, but they would be easily dealt with. On their bellies, the band peered down at the camp from the cliff-top. There were perhaps a couple of hundred humans present, mostly uniformed. Three covered wagons stood to one side of the clearing, and a carriage, presumably Jennesta's, was parked near its centre.

'How we going to deal with that many, Stryke?' Coilla said.

'We've faced bigger odds.'

'Hmm. Something wily might be better.'

'You're our Mistress of Strategy. So strat.'

She smiled. 'I'll think of something.'

Stretched out full-length nearby, Spurral idly worked her fingers into the grassy sward. She closed her eyes.

'*Shit!*' The ground could have been boiling hot going by the speed she pulled out her fingers.

'*Ssshhh!* Keep it down,' Jup whispered. He saw how she looked. 'What is it?'

'I just used the sight. Think I picked up what you did, only this seems a hell of a lot stronger and closer. It's really intense, Jup.'

'Where?' Stryke demanded.

She turned and pointed to the darkening plane behind them.

Stryke looked up and down the Wolverine line. 'Anybody see anything out there?'

Nobody could.

'If that's another bunch of Jennesta's supporters,' Coilla speculated, 'it could be a flanking action.'

'That makes us sitting ducks. All of you: back from the edge and down to the plain.'

They withdrew, moving furtively. They knew Jennesta would have more guards stationed around the camp, and probably patrols. The last thing they needed was to alert them.

Back on the plain, they peered into the gathering gloom.

Haskeer glared at Jup. 'You sure your female's right about this? I can't see a fucking thing.'

'*His female*,' Spurral told him, 'is quite capable of speaking for herself; and yes, I'm sure.'

Haskeer grunted but otherwise kept quiet.

They all stood motionless for several silent minutes, surveying the plain. Stryke wasn't alone in starting to think it was some kind of mistake.

It was Pepperdyne who pointed and said, 'What's that?'

Stryke strained his eyes. 'Can't see anything.'

Coilla chimed in with, 'I can! Look, just to the right of that stand of trees.'

Something was coming out of the murk. As it got nearer they realised it was someone mounted on a white horse. A slight figure, lean and straight-backed.

It came near enough for them to make out what kind of being it was.

'What the *fuck?*' Haskeer exclaimed, voicing the amazement they all felt.

The rider was unmistakably of a race that didn't exist on Acurial.

Halting just short of the band, the rider lifted her hand in a gesture of greeting. 'I'm here in peace. I intend you no harm.'

Stryke found his tongue. 'Who are you?'

'My name is Pelli Madayar.'

'You're an elf.'

'Very observant of you.'

'What the *hell* is—'

'There are some things you'll have to take on trust.'

'Like a member of the elven race turning up here?' Coilla said. 'We need more than trust to take that in our stride. Where are you from?'

'That's not important.'

'Is there a tribe of elves living in Acurial we didn't know about?' Stryke persisted.

'As I said, that's not important.'

'If you're not from this land you must have come from . . . elsewhere.'

'As you did.'

Stryke was taken aback by that, as they all were. 'You seem to know a hell of a lot about us.'

'Perhaps. But I repeat: it's not my intention to do you harm.'

Jup said, 'You wouldn't have come from Maras-Dantia, would you?'

'No. My kind are not confined to any one world. No more than orcs are, as you have found.'

'You with Jennesta?' Stryke wanted to know.

'No. My allegiance lies elsewhere and shouldn't concern you.'

'Helpful, ain't she?' Haskeer muttered.

'There are some things it's better you should not know.'

'Is that so? So how about we beat it out of you?'

The elf was unruffled. 'I wouldn't advise you trying that. We don't want to hurt you.'

Haskeer laughed derisively. 'Hurt us? You and whose army?'

No sooner had he spoken than some of the grunts started shouting and pointing along the plain. A group of riders, about equal in number to the Wolverines, was emerging from the shadows. Many in the band went for their swords.

As they slowly advanced, the nature of the newcomers could be seen. There were goblins, trolls and harpies in their ranks, along with centaurs, gremlins, gnomes, satyrs, kobolds, were-beasts, changelings and individuals from many other races, including some the orcs hadn't seen before.

'This just gets creepier,' Jup remarked, clutching his staff with rapidly whitening knuckles.

'Who the hell are you, Madayar, and what do you want?' Stryke demanded.

'We've come to parley.'

'About what?'

'You have certain things that don't rightfully belong to you. Our duty is to retrieve them.'

'What things?'

'She means the stars, Stryke,' Coilla reckoned.

'Yes,' the elf confirmed. 'The artefacts more properly known as instrumentalities. They cannot stay in your possession.'

'They're ours by right!' Stryke thundered. 'We fought and bled for them. Some of us died on the way.'

'Yeah,' Haskeer added, 'you want 'em, you rip 'em from our corpses.'

'You have no understanding of their power.'

'We've got a pretty good idea,' Stryke said.

'No, you haven't. Not their *real* power, and what they represent. What you've seen so far is just a fraction of their true potential.'

'All the more reason not to hand them over to the first bunch of strangers who come begging.'

'We're not begging, we're asking.'

'The answer's no,' Haskeer told her. 'Now fuck off.'

She ignored that. 'The instrumentalities pose a terrible threat. Our task is to make sure they don't fall into the wrong hands.'

'And yours are the right hands, are they?' Stryke came back. 'I don't buy that.'

'In the name of reason, consider what I'm telling you. If you knew what you were meddling in—'

'So tell us.'

Pelli faltered. 'As I said, some things must rest on trust.'

'Not good enough. You want something from orcs, you've got to take it. If you can.'

Her tone took on a more conciliatory note. 'The ferocity of the orcs, and their bravery, are well known, for all that so many malign you. I know your tenacity and of your valour. But you can't hope to prevail against us.'

Stryke looked to the rest of her group, now at a standstill a short arrow's flight away. 'In our time we've killed many from just about all the races in your ranks. Nothing I see makes me think you'd be any different.'

'Don't judge us by your past experience, Stryke. Your instinct is to fight, I understand that. It's your birthright. But you don't have to surrender to that impulse this time. Rather than lift your blades against us, try thinking instead.'

'You saying we can't think?' Haskeer rumbled.

'I'm saying that in the end you have no choice but to surrender the instrumentalities.'

'Surrender's a word we don't grant,' Stryke replied icily.

'Don't see it as surrender, but rather as a triumph of good sense.'

'And if we don't?'

'Then I have to demand that you turn over the artefacts. Now.'

'We don't take demands either.'

'This is pissing me off,' Haskeer fumed. 'You're *pissing me off*, elf!'

'That's your final word?' Pelli asked.

Stryke nodded. 'Any other parleying gets done with blades.'

'I'm sorry we couldn't reach an agreement.'

'What you going to do about it?'

'Reflect, and consult with my companions.' She turned her mount and began to leave.

'You reflect away!' Haskeer shouted after her. '*And all the fucking good it'll do you!*'

In common with others in the band, several of the new intake had nocked arrows when the strange group appeared. Now one of them, raw and jumpy, accidentally let loose his string. The arrow shot past the retreating elf's head so close she felt the air it displaced.

Pelli Madayar swung about to look their way.

Stryke started to shout. He wanted to say that it was an accident. That the band would fight to the last drop of blood and without mercy, but had no need to put an arrow in the back of anybody under a truce. He didn't get the chance.

The elf pointed her hand their way, then swept it left to right, rapidly. A wave of energy, red-tinged, flew at the band as fast as thought. It hit them with the force of a tempest. All of them. The entire company went down, knocked off their feet as surely as if they'd been struck with mallets. With it, the wave brought pain that coursed through their bodies for a good couple of seconds.

'Gods,' Coilla groaned as she struggled to get up.

'*Stay low!*' Stryke hissed. 'All of you: head for the tree-line. But keep down!'

They scurried for the trees, bent double, trying to zigzag and make themselves harder targets. Halfway there, the air above them lit up with intense, multicoloured beams of light. Rays crackling all around them, they put on a burst of speed and made it into the tiny wood.

'Anybody hit?' Stryke panted.

Miraculously, it seemed no one had been.

'Who the fuck *are* this bunch?' Haskeer said.

'Doesn't matter. Main thing is getting out of the way of their magic.'

'A frontal assault's not on then?' Coilla ventured.

'What do you think? Magic that strong, we'd be lucky to get ten paces.'

'They're coming!' Dallog warned.

The bizarre multi-species company was approaching, riding in a line, steadily.

'We'll get to safer ground and figure out how to fight this,' Stryke decided.

Jup, who with a couple of scouts had penetrated the wood further than the others, came dashing back. He was breathing heavily. 'Not that way. Jennesta's troops.'

'Shit,' Coilla cursed. 'They must have picked up on the racket.'

'Great,' Haskeer grumbled. 'Jennesta and a couple of hundred humans that way, the freak circus over here, and us in the middle.'

'What do we do, Stryke?' Pepperdyne badgered.

'Depends how you want to die.'

Coilla shook her head. 'No, Stryke. There's one other course.'

He didn't have to be told what that was. But he hesitated.

They could hear Jennesta's army now, tramping through the wood and making no effort at furtiveness. The riders were much nearer, too.

'Hurry up, Stryke!' Coilla pleaded.

He reached for the pouch where he kept the stars.

Standeven stared, open mouthed. 'Surely you're not going to—'

'*Shut it*,' Stryke told him as he began pulling out the artefacts. His other hand went to the amulet at his throat.

'There's no time!' Coilla yelled.

The Gateway Corps had reached the tree-line. In the other direction the foremost of Jennesta's troops could be seen moving through the wood, a spit away.

Stryke let go of the amulet and concentrated on the stars, quickly slotting them together in a random pattern.

The whole band instinctively gathered about him.

Standeven started to shout. The words were unintelligible and slick with panic. It almost drowned out the noise Wheam was making.

Stryke took one last look at the comet through the branches overhead. It shone like a night-time sun.

Then he clicked the final instrumentality into place.

13

The bottom had dropped out of the universe.

They were living sparks, sucked through an endless, serpentine tunnel of light. On its supple walls flashed endless images of other realities, moving so fast they were almost a blur. And beyond, outside that terrible shaft, an even more breath-taking actuality; a limitless canopy smothered in countless billions of stars.

The band's only sensation was of helplessly falling. A ceaseless and unremitting plunge into the black maw of the unknown.

Then, after an eternity, they dropped towards a particular chasm, a whirlpool of sallow, churning light.

It swallowed them.

They landed hard. The collision with what seemed to be solid ground was bone-shaking. But they had no leisure to recover from the impact. Wherever they had fetched up was hostile. Murderously so.

The place was in the grip of a violent sandstorm. Trillions of grains of sand lashed them like shards of glass or tiny diamonds, bathing them in pain. The sand not only pummelled them, it all but blinded them; they could see practically nothing. It was hard to stand, let alone walk. The heat was terrific, and in no way mitigated by the never-ending, roaring wind. Even for a group of warriors as toughened as the Wolverines, it was intolerable.

Coilla was vaguely aware of other figures clustered about her. She happened to be standing next to Stryke when he slotted the instrumentalities together. If she hadn't, she probably wouldn't have been able to find him now. But by luck, when she stretched out her hand she brushed his arm. She took it in an iron grip.

Thrusting her mouth to his ear, she bellowed, '*Get us out of here!*'

Coilla had no way of knowing that was exactly what he was trying to do. The cluster of stars was still in his hands, and hampered by being unable to see what he was doing, he was battling to rearrange them.

After what seemed an agonisingly long time, choking with the sand filling his mouth and nose, he managed to slot them into another random assembly.

The void snatched them again. They were back in the swirling, never-ending spillway, taking a stomach-churning tumble to another unknown goal.

The band was pitched into a blizzard, exchanging insufferable heat for unspeakable cold. All they could see was white. Stinging snow pricked them like innumerable needles. The temperature was so low they found it difficult to breathe. Stryke's fingers froze instantly, and it was all he could do to manipulate the stars. Teeth chattering, hands shaking uncontrollably, he finally altered them.

Once more, the cosmic trapdoor flipped open.

They were standing in torrential rain in a landscape that seemed to consist solely of mud that was nearly liquid itself. The air was uncomfortably humid. In seconds they realised that the rain was corrosive. It nipped at their flesh and singed their clothing as though it was vitriol. Stryke manipulated the stars.

A jungle embraced them. At first it seemed endurable. Then gigantic swarms of flying insects appeared, tenacious and hungry. They covered the band, fibrous wings beating, stingers seeking unprotected skin. Stryke manoeuvred the stars into another configuration.

They were deposited on a vast, featureless plain, the only variation being a distant range of blue-black mountains. Three suns beat down, one of them bloody red. Of more immediate import were the two armies the Wolverines found themselves between. One consisted of creatures resembling giant lizards, with purple hides and flicking, barbed tongues. The other was made up of beasts that seemed to be a cross between bears and apes, only with four arms. Each horde numbered in the hundreds of thousands, and they were moving rapidly forward, with the warband squarely in their path, like a nut in a vice. Stryke fiddled with the instrumentalities.

Icy salt spray splashed their faces. They were on a tiny rock in the middle of a turbulent ocean, battered by winds and towering waves, beneath an angry sky. The rock was jagged and slippery, and the band clung on to each other for fear of falling and being swept away. Stryke acted.

He kept on readjusting the stars as they were transported from world to world in search of somewhere bearable.

In dizzying succession they flashed in and out of lands of startling diversity, including some they found incomprehensible as well as hostile. In one, they were attacked by carnivorous birds; another was an environment that had a noxious gas for its atmosphere that they were lucky to escape in time. They witnessed abundant orc-sized fish emerging from a huge lake, revealing legs, and jaws bristling with fangs; sentient snakes as big as elephants, devouring each other; a land of perpetual earthquakes where enormous fissures opened and closed with frightening rapidity; a world stifled by sulphur and riddled with blue lava flows; a mighty river inhabited by multi-tentacled beasts with the faces of rodents; gigantic flies that supped on struggling spiders in sticky webs that spanned valleys; a place where great prides of felines waged war amongst themselves; rampaging worms as large as mature oaks; dominions ruled by plagues of rats, and on and on.

Eventually they materialised somewhere that didn't seem immediately threatening. It was a dead world. They couldn't tell if the desolation was the result of war or natural disaster, but it seemed complete. Not far away stood acres of debris and twisted uprights, just recognisable as the ruins of a city. There was no sign of life anywhere, not even vegetation, which the soil looked incapable of supporting in any event. Everything was grey and spent.

The Wolverines stood wordlessly for several minutes, in anticipation of something unfriendly happening. When it didn't, they did more than relax. They collapsed exhaustedly. They were in a sorry state; drenched, tattered, bruised and bleeding. The tyros were near unhinged, and Standeven was a wreck. Some of the band were vomiting. Others nursed wounds or crouched with their heads in their hands.

'*That was . . . one . . . hell of a . . . ride,*' Coilla said when she stopped fighting for breath.

'*Couldn't. . . set the . . . stars . . . properly,*' Stryke gasped back. '*No . . . chance to.*'

She started to pull herself together, as most of the others were. 'I . . . know. Who would . . . have thought. . . so many . . . of the worlds were . . . so shitty?'

'Least it looks safe here.'

'Maybe.' She surveyed the barren landscape suspiciously.

'We'll rest for a bit, tend wounds. Then I'll fit the stars for Ceragan.'

She nodded and perched herself on a half-melted rock, head down, arms dangling.

As soon as he could, Stryke got some of the recovering grunts to mount guard. He had Dallog look at injuries, none of which fortunately called for major treatment, and ordered iron rations to be broken out.

They spent the next hour or more recuperating and getting their heads straight. During which, Jup came to Stryke with a question.

'What do we do about the humans?'

'Do?'

'Yeah. You planning on taking them back to Ceragan with you? Come to that, what about me and Spurral?'

'I've not been thinking straight,' Stryke confessed. 'That's a problem I hadn't weighed.'

'Can't be blamed for that. But what *are* you going to do with us non-orcs?'

'You and Spurral are welcome to join us in Ceragan. You'd be the only dwarfs, but you wouldn't be without comrades.'

'That's a generous offer, Stryke, and I thank you for it. But I'm guessing it's not one you'd be happy making to Pepperdyne and Standeven.'

'No, there'd be no place there for *them*. But suppose we took them back to Maras-Dantia?'

'*That* I hadn't thought of. Seems right, seeing as it's where you picked them up in the first place.'

'We could do the same for you. Get you back to your own kind.'

Jup sighed. 'I dunno, Stryke. We had good reasons for leaving. I'm not sure either of us would relish going back, for all that we were born there. Maras-Dantia's fit only to break hearts these days.'

'Then my offer of Ceragan stands. Who knows? Maybe we can figure out how to use the stars to find a dwarf world for you.'

Jup grinned. 'Trying to get rid of us already and we're not there yet. But I reckon we've got no real option. Though I've doubts about us ever finding a dwarf needle in that haystack of worlds we've just seen.'

'Maybe. Anyway, that's settled. Maras-Dantia for the humans and you two with us.'

'I'll have to talk it over with Spurral, mind. But I reckon she'll agree with me.'

Stryke nodded. 'Don't be too long about it. I want to get out of this place.'

The dwarf glanced at the bleakness surrounding them. 'You're not alone.'

He left.

Coilla took his place. 'Had any ideas on who they might have been?'

'Who?'

'You're not working with a sharpened sword yet, are you, Stryke? Who do you think I mean? That mixed bunch of races that tried frying us, of course.'

'No. We've seen a lot we can't explain these last few hours; they got kind of pushed out of my head.'

'But what do you reckon? Bandits? Mercenaries?'

'With the way their ranks were made up? And with magic? Really *powerful* magic? I've never seen any marauders like them before.'

'And all they wanted was the stars. Why?'

He shrugged. 'Damned if I can figure it.'

'Know what I can't understand? Why didn't that elf . . . what was her name?'

He thought about it. 'Madayar. Pelli Madayar.'

'Right. Why didn't she kill us when she had the chance? I reckon she could have, with magic that strong. Don't you?'

Stryke nodded.

'Yet she just gave us a bit of a knock. And those magic beams or whatever they were; funny how none of them took any of us out, isn't it?'

'It does seem . . . odd,' he conceded. 'Maybe she lied about being with Jennesta, or maybe they *were* mercenaries who saw the value of the stars.'

'How did they know we had them? Or even that they existed?'

'I . . . don't know. But does it really matter? How likely is it we'll run into them again?'

'There's something you're forgetting. That Madayar more or less told us they'd come from somewhere else, *like we did*. That can mean only one thing, Stryke. They can world-hop, too.'

'But they'd have to have stars to do that.'

'Unless there's another way we don't know about. Mind you, who says we've got the only set there is?'

'If they've stars of their own, why did they want ours?'

'Search me. Maybe they collect the bloody things. What I'm trying to say is that if they have stars, could be we haven't seen the last of them.'

She left him to ponder that.

Shortly after, he gathered the band.

'We've had an interesting day,' he told them, raising a few wry laughs. 'But now we've had a chance to steady ourselves I can use the stars to take us where we want to go.'

'Where's that?' Standeven asked.

'Us and the dwarfs to our world, Ceragan. You two back where we found you.'

'Centra— Maras-Dantia?'

'Unless you want to stay here.'

'But . . .'

'But what? Enjoy our company so much you can't leave us, is that it? Or maybe you'd prefer being taken back to Acurial. I'm sure the orcs there'd be glad to see you again.'

'Don't we get a say in this?'

'What say do you want? Stay here or go back to Maras-Dantia. That's your choice.'

'I think you're being very high-handed,' Standeven protested, 'and you should at least—'

'Let it go,' Pepperdyne told him. He knew his one-time master still harboured thoughts of gaining the instrumentalities, and thought even less of the idea now than he had originally.

'When I want *your* opinion—'

'*Let it go*,' Pepperdyne repeated coldly, laying an emphasis on the words that he hoped would convey to Standeven exactly what it really was he should let go of. 'We're lucky Stryke doesn't leave us here. Or somewhere worse.'

'Too fucking right you are,' Haskeer interjected. 'Though I reckon it's what we ought to do.'

'We do things my way,' Stryke reminded him. 'Maras-Dantia it is.' He took out the instrumentalities and laid them on a rock beside him. Then he reached into his shirt for the pendant. 'Get ready to brace yourselves.'

He was becoming more adept at fitting the stars together, and now he did it with great care, careful to follow exactly the order that would get them to their old home world.

Just before he clacked the fifth one into place he took a look at the faces staring at him. Many were apprehensive. Several, notably Standeven and Wheam, wore expressions that were positively sickly. Stryke couldn't altogether blame them. He wasn't looking forward to what came next himself.

He slammed the star into position.

Reality instantly dissolved and the now familiar, dread sensation of falling was on them again. They were drawn through the hellish kaleidoscope with no more means of controlling their passage than if they had been leaves in a gale. The only scrap of comfort they had was knowing where they'd end up.

Several lifetimes later, as it seemed, they came to themselves in another actuality.

They were standing on a large circular rock that had been raised like a dais and smoothed flat. The rock was inside a colossal cavern. Surrounding it were a hundred or more startled dwarfs, apparently in the throes of some kind of ritual. Stryke began fumbling with the stars. The dwarfs moved faster. Scores of them swarmed up onto the rock podium, and in a second the tips of multiple spears were pressing against the Wolverines' throats.

'I don't think this is Maras-Dantia,' Coilla said.

14

Two things saved the Wolverines' lives: their seemingly miracu-lous arrival and the presence of Jup and Spurral.

All the dwarfs surrounding the warband were male. They wore kilts woven from coarse material, and sandals, but were bare-chested. Many had necklaces of animal teeth, and a few sported brightly coloured feather headdresses. They were armed with daggers and the stout, bone-tipped spears that currently menaced the warband.

It was obvious that the dwarfs had never seen anything like orcs before, and regarded them with open amazement. The humans they looked upon with disdain, if not actual hatred. But they were confounded most by Jup and Spurral, and it was apparently because of them that they stayed their hand. They either gaped at the couple with something like awe or avoided their gaze almost shyly, keeping their eyes downcast.

'They seem 'specially taken with you and Spurral, Jup,' Stryke said, a spear pressing against his throat. 'Talk to them.'

Jup looked doubtful but gave it a go. 'Er . . . We come in peace.'

'That was original,' Coilla muttered.

'Doesn't look like it worked,' Stryke said.

The dwarfs had blank expressions.

Jup tried again, carefully mouthing, 'We are friends. There's no need to fight us.'

'Kill us, you mean,' Coilla remarked under her breath.

Still the dwarfs were baffled.

'Try Mutual,' Stryke suggested.

Jup raised a sceptical eyebrow. 'Really?'

'Got a better idea?'

'We mean you no harm and we're here as friends,' Jup said in Mutual, the common tongue used by most of the races of Maras-Dantia.

Comprehension dawned on the dwarfs.

One of them, an older individual with a particularly impressive headdress, and presumably some kind of elder, replied in Mutual, 'You come from the sky?'

'Well, what do you know,' Haskeer whispered hoarsely.

Jup glanced Stryke's way for a lead. Stryke managed to give him the tiniest of nods.

'Yes,' Jup announced, feeling faintly ridiculous. 'Yes, we are here from the sky.' He raised his eyes heavenward, theatrically.

A chorus of gasps and exclamations of wonderment came from the dwarfs.

'These are your servants?' the elderly one asked, indicating the band.

'Oh, yeah,' Jup confirmed. 'They serve my every need.'

'And these?' He pointed his spear at Pepperdyne and Standeven. 'They are your prisoners?'

'Uhm. Well . . .'

'Do you want them executed now?'

'Exe— No. *No.* They're . . . I've decided they should be my slaves.'

'It's never wise to allow these creatures to live.'

'With you there,' Haskeer agreed in an undertone.

The humans, unfamiliar with Mutual, hadn't a clue about what was being said.

'What's going on?' Pepperdyne asked Stryke softly.

'Don't worry about it,' he mouthed back.

Jup having faltered somewhat, Spurral decided to push their luck, and took a hand.

'We choose to allow them their lives,' she told the elder imperiously, 'for the time being. Now release us. *Immediately!*'

The elder flinched, then looked alarmed. He snapped something to his fellows in their own, slightly guttural tongue.

The spears were lowered and the dwarfs stepped back from the Wolverines. The dwarfs moved away from the two humans more reluctantly, and carried on eyeing them with suspicion. Stryke quickly stuffed the instrumentalities into his pouch, hoping no one had noticed.

'You must crave sustenance after your journey,' the elder stated ingratiatingly. 'Please allow us to lay humble offerings before you.'

'Let us at it,' Jup replied, trying for an air of command.

The elder ushered them down from the dais and led them away from it. To the band's bemusement, dwarfs bowed as they passed. Not a few prostrated themselves. Pepperdyne and Standeven were viewed less respectfully. They got glares.

'They think we're gods,' Coilla whispered.

'Band of heroes,' Haskeer boasted, 'that's us.'

'Don't get above yourself,' Jup said. He gave Spurral's arm a pat. '*We're* the gods. You're just a servant.'

Powerless to start anything, Haskeer clenched both his teeth and his fists.

It was obvious that the cavern was a natural formation. Enormous and cone shaped, it had a round opening in its roof, far above. They could see blue sky through it.

They were taken to one of a number of tunnel openings. The passage was wide and sloped upwards. Their way was lit by flaming brands fixed to the walls. Soon they came to where two tunnels crossed, and they turned right, still climbing. Several more twists and turns brought them to daylight.

They emerged at a high point, giving them a perfect view of where they were. It was a tropical island; sizeable, but not so big that they couldn't see its limits. Around two-thirds of it was swathed in lush jungle. There were white beaches against which an azure sea gently lapped.

The dominant features were a pair of volcanoes towering out of the jungle. One was considerably taller than the other, and strands of grey smoke rose from both. Looking back, the band realised that they had just come out of a third volcano, bigger than either of the other two. The only difference being that it was extinct.

The day was warm, getting on for hot, and no cloud marred the sky. As the Wolverines followed their elderly guide they started to attract a retinue of dwarfs. There were gangs of children, and for the first time, females. Like their men-folk, they went bare-chested. Jup found that of particular interest until Spurral elbowed him sharply and cooled his ardour.

Coilla gave Stryke a nudge too, but more gently and in order to draw his attention to something. He followed her eyes. High up on the volcano they'd just exited there was a broad ledge on the seaward side. Standing on it was a line of five or six trebuchets. The catapults were large, similar to ones the orcs had seen, and used, in sieges.

A little further on they passed a low wooden structure not unlike a squat barn. Its doors were closed and half a dozen stern-faced dwarfs stood guard outside.

The crowd stared, grinned, laughed and shouted as the procession made its way to a clearing. Dozens of huts of various dimensions stood there. They were taken to the biggest, a one-storey affair on piles, with a porch on its front. The elder threw open its door and welcomed them in.

The longhouse was generous enough in size that even the Wolverines and their hangers-on didn't overfill it.

'My own dwelling,' the elder explained. 'I trust it isn't too humble for you.'

'It'll do,' Jup said.

There was a gaggle of females present. Members of the elder's family perhaps, or his wives or servants. They were gaping open-mouthed at the strange visitors. The elder snapped something at them and they fled, giggling, out of the open door.

'I will send you refreshments,' the elder told them. 'Is there anything else you need?'

'No,' Spurral replied in her queenly tone. 'You may leave us now.'

The old dwarf bowed awkwardly and backed out.

When he'd gone, Haskeer said, 'Fuck me.'

'You've a skill, Spurral,' Stryke told her. 'You should have been a troubadour.'

'They seemed to think we were somebody important. I just played on it.'

Haskeer took in their surroundings. 'Not bad, this place. Better than some of the shit-holes we've seen lately.'

'Yes, it's all very fine,' Coilla said, 'but what the *fuck* are we doing here? Stryke, how come we're not in Maras-Dantia?'

'I don't know.'

'Did you make a mistake setting the stars?'

'I'd swear I didn't.'

'One way to be sure,' Dallog offered. 'Try them again now.'

'No,' Stryke decided. 'If they got it wrong this time they could again.'

'And we might not end up somewhere as sweet,' Jup finished for him. 'There are worse places for a billet.'

'Maybe it's not as sweet as you think,' Coilla argued. 'Did you notice those catapults? They have to be here for a reason.'

'And they've got something in that hut back there they don't want us to see,' Pepperdyne added.

'I agree with Jup,' Stryke declared. 'We'll hold up here.'

'How long for?' Coilla wanted to know.

'For as long as I need to think about why the stars got it wrong. We're all bushed. It won't hurt us to take a furlough here.'

The door opened and a multitude of female dwarfs came in bearing platters of food. They laid out a feast for them and withdrew bowing. The timber dining table that dominated one end of the room was laden with breads, fish and fruit, much of a kind none of them recognised. There were also flasks of something that resembled rice wine. Pepperdyne, born an islander, told them he was pretty sure it was distilled from seaweed. That made some of them doubtful, but it tasted good.

Sitting at the table eating their fill, which was considerable, they allowed themselves to relax a little. Though Stryke did take the precaution of stationing privates by the door and the several windows. The guards took heaped dishes of food with them and stuffed themselves as they stood watch.

'What do you think of this as a dwarf world?' Dallog asked of Jup and Spurral.

'Well, they don't seem as advanced as our tribes in Maras-Dantia,' Jup replied, 'but it's pleasant enough.'

'If you happen to be a fucking god,' Haskeer murmured.

'Any more of your insolence and I'll have you whipped, underling,' the dwarf teased.

'We're not gonna be here for ever,' Haskeer promised darkly. 'Just you wait.'

Jup laughed in his face.

'That language you were speaking,' Pepperdyne said. 'What was that all about?'

'In Maras-Dantia, or at least what used to be our part of it,' Stryke informed him, 'just about everybody spoke Mutual. How else would so many different races figure out each other?'

'And now we've found it here,' Coilla remarked. 'How can that be?'

'Looks like there's more moving between worlds than we thought.'

'How long was it used in Maras-Dantia?' Pepperdyne asked.

'For ever,' Coilla told him. 'Nobody knows who first thought of it.'

'So maybe it didn't start there. If the worlds have bled into each other more than we know, it could have originated anywhere.'

'Possible, I suppose.' Coilla knew that the elder races weren't native to Maras-Dantia; it was the humans' world by birthright. It seemed logical to her that when the various races were inadvertently deposited there, long ago, they might well have brought something like Mutual with them. But she didn't mention any of that. Instead, she said, 'From what we heard, it seems humans aren't too well liked in these parts, Jode.'

'We gathered that much.'

'Yeah, well, I think it goes a bit deeper than a tiff. Take care.'

'Ahhh, ain't it cute?' Haskeer mocked. 'She's worried about her little pet.'

'You'll be worried about the one between your legs if you don't pipe down,' she promised him.

Nobody spoke for a moment until Wheam wondered, 'How do you think they're getting on in Acurial?'

'Just fine, I should think,' Stryke reckoned.

'You can't help thinking what they made of us, can you?' Dallog speculated.

'Maybe we'll go down in their history books,' Coilla said, only half seriously.

'Yeah!' Haskeer enthused. 'As a band of legendary heroes who—'

He was drowned out by the catcalls of the rest of the band.

'I think you're right about the resistance winning out there,' Pepperdyne said when it quietened. 'I'm more puzzled by who that bunch were who wanted your stars, Stryke.'

That put a damper on the band.

'Damned if we can figure it out,' Stryke confessed. 'But if they really did come from somewhere other than Acurial, like that elf said, they could turn up here. We're going to have to be alert for that.'

'Not much of a furlough then,' Coilla came back dryly.

'If these dwarfs don't try to stop us we'll find ourselves a good defensible hold-out first thing. We'll be better prepared if they come again.'

'Against the magic they have?' She paused a moment before braving the next thing she wanted to say. 'Stryke, about the stars . . .'

'What about them?'

'Given they're precious, and now we might have this new bunch trying to get their hands on them, why don't you divide them up between five of us and—'

'No.'

'Don't just dismiss it, Stryke. It could be a good way of protecting the things.'

'If we lost just one, that's enough to make the others useless.'

'This isn't just about you, you know. The stars are our only way home too.'

'No Coilla. Not after what happened last time.'

'You're blaming me for that, are you?'

'You know I'm not. How could I when I lost four of them to Jennesta myself?'

'So you won't consider it?'

'It's better my way.'

'You can be such a stubborn pig sometimes!' she flared. 'When are you going to get it through your head that—'

There was a commotion outside. They heard shouts and screams.

Rushing to the door, they saw dozens of dwarfs running in all directions in panic.

The band flooded out of the longhouse. At sea, a flotilla of small boats was heading for the shore. In the distance, a ship was at anchor.

The Wolverines headed for the beach. There were more dwarfs there, desperate to get away from the advancing boats. They stopped a few to ask what was going on, but got no sense out of them.

'Look!' Coilla yelled, pointing at the nearest boats.

They were manned by humans.

'I'm guessing it's not a social visit either,' Stryke observed.

'Now we know why the dwarfs aren't keen on Jode and Standeven.'

A number of male dwarfs were now running onto the beach as opposed to away from it. They were armed with their spears.

'What do we do?' Dallog asked.

'We make a stand with them,' Stryke replied, 'what else?'

'Pity they've got nobody operating those trebuchets.' The corporal pointed to the ledge on the volcano.

'No time. They've been caught unawares.'

'Yeah,' Coilla agreed, 'probably because they were too concerned with us.'

'Here they come!' Haskeer bellowed.

The first of the humans were wading ashore.

'So let's get to it,' Stryke ordered, drawing his sword. '*Come on!*' He led them into the surf. Only Standeven held back, skulking far up the beach.

They met the invaders in knee-deep water and laid into them. The humans were shocked to be facing an unknown race, and one so ferocious, and were equally dismayed to find Pepperdyne among their attackers. That gave the band an initial edge. Soon, the surf was stained red.

But it didn't take long for Stryke to realise he'd made an error. This wasn't the incomers' main or only force. Further along the shoreline more boats had come round the island's curve. Humans had already got well inland in that direction. They were fighting dwarfs on the beach, and the dwarfs weren't coming off best.

Stryke ordered some of the band to stay where they were and finish off the dwindling number of humans still exchanging blows. He took the rest up the beach to confront the bigger influx happening there. Spurral, who proved a good runner, had seen what was happening and streaked off even before he issued the order. She was well to the fore and not far short of a group of humans wading ashore.

Running abreast with Haskeer, Jup and Coilla, and the other band members on their heels, Stryke yelled a warning. A party of humans who must already have penetrated the island's interior were returning to the beach, and their path crossed the Wolverines'. The humans, perhaps twenty strong, were dragging and carrying screaming dwarfs towards the waves.

Stryke's band and the kidnappers all but collided. Startled by the sudden appearance of a group of creatures they were unlikely to have encountered before, the humans let go of their captives to defend themselves. The freed dwarfs, most of them young, began fleeing back into the jungle.

The warband tore into the boatmen, savagely hacking them down. Pepperdyne, taking a great swipe with his blade, parted one of them from his head. Haskeer, employing both hatchet and knife, hurtled into a duo simultaneously, stabbing one and braining the other. Dallog plunged his spear into a foe with such force it lifted the man off his feet. Even Wheam gave a good account of himself, in Wheam terms. He managed no fatalities, but attacked with gusto and inflicted mean wounds on a couple of opponents.

They worked as fast as they could to get through the obstruction and reach the greater number of humans beyond, where more struggling dwarfs were being hurled into the humans' bobbing craft.

As the last man in their path was downed and dispatched, several of the grunts started raising a clamour. Stryke and the others looked to where they were frantically pointing.

Out in deep water, Spurral was grappling with three men. As the band watched, they pummelled her senseless and flung her into a boat, then hauled themselves aboard.

'*Shit!*' Jup cried. He began running.

The band took off in his wake, arms pumping, heads down.

A burly human tried blocking Jup's way. He cracked the

man's skull open with his staff while barely breaking step. He ran on, splashing into the water.

'Spurral!' he shouted. '*Spurral!*'

The boat she was in had begun moving away, four men pulling mightily on the oars.

Jup was wading now, finding the going increasingly harder the further he got. Breakers battered him and he almost lost his footing.

The others were close behind. By the time they caught up with him he was more than chest high and battling impotently against the water's sluggish impediment.

They saw Spurral's boat, along with dozens of others bearing snatched dwarfs, rapidly departing.

All they could do was watch helplessly as it headed for the ship waiting on the horizon.

15

Jup was frantic, and seethed with a cold fury, but knew that keeping his head was the best hope of finding Spurral.

Stryke did the logical thing and ordered the band to find a boat. They scoured the shore and came up with nothing except small canoes, totally unsuited for venturing out to sea. He considered building a boat, or possibly a raft. But with time at a premium, and his doubts about whether they could construct something truly seaworthy for who knew how long a voyage, that looked impractical.

Boat or no, their biggest problem was finding out where Spurral might have been taken. Jup's farsight was useless because a vast body of water like the ocean, he explained, gave off an energy of its own that swamped the pinpricks generated by living beings riding it. So they needed the dwarfs' help. Which proved harder than they first thought, simply because the natives seemed to have disappeared. Some had obviously been taken by the raiders. They could only guess that the rest had gone into hiding, probably in the depths of the jungle, or perhaps in the labyrinth of tunnels that riddled the dead volcano.

Stryke decided to concentrate their efforts on finding them. Surveying the terrain from the highest point they could easily get to, which turned out to be the outcropping where the catapults stood, he hastily scrawled a crude map of the island. This he divided into more or less equal segments. Then he split the band into eight groups of four or five members each and allotted them a segment to search.

His own group included Jup, Coilla and Reafdaw, who was one of the Wolverines' more experienced scouts. Stryke made a point of having Haskeer lead one of the groups assigned to the farthest tip of the island. He wanted to keep him and Jup apart for now, given their tendency to aggravate each other. That was a complication they could do without.

Stryke's team had an area of jungle to search. It wasn't one of the densest parts, and they were able to pace out most of it, looking for any sign that might betray the dwarfs.

'Those humans had to be slavers,' Coilla said as they trudged. 'No other reason I can see for taking prisoners alive.'

'Oh, great,' Jup groaned. 'And that's supposed to cheer me, is it?'

'Yes. Slaves have a value. It doesn't serve the slavers to be careless with their wares.'

'Assuming they *are* slavers. Who knows what goes on in this world?'

'I think Coilla's right,' Stryke said. 'They sought out the young and fit, so it figures. Spurral might not be having too good a time of it, but they don't gain by harming her too much.'

'Not *too* much,' the dwarf repeated bitterly. 'This isn't lifting me, Stryke.'

'I know. But don't we like to try working out the odds before any mission?'

'Yes,' he sighed, 'I suppose we do.'

'Well,' Coilla remarked by way of steering the subject elsewhere, 'one thing we've found is that this world isn't made up of just dwarfs.'

'Worse luck.'

'And if there's humans here too,' she went on, 'there could be other races.'

'Like Maras-Dantia?' Stryke said. 'The way they got here, I mean.'

'Could be. From what we know, Maras-Dantia was like a big sink hole once, sucking in all those races, including ours. Could have been the same here.'

'Why does it have to have been once?' Jup wondered, taking an interest despite his worry. 'You mean some time in the past, right?'

She nodded. 'Has to have been. All the races were too well rooted. That must take time. Other thing is, no new races were turning up out of nowhere. We never heard of anything like that, did we?'

'Doesn't mean to say it only happened way back in the past and can't happen now. Why did it stop?'

'It'd take better heads than ours to know that.'

'Maybe it's happening all the time,' Jup persisted. 'If not in Maras-Dantia, in other places. Like here.'

'Could that have been how that crew who wanted the stars got to Acurial?' Coilla wondered. 'By chance? You know, perhaps they fell into—'

'Don't think so,' Stryke interrupted, 'not from what Pelli Madayar said. I got the sense they weren't the sort to be tossed around like corks.'

Reafdaw had been walking ahead, scanning the greenery. Now he stopped and held up a hand. They cut the talk and froze. He used gestures to indicate a point on the jungle floor that to them looked no different to any other. They quietly caught up with him.

He pointed downward. Two things became clear with scrutiny. There was trampled vegetation in a particular spot. And when they grew accustomed to the scene they could make out a patch of ground that had a phoney look to it. It was just about possible to see the lines that hinted at something like a trapdoor. They silently positioned themselves around it, weapons drawn. Stryke began issuing orders via signing.

Jup and Reafdaw crouched and inserted their blades into the

almost invisible slits. On a signal they levered the trap out of true, and with Stryke and Coilla's help, lifted and tossed it aside.

A piercing scream came from the pit they exposed.

They looked down. A young female dwarf was cowering below in a hollow not much bigger than herself. She wasn't alone. Three dwarf children, all males, clung to her. Their dirty, upturned faces were terrified.

Jup spoke softly to them in Mutual, assuring them they were safe. The orcs stepped back out of sight while he did it, to save spooking them. At last Jup won their confidence, and got them to accept that the orcs were friendly. They were helped out of their dank pit and given water, which they bolted.

Stryke judged it best to take them to the elder's longhouse. On the way they were silent, and noticeably still fearful. But the orcs, and even Jup, despite his anxiety, held back on questioning them.

Being in the more familiar surroundings of the village, and then the longhouse, seemed to reassure the quartet. If not exactly relaxing, they at least became easier in themselves. They were given food, and more to drink.

The girl's name was Axiaa, or something very much like it, and she was related in some obscure way to the three children. Obscure because, as she haltingly explained, in the closed community of an island, everyone was related.

The boys were called Grunnsa, Heeg and Retlarg, as far as Stryke and the others could nail it. Their names didn't translate to Mutual, and the dwarfs' throaty first language made understanding no easier. Grunnsa was the oldest, at ten or eleven seasons. Heeg and Retlarg were perhaps seven or eight, and brothers. Grunnsa was their cousin, and possibly their uncle too, such were the island's tangled relationships.

It seemed that the brothers' parents had been taken by the humans. Grunnsa's might have been too, or could be in hiding somewhere. It was unclear.

'Who were those raiders, Axiaa?' Stryke asked.

Being addressed by an orc, and the servant of a god to boot, made her a little shy, but she answered, 'Gatherers.'

'Seen them before?'

'Oh, yes. They come from time to time and take away some of our kin. Never all. They like for there to be more when they return.'

'Why do they take you?'

'To trade. Sell. For work on other islands.'

'Are there many other islands?'

'Yes. Many.'

'The dwarfs have visited them?'

'A few have. The brave ones. But most of us never leave here.'

'Why?'

'Outside—' she waved a hand in the direction of the sea '—is death.'

'Oh good,' Jup said.

'Axiaa,' Coilla asked, 'do you know where our friend was taken? The she-dwarf we came with?'

'The goddess.'

'Er, yes, that's her. Where did she go?'

'Bad place.'

'But do you know *where*? How could we find it?'

The girl didn't seem to grasp that.

'We know!' Retlarg piped up.

Coilla turned to them. 'You do?'

'Yes,' Heeg confirmed.

'The grown-ups don't know we know,' Grunnsa confided. 'But we found out.'

'How?'

'Show you?' Retlarg asked.

She nodded, puzzled.

The three youngsters leapt to their feet and tore to one side of the spacious room. They fell upon a piece of furniture not unlike an ottoman; a couch that doubled as a storage chest. Throwing aside its coverings, they raised the top. There was a jumble of household possessions inside, which they cheerfully tossed onto the rush-matted floor as they burrowed. At last they retrieved a rolled, yellowing parchment, about the length of an orc's arm, secured with a round of smooth twine. They ran back to Coilla and gave it to her.

Along with Stryke, Jup and Reafdaw, she took it to the feasting table. Sweeping aside the remains of their earlier meal, she unfastened the scroll and rolled it out. They weighed down its corners with coconut drinking vessels and fat candles.

It was a chart. Whoever drew it, quite a while ago from its state, had a fine hand. It had been executed in different coloured pigments, now much faded.

The map showed a world dominated by ocean. But sprinkled with islands of all shapes and sizes, some in close clusters, others alone, a few isolated. There were hundreds of them.

'I'm guessing the one we're on,' Stryke said, 'is here.'

He pointed to a shape quite far south, but reasonably close to a number of others. A red cross had been drawn inside its outline, and there were some crude symbols underneath. None of the others had that, save one. This bore a stylised skull in its centre and it had been circled in black. It was north-west of the first, and without knowing the chart's scale, they thought it looked not too far away.

'Gotta be that one,' Jup reckoned.

The three kids clamoured to see, the table being too high for them. They were hoisted up onto chairs.

'Is this where we are?' Coilla wanted to know, pointing at the island with the cross.

They confirmed it.

'And the place these Gatherers come from?'

'*There!*' they chorused, plonking grubby fingers on the island with the skull.

'That clinches it,' Stryke said.

'Now how do we get there?' Jup inquired gloomily.

'In a boat,' Grunnsa suggested.

'They're all too small,' Coilla reminded him.

'*No*,' Heeg insisted. 'The *big* boats.'

'There are big boats? Where?'

'In the boathouse, of course,' the boy replied in a way that sounded like he was the adult and she the child.

'Where is this boathouse?'

'Outside the village.' Grunnsa pointed vaguely in the direction of the extinct volcano.

'Must be that place we saw them guarding,' Stryke reasoned.

'So what are we waiting for?' Jup said.

At that point the longhouse's door opened. Haskeer and a pair of grunts came in. They had the elder with them.

'Found him and a couple of others hiding in the tunnels,' Haskeer explained. 'He's pissed off with us.'

The elder's angry expression verified that.

'Why?' Jup wanted to know.

'Ask him yourself. He doesn't talk to mere *servants*.'

Jup addressed the elder. 'We're sorry about your trouble with the Gatherers. What can we do to help?'

'Your offer comes too late. You should have stopped them.'

'We tried.'

'Those who fall from the sky must be more powerful than the Gatherers. Yet it seems you are not.'

'We want to avenge you, and to get your islanders back. But we need your help.'

'*Our* help? What can we do that those who come from the sky cannot?'

'We need boats that can put to sea, so we can pursue the Gatherers and punish them.'

The elder became tight-lipped.

'We know you have such boats,' Stryke told him. 'And where the Gatherers are to be found.'

The elder shot the children a sharp, disapproving look. 'It is forbidden.'

'What's forbidden?'

147

'Our customs forbid any from leaving here and voyaging to other islands. It brings wrath upon our heads. We believe the Gatherers would not have known of us if some of our kin had not ventured out and been captured.'

'We understand,' Jup sympathised, 'but we aren't bound by your customs. And one of our number was taken by the Gatherers. We want her back.'

'It isn't just the Gatherers. There are other dangers on the outside. Great dangers.'

'We can deal with them,' Stryke came back harshly. 'But what about the *boats*? Do you hand them over or do we take them?'

He said it with sufficient force to give the elder pause. 'There are two,' he admitted. 'We took them from certain of our kin who were building them secretly, in defiance of custom. They would have used them to leave here and try to make a new home free of the Gatherers.'

'Might not have been a bad idea.'

'Did you not survey this world from your vantage point in the sky? You seem to know little about it. For all that we suffer from the Gatherers, this island is safe compared to what dwells beyond it.'

'We'll take our chances.'

'When we seized the boats they were incomplete. They are not yet seaworthy.'

'Would it take much to finish them?'

'I think not.'

It occurred to Coilla to ask, 'If you don't allow sea-going craft, why did you keep them?'

'We had no intention of keeping them. They were to be publicly burnt, as a warning to any who would try the same foolishness. But then you arrived.'

'Lucky we came when we did.'

'Can we get any of your islanders to help us make the boats ready?' Stryke said.

The elder shook his head. 'It would go against our customs and stir up unrest.'

'And the same goes for any of you helping us sail them?'

'It does.'

'To hell with your stinking customs then. We'll manage alone.'

'Not quite,' Coilla said. 'Jode was island-born, he told me so. He'll have sailing skills.'

'You seem to know more about those humans than we do,' Haskeer jibed.

'Good thing I do, isn't it?'

'That's settled,' Stryke decided. 'We'll start work on the boats right away. As to you.' He fixed the elder with a hard look. 'Forget any idea you might have about taking it out on these kids for aiding us. Or we'll bring wrath down upon *your* head.'

'Have we done chin-wagging?' Jup pleaded. ' 'Cos while we're standing here flapping our tongues there's no saying what Spurral's going through.'

16

Spurral had been knocked cold by the blows she took on the beach. When she came to, in the rowing boat, the island was just a speck in the distance, recognisable only by the columns of smoke curling from its pair of active volcanoes.

There were five humans in the boat; four rowing, one at the helm. Three dwarfs, apart from herself, were aboard, lying on the boat's deck. Two male, one female, all young. Like her, their hands were tied. The humans said nothing, contenting themselves with scowling at their captives from time to time and raising a sweat at the oars. When Spurral tried to speak to them they told her to shut up in coarse terms.

They were hardy, weather-beaten men, with skin the colour of old hide from a life under the merciless sun. Most were bearded, and several bore scars. Their clothing suited the needs of fighting and sea-going.

Cautiously lifting her head, Spurral looked over the rail. She saw that their boat was one of dozens of identical craft heading in the same direction, and she guessed they held dwarf captives too. The boats were making for a large triple-masted ship whose sails were being run up as they approached.

When they reached the ship it towered over them like a cliff-face, making the row-boats toys by comparison. Rope ladders dangled from its side. Spurral and the others had their bonds cut, amid threats against misbehaviour, so they could climb them. The ascent was precarious, and as she made her way up she could hear the ship's timbers creaking and the waves lapping against its hull.

On deck, they were herded together facing the bridge. Spurral estimated there were forty or fifty dwarfs present. The humans numbered about the same, and most of them set to hauling aboard the boats for stowing, or making them fast to be towed. Nine or ten men kept an eye on the dwarfs. Not that they were troublesome. They were browbeaten, and some of the females were weeping. And apart from the occasional whispered exchange, they were silent.

A man appeared on the bridge. He was younger than the majority of the crew, surprisingly so for someone Spurral took to be their skipper. His face was hairless, his head was a mane of black curls. There was something about the way he looked and moved that was almost sensuous, calling to mind a predatory feline eyeing its next meal. Of his robustness there was no doubt, and even from a distance he radiated a vitality that spoke of harsh command.

He rapped loudly on the bridge's balustrade with the hilt of his richly embellished sword. There was no real need. He already had their attention.

'I am Captain Salloss Vant,' he announced in a strong, carrying voice. 'It's normal for the master of a vessel to welcome guests aboard. But I've a feeling you'd find it hard to take my words to your hearts.' The crew laughed. He smiled at his quip, then turned stern. 'But take *this* as holy writ. If you have any other gods, forget them. *I* am your deity now.'

Spurral was aware of dwarfs giving her furtive glances. She began to regret the band letting them believe something so fanciful.

'As far as you're concerned,' Vant went on, 'I am the god of this vessel for as long as you're on it, and my word is your only law. And have no doubts that law-breakers will feel a wrath that only a god can bring about.' His expression slid to ersatz amiable. He spread his hands in a gesture of reasonableness.

'We are Gatherers. You are the gathered. Accept your fate and allow us to fashion ours. And don't look so glum! Your new lives as servants, oarsmen, menials and the like will no doubt bring you great satisfaction.' The crew laughed again. 'A pleasure you can begin practising for straightaway,' he continued, the mask going back to severe. 'There are no passengers on this ship. You will work.'

With no further word he turned his back on them and strode away.

'That's one god I can't wait to see fall,' Spurral said, just loud enough for those nearest to hear.

Twilight on the island brought cool breezes, along with a reminder that time was getting on.

The pair of boats the elder surrendered were quite large. Big enough between them to take the whole warband and their provisions, with a little room to spare. They were essentially oversized rowing boats or undersized galleys, depending on how it was looked at. Both were fitted out for between eight and ten rowers. In addition they had a short mast to add the power of a sail. The rudders were a mighty affair, and would need two pairs of hands in rough weather. There were no covered areas on the boats, but lockers had been built in.

They needed most work on their hulls, which were unfinished, and both craft lay keel up, with the band swarming about them. Wood was shaped, twine woven, tar boiled. Hammering, sawing and chiselling filled the air. Supplies were being gathered for the voyage; water, and such food as they thought might keep.

True to their elder's word, the dwarfs didn't assist. But many looked on, some in open curiosity, a few disapproving. The three children, Grunnsa, Heeg and Retlarg, were the band's shadows, though even they were wary of being seen to actually help.

Under the pressure, from time and Jup's growing unease,

tempers were wearing thin. As Pepperdyne, the only one with any real experience of seamanship, was effectively in charge of getting the ships ready, he was the lightning rod.

'Can't you get them to work any faster?' Jup demanded.

'They're performing miracles as it is,' Pepperdyne assured him. 'Be patient.'

'That's easy for you to say. Your woman's not out there somewhere, suffering the gods know what.'

'Trust us, Jup. We want Spurral back as badly as you do.'

'I doubt that!' He checked himself, and relented. 'Sorry. I know you're doing your best.'

'And we'll keep on doing it.'

'It's funny. I never thought I'd be making common cause with a human, let alone over something as important as this. No disrespect.'

'None taken. Life has its little ironies, doesn't it?'

'Never thought I'd be bossed again by a human either,' Haskeer muttered darkly as he worked nearby.

'Jode's not bossing us,' Jup told him. 'He's helping.'

'Oh, so it's *Jode* now, is it? That's what Coilla calls him. Seems to me some in this band are getting a bit too pally with his kind.'

'Jode happens to be his name. And I reckon he's earned his part in this.'

'You know where putting your trust in humans gets us. Or is your memory as short as your legs?'

'I've not forgotten. But when somebody proves their worth—'

'Know what humans are worth? *This* much.' He spat.

'Nobody's saying you have to like me, or my kind,' Pepperdyne said. 'Or that I should have any great regard for you. None of that matters. Fact is, we need to work together.'

'It might not matter to you—'

'For fuck's *sake*,' Haskeer,' Jup butted in, growing incensed. 'Won't you rest it? This isn't about you. It's about finding Spurral.'

'Yeah. Right.'

'What's *that* supposed to mean?'

'All this fuss for a mate.'

'*What?*'

'They come along regular as whores. You can always get another one.'

'*You bastard!*' the dwarf exploded, leaping forward.

He delivered a couple of low punches in quick succession, and while Haskeer was still reeling, seized him by the throat. He hit back with a vicious kicking at the dwarf's legs.

Then Stryke and Dallog were there, grabbing Haskeer from behind. Pepperdyne did the same to Jup, and the pair were pulled apart.

'*Are you two insane?*' Stryke bellowed. 'There's no time for this shit!'

Jup glowered. 'He said—'

'Do I look like I care? You're sergeants in this band. *Sergeants.* But you're going the right way to getting yourselves broken to the ranks. Understand?'

'Yeah,' Jup muttered, and Pepperdyne let him go.

Haskeer didn't respond.

'Haskeer?' Stryke said. He and Dallog still had hold of him. Stryke applied a little less than gentle pressure.

'*Yes!*' Haskeer replied. 'Yes, damn it!'

They released him. He was enraged, and gave Dallog a particularly poisonous look, but curbed himself.

'Spurral's one of our band.' Stryke directed the statement at Haskeer, suggesting he *had* heard what was said. 'And this band sticks together. If any of us is in a fix, all of us get them out of it. *Whoever* they are,' he added pointedly. 'Now get this job finished.'

They went back to work. Some with better grace than others.

When he'd moved away from the rest, Coilla went to Pepperdyne. 'Don't take it too personal. Haskeer can be a swine, but he comes through when it counts.'

'What's his beef?'

'It's a thing between him and Jup. It goes way back.'

'He wants to watch his mouth. I thought Jup was going to kill him.'

'Nah. Cripple him maybe.'

Pepperdyne had to grin.

'Seriously,' Coilla asked, 'when do you think we're going to get these things launched?'

'They might be finished tonight. But no way should we put to sea in the dark. So first light, I guess.' He glanced Haskeer's way. 'Let's hope we all hold together that long.'

'Yeah, and we need to. These islanders don't say much, but from what I've picked up we could run into anything out there.'

They gazed at the vast expanse of water and the disappearing rim of the sinking sun.

Pelli Madayar stood on the peak of a hummock and watched as day began slowly turning to night.

Her second-in-command, Weevan-Jirst, was by her side. A member of the goblin race, his kind were known to be nimble and tough. He had a gaunt build, almost sinewy, and the texture of his knotty, jade-coloured flesh resembled taut leather. His elliptical head had no hair. His ears were tiny and half enclosed by flaps of rough tissue. His mouth was little more than a slit, and his compressed nose had nostrils like slashes. His eyes were disproportionately large, with inky black orbs and sallow surrounds.

The foreboding appearance of goblins often led other species to assume they were hostile; an impression not always without foundation, though unjust in Weevan-Jirst's case. He had devoted his life to the Gateway Corps, and met the high standards of probity the Corps demanded. Which was not to say that he was incapable of performing acts of violence in pursuit of their cause.

'I communicated with Karrell Revers again,' Pelli revealed, 'shortly after we got here.'

'And what did the leader have to say?' The goblin's inflection was sibilant, containing traces of a throaty hiss that formed the greater part of his native tongue.

'More or less what I expected. He was unhappy with the outcome of our first encounter with the orcs.'

'It would be difficult to count that as a triumph.'

'I know. But Karrell gave me a free hand on this mission, and he knew I wanted to try dialogue before force.'

'No one could argue against that being the ideal. But I've yet to see a world where ideal is the norm.' He grew reflective. 'It occurred to me that it could have been the goblin presence in our party that enraged them.'

'How so?'

'Traditionally, goblins and orcs haven't seen eye to eye, shall we say. And not always without good reason.'

'I don't think it was that. The fact is I handled it badly.'

'You're too hard on yourself.'

'No harder than our cause demands. This is my first real mission; I'd hoped to have made a better start.'

'There are few precedents to guide us, Pelli. Instrumentalities being so rare, these assignments are very uncommon. Some go their whole lives without having to do what the Corps has asked of you.'

'That's hardly an excuse.'

'Perhaps not. But it serves as a reason. What conclusion did Karrell reach?'

'He's still content to leave it to my discretion. Just. But he warns that, given the nature of the race holding the artefacts, force is probably the only option.'

'He could well be right. Can anybody negotiate with orcs?'

'I'm starting to think not.'

'Then what choice do we have?'

'There's something else. Karrell warned me earlier that

another force had entered this game. Some individual or group with command of the portals. Their presence was detected in Acurial. And if they were there—'

'I take your point. Do we know more than that about them?'

'No. Which is worrying. To have one set of instrumentalities in irresponsible hands is bad enough. To have two—'

'Must surely be unprecedented.'

She nodded. 'This is a dangerous enough world as it is without another variable being thrown in.'

'All the more reason for us to bow to the leader's wisdom in the matter of the orcs.

'Yes, I suppose it is.'

'Do we have any idea where they might be?'

'We do now. Or at least we do roughly. Karrell gave me coordinates.'

'So your orders are . . . ?'

'We go after them at dawn. And when we find them, we hit them hard this time.'

They watched the last fragment of the sun vanishing below the horizon.

The patchwork of islands spread out before them fell into night.

17

It wasn't long before Spurral witnessed the nature of Salloss Vant's justice.

The captives had immediately been given various onboard chores, most of them mindless and all of them hard work. Spurral was put with five other dwarfs in an ill-lit, dank area below decks containing enormous lengths of unyielding rope, thick as her arm. They had to roll it into coils on great wooden cylinders that took two to turn. Spurral's job was to guide the rope onto the drum so that it wound neatly. In no time they all had bleeding, blistered hands.

There was a single crewman overseeing their labours. After an initial bout of shouting and threats he deposited himself on a heap of filthy sacking and promptly dozed off. Spurral took the opportunity to try to engage the others in whispered conversation. Most were too frightened to respond, but two answered, and they got a conversation going, of sorts.

One was male and a bit older than the majority of prisoners. He seemed to be called Kalgeck, and Spurral thought he had spirit. The female was in some ways his opposite. Her name was something like Dweega. She was among the youngest on board, and timorous, yet found the guts to reply, which Spurral had to give her credit for. It was only later that Spurral discovered Dweega had spoken not out of courage, but desperation.

Several hours of hard labour passed before a bell sounded somewhere. The guard woke up, ran a quick eye over what they'd done and ordered them out. As they shuffled forward, Spurral saw that the girl was having trouble walking. But before the crewman noticed, several others, principally Kalgeck, crowded round and hid her limp from view.

By now, night had fallen. The captives were herded into the ship's hold, and when it was Dweega's turn to descend the ladder, Kalgeck kept close enough to disguise her faltering progress.

For the first time since being seized, they were given sustenance. It was hard, stale bread and suspect water. The hold was badly crowded, but Spurral made sure she got floor space next to Dweega. She noted that Kalgeck had bagged the space on the girl's other side.

The prisoners were forced to keep silence throughout. But once the few meagre candles had been snuffed, and the hold was locked down, whispers were exchanged. Though quiet weeping was more prevalent.

Spurral wriggled nearer to the girl and spoke low. 'You all right?'

'Are any of us?'

'You in particular. What's wrong with your leg?'

Dweega didn't answer. But Kalgeck leaned in close and said, 'She's lame.'

Spurral sensed the girl stiffening at the words.

'It happened when they caught us?' Spurral asked.

'No,' Dweega said. 'I've always . . . been like this.'

'And you don't want the Gatherers knowing.'

'They can't get a good price for damaged goods,' she mouthed bitterly.

'You've been lucky so far. How much longer do you think you can hide it from them?'

'I was hoping that when we get to wherever we're going I might slip ashore and—'

'Can't see that happening. Not the way they've got things set up.'

'I thought you might be able to help.' There was anger in Dweega's voice, and obvious despair. 'You're supposed to be some kind of god.'

'She can't be,' Kalgeck whispered, 'or she wouldn't be here.'

'It was your elder who assumed we were gods,' Spurral told them. 'I'm flesh and blood, just like you.'

Dweega sighed. 'Then that's our last hope gone.'

'You don't have to be a god to do something about our situation.'

'Like what?' Kalgeck wanted to know.

'There are as many of us as there are of them. If we could overpower a few of them and get hold of their weapons—'

'*Mutiny?* We wouldn't stand a chance.'

'What's our choice? We can go meekly to our fate or make a stand. I know which I'd prefer.'

'Then you go ahead,' Dweega said.

'I can't do it alone. We need to organise ourselves.'

'You don't know the Gatherers like we do,' Kalgeck rasped. 'They'd show us no mercy.'

'They'll certainly show none to Dweega when they find out she's lame. Isn't that reason enough to strike at them first?'

'And assure our deaths. Maybe she can get off this ship; and at least the rest of us will be alive as slaves.'

'You might call it a life. I don't.'

'I don't relish it either. And if I thought we had a hope of overcoming the Gatherers I'd be with you. But I can't see the others having much of an appetite for taking them on.'

'What about you, Dweega?' Spurral asked her. 'How do you see it?'

'I'll take my chances.' She turned over and showed Spurral her back.

Nothing more was said, and exhausted, they gave in to fitful sleep.

*

It seemed no time at all before the morning came.

At first light they were roughly roused with kicks and curses, and allowed a little of the brackish water to gulp. Then they were steered to their labours.

But this time they were given different tasks. Instead of working with the rope, Spurral's group was set to scrubbing the decks. Again, Kalgeck and some of the others did their best to shield Dweega, but it wasn't as easy as when they were working in the dimly lit winding room.

Inevitably, something happened that made it impossible for Dweega to hide her disability.

One of the crewmen ordered her to move away from the small cluster of companions trying to shelter her, and swab a different part of the deck. Dweega wavered, which only attracted more attention to her. Under an impatient tirade from several of the crew, she finally rose, and clutching her pail made her way to the indicated place. She did her best to walk normally, but was obviously struggling, and the effort could plainly be read on her face.

It was only a short distance, but it was an ordeal for her. Doubly so as everyone watched her progress in silence. As she knelt, painfully, one of the crew slipped away. A moment later he returned with the captain.

Salloss Vant went to Dweega and towered over her, sour faced.

'Stand up,' he ordered coldly.

She did it, although awkwardly.

'Now walk,' he said. 'That way.' He pointed to the spot she had just come from, where Spurral and the others were standing.

The deficiency in her leg was apparent, and when she got there she all but collapsed into Spurral's arms.

'We've no room on this ship for any who can't pull their weight,' Vant boomed, 'or who have no value to us! They're a waste of precious food!'

'I can work!' Dweega pleaded.

'But not very well, it seems. We Gatherers aren't a charitable trust, and we carry no passengers.' He nodded to several crewmen, and started to walk away.

The men advanced on Dweega. A tussle developed as they tried to prise her away from Spurral. None of the other dwarfs did anything except look horrified.

'*Captain!*' Spurral shouted.

Salloss Vant stopped in his tracks and turned, a look of surprise on his face that one of his chattels should dare address him.

'You don't have to do this,' Spurral told him. 'We can do her work for her. She doesn't have to be a burden on you.'

Vant gave the crewmen another curt nod. One of them landed a heavy blow to the side of Spurral's head with a linchpin, breaking her grip on Dweega and knocking her down. Then they began dragging the girl away.

At that point Kalgeck came alive and tried to intervene. He rushed forward, shouting, '*No! No!*'

He, too, was viciously downed.

'*I'll have no defiance on this ship!*' Vant roared, glaring at the captives.

None of them moved as Dweega, screaming now, was forced to the ship's rail.

'Heed this well!' Vant said. 'And be certain that the same fate awaits any who challenge my authority!'

The crewmen lifted the struggling Dweega by her arms and legs. They swung her back and forth a couple of times, building momentum, then tossed her over the rail. There was a shriek as she fell, followed by a distant splash.

Gasps and screams came from the horrified dwarfs.

'*Bastards!*' Spurral yelled. '*Stinking, cowardly bastards!*'

Vant turned his attention to her, and to Kalgeck, quaking beside her on the deck.

'Spirit's a good thing,' he stated, looming over them. 'Slaves with grit usually make good workers, and that increases the price we'll get for you. Once you've been broken, that is.'

'Go to hell,' Spurral spat.

'We're already there. And should you doubt that, I'm happy to underline the point.' He gestured to the crewmen who threw Dweega overboard.

They hoisted Spurral and Kalgeck to their feet, and shoved them to the central mast. Chests to the column, arms hugging it, their wrists were tied. The backs of their shirts were ripped open.

All the other captives were gathered and made to watch what happened next.

Vant barked an order. A muscular crewman stepped forward, unfurling a leather whip.

'Six for a start, I think,' the Captain decided.

The whip cracked across Spurral's back. She felt indescribable pain, but was damned if she was going to cry out. The next lash was for Kalgeck. Agony racked his body, but he followed her lead and kept silent.

They were beaten alternately, with lingering pauses between the blows, until each had received their six strokes. Neither made a sound throughout. Trickles of blood ran from their lips due to them clenching their teeth so hard.

Somebody doused their gore-clotted backs with buckets of sea water. The salt stung like fire. Then they were left there, still tied, as examples to the rest as they filed past on the way to their labours.

At length, Kalgeck whispered, 'That . . . mutiny.'

'What . . . about it?' Spurral managed.

'How do we . . . start?'

The Wolverines finished work on the boats during the night. They were up again as soon as the sun rose, lugging the vessels down to the water's edge and loading provisions. The day was already warm.

The band was fatigued, and tempers were still taut, particularly in the case of Haskeer and Jup. Given the tensions, Stryke had the additional problem of carefully choosing who went on which boat. He decided that Jup, Dallog and himself would represent the officers on one of them, along with Pepperdyne as a sort of unofficial master. He thought it best to have Standeven along too, so he could keep an eye on him. The second boat had Haskeer and Coilla aboard, with the latter put in charge. Haskeer didn't like a corporal being given primacy over a sergeant, but Stryke couldn't risk him being in command when he was in such a volatile mood. He did take a chance by including Wheam on the second boat, however, in the hope that Haskeer wouldn't find that too provoking. The tyros were just about evenly distributed between the two craft, as were the Wolverine privates. Turns would be taken at the rowing, and with operating the rudders.

The trio of dwarf children, Grunnsa, Heeg and Retlarg, were also up with the dawn, if they had slept at all. When the final preparations were being made, they shyly approached Stryke and Coilla.

It was Grunnsa, the oldest, who came right out with, 'Can we go with you?'

'No,' Stryke told him. 'Sorry.'

The children chorused their disappointment.

'It'd be too risky,' Coilla explained patiently. 'Besides, you're needed here to lend a hand getting things back in shape after the raid.'

'Will you see our parents?' Retlarg said.

'I don't know,' Stryke admitted. 'But if we do, I promise we'll help them if we can.'

Heeg put a question they'd rather wasn't asked. 'When will you be back?'

Stryke and Coilla knew that for good reasons or ill, they might never return.

Coilla softened the blow. 'It could be soon. So look out for us, won't you?' She felt bad giving them what could well be a fruitless task, but didn't want to dash their hopes completely.

'Thanks for your help,' Stryke told them. 'We couldn't have done this without you.'

Grunnsa beamed. 'Truly?'

''Course.' He brandished the chart. 'How else would we know where to go?'

'Time for us to get on,' Coilla announced. 'And you three should be getting back to your duties.'

The kids puffed their chests at the implication of their importance and ran back up the beach shouting.

'Talking about the chart,' Coilla said as she watched them go, 'how do we know these Gatherers are heading for their base? Maybe they've gone straight to whoever they want to sell the islanders to.'

'*It's all we've got to go on. If they're not there, we'll be waiting when they get back.*'

'That won't be much use to Spurral.'

'I know. But like I said, we've no other option.'

Before they left, Dallog performed a short ceremony invoking the Tetrad, commonly referred to as the Square, the four principal orc deities. He called upon Aik, Zeenoth, Neaphetar and Wystendel to favour their voyage and keep their blades keen. It wasn't something the band normally did, except before major engagements. But Stryke had given permission for morale's sake, and because he thought they could use all the help going.

As Dallog recited the simple ritual, the band veterans remembered Alfray, his fallen predecessor, who always undertook the same duty. A very few, Haskeer among them, wore expressions that showed they considered the comparison unfavourably.

When it was done, Stryke ordered everybody to board the boats. It looked as though all the islanders had gathered, the elder at their forefront, to watch the warband depart. They took in the scene in complete silence.

Stryke stood at the bow of his vessel. Almost without thinking, he patted his pouch containing the instrumentalities.

Then the oars cut into the foaming water and they set off.

18

The young officer who brought Jennesta the news had been part of the retinue that accompanied her from Peczan. So he knew her temper, and dreaded her reaction.

When he presented himself at her tent in the makeshift camp near the coast in Acurial she was alone. At least as far as other living beings were concerned. As usual, several of her undead bodyguards were present, shuffling vacantly in the background.

'What do you want?' she asked languidly as he entered. She didn't bother looking up.

He bowed. 'M'lady, I've word of the hunt for the Wolverines you ordered.' She said nothing so he ploughed on. 'I regret having to tell you that they . . . got away.' He braced himself for the storm.

But she was calm. 'How?'

'That's what's extraordinary, my lady. We had them in sight, in the woods. Then they . . . somehow they . . . *vanished*. Or not quite vanished. They . . . I have no words to describe it, m'lady.'

She didn't seem surprised. 'Then don't try. It's obviously beyond you.'

'There's more, ma'am, if it pleases you.'

'We'll have to see, won't we? What is it?'

'Ours wasn't the only force out there. There was some other group. Small, but possessing powerful magic. They seemed to be after the orc band, too. ma'am. And once the orcs . . . went, we were anxious this group might have turned their magic on us.'

'How was this group made up?'

'That's another strange thing, ma'am.'

'It has been an unsettling night for you, hasn't it, Major?'

'We didn't get too close a look at them, my lady, but many of the men swear they weren't human. Not like orcs or—' He was about to say *you*, and thanked the gods he checked himself. 'Not like orcs. These were many different kinds of creatures, unlike anything we've ever seen before.'

'If you're to thrive in my service you'll learn to take *strange things* in your stride. Is that all?'

He was surprised, if not shocked, that she took what seemed to him bad news so evenly. 'We've also had reports that bands of liberated . . . that's to say *rebellious* orcs are roaming this area. We're not in the most secure of positions, ma'am.'

'We won't be here long.'

'What are your orders, my lady?'

'My intention is to follow them.'

'My lady?'

'The band of orcs. The *Wolverines*.'

He was baffled. 'Begging your pardon, my lady, but . . . how? By ship?'

'No, you fool. There never was a ship expected. And no vessel could follow where they went.'

'Then, my lady, how . . . ?'

'I have the means. Though I warn you that you might find the journey a little . . . exhilarating. What's the matter, Major? You look uneasy.' She was poking fun, not inquiring after his well-being.

'Nothing's wrong, thank you, ma'am.'

'Good. Because if I thought that you or any other of my followers might baulk at the manner of our going from this place . . . Well, perhaps an illustration will serve.' She reached for a small silver bell standing on the arm of her couch. It tinkled lightly.

In response, the tent flaps rustled and were clumsily pulled aside. A figure lumbered in. It was another of her zombie slaves. Superficially, it looked like all the others the major had encountered. Its eyes were glassy, and lacked any hint of compassion. The skin that could be seen, on the face and hands, had the sickly pallor of a long mummified corpse.

The being lurched forward a few steps, then halted, adopting a grotesque parody of standing to attention. And the major couldn't help but notice that it gave off the vile odour of decomposing flesh.

'The latest of my attendants,' Jennesta explained. 'Study him closely. I think you may have been acquainted, albeit loosely.'

He stared at the swaying abomination.

'Come on, Major!' she urged. 'There's enough of the original features left for you to make out who this is, surely? He was a man of some distinction, for a while.'

Realisation began to dawn. The major's face took on an appalled expression.

'Ah, I see you *do* recognise our visitor. But let me formally introduce you. Say hello to General Kapple Hacher, late governor of this province.'

The creature that had been Hacher was drooling.

'Consider him closely,' Jennesta said, icy now. 'Because in him you see the destiny of any who would seek to thwart me or disregard my wishes. Make no mistake, Major; I could as easily command an army of his kind as a rabble of free-thinkers. Make sure you and your comrades give me no reason to do so.'

He nodded, words being hard for him to summon.

'Prepare for our departure,' she ordered. 'Oh, and do spread the word about the general's new status, won't you? Now leave me.'

He bowed and turned to go.

'And, Major.'

'Ma'am?'

'See to it that I'm not disturbed.'

The officer gave another quick bow and departed, ashen-faced.

Ignoring the undead Hacher and her other flesh puppets, she stooped and pulled a small chest from under the couch. It was steel-banded and had an elaborate lock, but its real protection lay in the enchantment Jennesta had cast upon it; a spell only she could negate without fatal consequences. Inside the chest was another, slightly smaller, fashioned from pure silver. This, too, was bound with a charm. Once opened, she gazed at her greatest treasure.

The instrumentalities were identical to the ones she had purloined from the Wolverines: sandy coloured, green, dark blue, grey, red; each with varying numbers of projecting spikes. Knowing that even her magic wasn't powerful or subtle enough to create a set from scratch, she had studied and laboured for years to perfect a way of duplicating them. The faultless copies she now ran loving fingers over vindicated her efforts. She knew they would do everything the set the doltish orcs possessed. They could do *more*, given she was so better versed in their potential.

She looked forward with relish to pursuing the warband. But first she had somewhere else to go.

Beyond the veil of the worlds, the Wolverines' two sturdy boats sailed on.

They were lucky with the weather; the sea was calm and the sky clear, which meant the pair of craft could travel within a short hailing distance of each other. That was useful for Pepperdyne, who was able to bawl instructions to the second vessel when it was doubtfully handled. Coilla, in charge of the second boat, was grateful for the guidance. Haskeer was less enamoured of a human bellowing orders at them.

Stryke, Jup and Dallog were the high-rankers on the boat

Pepperdyne skippered. Standeven was aboard too, typically seated as far from the others as possible, and looking bilious despite the millpond sea.

Pepperdyne had been navigating by the sun, and earlier, by the fast fading stars as dawn broke, using a basic star chart he got from the elder. It was a crude method, and he was anxious for some kind of landmark to confirm their position. At around noon, he got it.

Jup pointed. 'There!'

Far off, they could just make out three or four dark bumps rising from the sea's otherwise featureless surface.

'You've good eyesight,' Pepperdyne complimented.

'But they are islands, right?'

'Have to be,' Stryke replied. He had the chart spread on a bench, and tapped a particular spot. 'These, I reckon.'

Pepperdyne leaned in for a look. 'I think you're right.'

'So we're on course?'

The human nodded. 'More or less.'

'But how much can we trust the map?' Jup wondered.

'It seems true so far. Though my hunch is that it covers just the immediate area.'

'Is that a problem?'

'Only if we have to go outside what the map shows, for any reason. Into what would be, for us, uncharted seas. If this world's all ocean there are probably a damn sight more islands than on here.'

'I heard one of those dwarf children come out with an old saying,' Dallog informed them. 'It was about there being as many islands as there are stars in the sky.'

'Poetic, but not very helpful if we have to travel further than this chart.'

'I don't see the need to,' Stryke said. 'The map tells us where we started and where we need to get to. Anything else happens, we'll deal with it.'

'Hope your right,' Jup remarked, 'For Spurral's sake.'

They had seen the chain of islands on the second boat, too.

Wheam was particularly excited at their first sight of landfall. 'This is an important moment. It should be celebrated. It will be, in the epic ballad I'm going to make out of this voyage.'

'Oh joy,' Haskeer intoned flatly.

'If only I had my lute. I always found it so much easier to word-weave with that in my hands. It was such a blow losing it.'

'Yeah, a real tragedy.'

'You'll just have to compose it in your head,' Coilla suggested.

'If there's enough room in there,' Haskeer muttered.

Wheam was oblivious to barbs. 'This ballad could be the making of me as a song-smith. Once I perform it—'

'You know,' Coilla told him, 'you really showed some promise back there in Acurial. When you lost your temper with that human over your lute.'

'He made me angry. But—'

'Exactly. It brought out your orcishness. Don't you think it's better to try being what you were born for than—'

'Poncing about like a limp-wristed fop with water for blood,' Haskeer finished for her.

'Not *quite* the way I'd have put it,' Coilla admitted, 'but not far off.'

'Why can't I be a warrior and a bard? A *warrior-bard*.'

'Don't think there have been too many of those among our race.'

'Then I'll be the first!'

'Just focus on the warrior bit. It's more likely to keep you alive.'

'I don't see why I—'

'Just a minute.' She was staring out to sea.

'But—'

'*Quiet*. Look.' Coilla stretched an arm to indicate something she'd seen.

'What?' Haskeer said. 'Another island?'

'No. Something small, and not far off. See it?'

He squinted, a hand shading his eyes. 'Yeah. What is that?'

'Dunno. Could be just a bit of flotsam. *Hang on.* Something moved.'

'I think it's somebody waving,' Wheam reckoned.

'You could be right,' Coilla agreed. She stood up and hailed the other boat, then gestured towards the object.

Stryke judged it something worth investigating, and ordered the boats to alter course.

As they got nearer, they saw that it was indeed a figure, clinging to a chunk of driftwood.

'It's a dwarf!' Jup exclaimed.

'And female,' Pepperdyne added.

When they reached the castaway, oars were upped on one side of Stryke's boat and she was hauled aboard. They laid her on the deck. She was obviously exhausted, and parched from exposure to the sun, but didn't seem to be seriously hurt. Though she was very frightened.

'It's all right,' Jup soothed. 'Here, drink this.' He pressed a canteen of water to her lips. 'Steady, steady. Not too fast.'

'I recognise her,' Dallog decided.

'I think I do, too,' Pepperdyne said. 'From the island.'

Jup grew animated. 'Then she must have been taken with the others.' He began lightly slapping the girl's cheeks. 'Come on. Wake *up.*'

'Go easy on her,' Stryke warned. 'She'll come out of it in her own time.'

'Here.' Pepperdyne handed Jup a brandy flask, 'Try her with a little of this.'

A trickle of the fiery liquid had the girl coughing, but it put some colour into her cheeks. Her eyes fluttered and opened, and she looked up at them fearfully.

'Everything's all right,' Jup assured her gently. 'How're you feeling?'

She groaned and tried to say something.

173

'What's your name?'

She managed, 'Dweega.' Then she focused and recognised him. 'The . . . god.'

'Well, not really.'

'I . . . know. She told . . . me.'

'She? Who told you? Was it Spurral, Dweega? Remember? She was with us on your island.'

Dweega nodded.

'She's alive?' Jup asked, not daring to hope.

'Yes.'

Jup punched the air. 'I knew it!'

'But. . .'

He sobered. 'What?'

'The . . . Gatherers . . . Salloss Vant . . .'

'Who?'

'She's done in,' Stryke declared. 'Let her rest for a while. At least we know Spurral's alive.'

'Or was when this one last saw her.'

'Which probably wasn't that long ago,' Pepperdyne offered. 'You don't get much time when you're adrift, what with the sun and lack of water. She might only have been out here for a matter of hours.'

'Which means the Gatherers' ship can't be far off.'

'Yes. Assuming that's where this girl came from, which seems a good bet.'

'But which direction?' Jup scanned the ocean.

'Our best plan's to keep going for the Gatherers' base,' Stryke decided. 'Chances are that's where they're heading.'

Jup nodded at Dweega. 'So how come this one ended up in the drink?'

'Noticed her leg?' Dallog asked.

They looked, and saw that one of the girl's legs was twisted and distended.

'That's not a recent injury,' Dallog continued. 'I'd say it's been like that for quite a while. Maybe she was born that way.'

174

Jup's face clouded. 'You're saying those bastards dumped her overboard because of it?'

'They're slavers. They've no use for faulty produce.'

'Shit. What's Spurral gotten herself into?'

'They've no reason to do the same with her,' Stryke reminded him.

'Far as we know. And she's not one to take bullshit from anybody. She could provoke them and—'

She's smart, Jup. Seems to me she'll know how to play it.'

The dwarf nodded, but looked doubtful.

'We push on,' Stryke said. 'Give this girl dry clothes and see if you can get some food down her. Once she rallies she might tell us more.'

It was about time to relieve the first set of rowers, so Stryke ordered the changeover. He got Coilla to do the same on her boat. With fresh bodies at the oars, they set off again at a clip.

A couple of hours passed before Dweega started to come to herself. Hesitantly, she told them what she knew about Spurral, and Salloss Vant.

'You know where they were going?' Stryke asked her.

She shook her head.

'Or where they are now?'

'Roughly. The course they were on, anyway.'

'Will you help us track 'em?'

'I'm . . . frightened. I don't want to go back to . . . *that man*.'

'It'll be different this time,' Jup promised. 'Nobody's going to hurt you.'

She looked around at the warband, taking in their weatherbeaten, scarred faces, and the flint in their eyes. 'All right.'

'So how far are we from their ship?' Stryke asked.

'Maybe closer than we think,' Dallog interrupted. 'Look.'

Well to their stern was a ship. It was distant enough for the details to be hazy, but the white of its sails was plain to see.

'Could that be them?' Jup wondered, a real edge in his voice.

'No,' Pepperdyne said. 'It's a different class of ship from the one they had.'

'What do you think, Dweega?' Jup said. 'Recognise it?'

'He's right. It's not the Gatherers' ship I was on.'

'Who says they've only got one ship?' Dallog speculated. 'Might be more of 'em.'

'Could be,' Stryke conceded. 'Then again, there must be lots of ships, this being a world of islands.'

'I don't think so,' Pepperdyne said. 'I've been watching it for quite a time, while you were tending the girl. It never varies its speed, never falls back or forges on. It's always at the same bearing. I'd say whoever that is, they're shadowing us.'

19

The casting overboard of Dweega galvanised many of the captive dwarfs. But they knew the Gatherers of old, and their terrible reputation. Angry as they were, and grief-stricken over Dweega, the dwarfs wanted to act but remained fearful. Spurral did her best to change that.

The whipping she and Kalgeck had taken left them pained and badly sore. There was no ministration from the Gatherers, not that they expected any, but their fellow captives rallied round. They had been stripped of their few miserable valuables, with the exception of a small number of items even the slavers thought worthless. These included certain herbs and salves the dwarfs habitually carried. They gave some relief, and speeded healing.

Although she didn't welcome the thrashing, Spurral was perversely grateful for it. It sharpened her appetite for revenge, and her fortitude earned her kudos among the other prisoners, making them more open to her whispered seditions. Kalgeck, too, seemed to find resolve in his punishment.

Spurral immediately set them to work making weapons. Nothing resembling blades could be pilfered. So they improvised bludgeons from pieces of timber and sacking. They made slingshots with strips of cloth, and sneaked peach-stones out of the crew's swill buckets, for shot. Part of the reason they got away with it was because the slavers had no regard for them. They were too used to plundering the dwarfs' island without opposition, and saw them as timid, unresourceful creatures. The Gatherers had grown complacent, which suited Spurral.

The only time they could really work on the weapons was at night, below decks in their makeshift dormitory. In almost complete darkness, by touch.

Satisfied that lookouts were posted, Spurral and Kalgeck, sprawled on their mean sacking, were busy fashioning wooden hatchets.

'How can we fight with these?' Kalgeck whispered, holding up his crude effort.

'They only need to work once or twice. To get us some real weapons.'

'Oh. Right. You know a lot about fighting, Spurral.'

'I've done a lot *of* it. You?' She knew he hadn't.

'Not really.'

'Then trust me.'

'I overheard something Vant said today.'

'What?'

'He said we'll be at our destination soon.'

'How soon?'

'Didn't say. But it sounded like very soon.'

'So the quicker we strike—'

'Wouldn't it be better to wait until we get wherever we're going? You know, and maybe make a break for it?'

'No. We don't know what we'll be up against when we dock. Here, we've got just the crew to deal with.'

'*Just?*'

'They're flesh and blood. They bleed and die like anybody else.'

'Including us.'

'Listen, Kalgeck; characters like Salloss Vant dominate others in two ways. First, by force. Second, *fear*. They trade on their victims being afraid of what they *might* do. To overcome the Gatherers you have to overcome the fear.'

'That's easy said.'

'What's the worst they can do?'

'Kill us?'

'That depends on whether you think death's worse than enslavement and misery.'

'And you don't.'

'I don't want to die any more than you do. But I like the idea of this scum staying alive even less.' She tried to make out his expression in the poor light. 'You are still with me on this?'

He was a moment answering. 'Yes.'

'And the others?'

'Most of them, I think. But all of us are . . .'

'Afraid? There's no shame in it, Kalgeck. It's something we have to get over.'

'Even you?' He sounded incredulous.

'Of course.'

'You credit us with more courage than we deserve. We're not known for bravado.'

'So-called courage isn't about doing something without fear. It's doing something *despite* fear. Show me somebody who doesn't feel dread in a fix like this and I'll show you a fool.'

'Can we hope for help? From those who dropped from the sky with you?'

She had to smile, though he couldn't see it. 'I know Jup and the others will be doing their best to find us. But we can't count on that. We have to suppose we're alone.'

'What do you want us to do?'

'We need to seize an opportunity, and soon. Pass the word for everybody to be ready to act, and watch for my lead.'

The sky was a breathtaking canvas of crystal clear stars.

Night had not deterred or slowed the ship stalking the Wolverines' boats. It maintained the same distance and rate of knots, and had no trouble staying on course despite the orcs' vessels being completely unlit. The ship itself did bear lights, or

179

at least gave off a soft illumination that couldn't be accounted for by lanterns. It progressed in an eerie glow, like a ghost ship.

On the first boat, Pepperdyne had managed to avoid contact with Standeven since they started out. Now he felt obliged to check with the man who, in spite of himself, he still thought of as his master.

Standeven remained in the seat he'd occupied since they began the journey. He hadn't exchanged more than a few words with anyone. It was a measure of how the others thought about him that, full as the boat was, he sat alone. He was staring at the ship trailing them when Pepperdyne perched beside him.

'Who do you think they are?' he asked in an undertone.

Standeven shrugged. 'Who knows? But it's obvious what they're after.'

'Is it?'

'Of course. What are the most valuable things on this boat?' He looked around furtively before answering his own question in an animated whisper. 'The instrumentalities!'

'How would they know we've got them?'

'How did that group that attacked us in Acurial know?'

'You reckon it's them?'

'Perhaps. Or some other. It doesn't matter. What's important is that they understand the worth of the artefacts.'

'What's your point?'

'We've let ourselves lose sight of what prizes they are.'

'I thought we'd seen the sense in abandoning that idea.'

'You might call it sense. I say anybody who turns their back on a fortune must be a fool.'

'You can't still be thinking they could be taken. From an orc's warband? That's *insane*.'

'Given the power at stake, and the riches, it'd be worth the risk.'

'Say we did get them. What then?'

'We'd use them to get out of this wretched world and—'

'How? We'd need Stryke's amulet too, and there's no way he'd let either that or the stars out of his sight.'

'There's always a means, Pepperdyne.'

'Like stealing them? The way the one Coilla had was taken back in Acurial?'

Standeven's face twisted. He raised his voice. 'How often do I have to tell you—'

'*Ssshhh!* Keep it *down*. If the others get a hint of what you're thinking . . .'

Heads had turned. Pepperdyne gave them a bland smile. When they lost interest he added, in an even lower tone, 'You're forgetting something. The damn stars aren't working properly anyway. So what are you going to do? Keep trying in the hope of them taking us home? And if by some miracle we got there, what do you do about the debt you owe Kantor Hammrik?'

'There'd be no need to pay debts with the instrumentalities in our possession. Or to go home. We could find ourselves a pleasant world somewhere. Maybe one where the natives are so backward we could rule them. We'd be *kings*, Pepperdyne.'

'Have you been drinking sea water? All this is crazy.'

'Only to someone with the imagination of a worm.'

'You're quite something, aren't you? It never entered your head that these orcs have become friends. Well, comrades at least. And you'd abandon them here.'

'Maybe they're . . . *friends* to you, but we've been in nothing but trouble since you got us tied up with them. And what are they dragging us into now?'

'We're trying to help one of our own. It's called loyalty, if the word means anything to you.'

'It means getting us killed.'

'Stryke said he'd take us home. I believe him.'

'Even if he kept his word, he'd still have the instrumentalities. I . . . we *must* have them.'

'Let it go. It's wild talk.'

Standeven didn't seem to be paying attention. He had a distracted look, and his head was half tilted, as though he was concentrating on something.

'What is it?' Pepperdyne asked.

'Can you hear anything?'

'Hear? Hear what?'

'I've been hearing a . . . melody. No, not that. It's faint but . . . it sounds like . . . voices, singing. *There*. Hear it?'

Pepperdyne listened. There was only the swish of oars cutting through water and the occasional murmur of other conversations. 'No, I can't hear anything.'

'You *must* be able to hear it.'

'There's nothing. It's just the sea. It can play tricks.'

He looked bewildered. 'Is it? Perhaps you're right. I can't seem to . . . I don't hear it now.'

'You've not been getting enough rest. None of us have. That probably accounts for it, and what you've been saying.'

'My judgement's sound,' he replied indignantly. 'I can see the logic of it even if you can't. I have to have the stars. They *want* me to.'

'What? Get a grip, Standeven.'

'You wouldn't have dared talk to me like that not long ago.'

'That was then. Now's a different game. I don't know what's going on in that devious head of yours, but understand this: if you do anything stupid you're on your own.'

'Obviously,' he sneered.

'Look, there's no way I'm going to—'

He stopped when he saw Stryke rise and make his way to them.

'Everything all right?' the orc said.

It could have been Pepperdyne's imagination, but he thought there was a hint of suspicion in Stryke's voice. He considered telling him what Standeven had just said, but decided against it. 'We're fine,' he told him. 'Just fine.'

*

On the Gatherers' ship, dawn brought another round of drudgery. The dwarfs were hurried through their usual meal of stale bread and water. Then they were steered, blinking, to the deck, for chores to be handed out.

The slavers had divided the prisoners into arbitrary work gangs when they were first brought aboard, and seemed content to let them carry on. So Spurral and Kalgeck were again in the same group, making intrigues easier. They were assigned to the galley.

It was sizeable, longer than it was wide, and oppressively hot, even so early. A row of wood-burning kilns occupied one side of the room. All were in full flame, with a variety of pans, pots and kettles on their tops, seething and steaming. The two biggest stoves were being used to heat cauldrons of water, vessels large enough to accommodate a crouching dwarf.

The not too clean work surfaces were littered with cooking utensils and victuals; principally fish, along with some doubtful-looking meat, wheels of rock-hard cheese and loaves of the musty bread. There were a few bunches of limp, shrunken vegetables.

It was among these that Spurral noticed the protruding hilt of a knife. There were no other blades to be seen. Presumably they had been hidden from the captives, and this one was overlooked. She nudged Kalgeck and indicated it with a subtle glance.

As the crewman watching them turned his attention to some bawling, Spurral whispered, 'Can you sidetrack him?'

Kalgeck was taken aback, then looked resolved and nodded.

While the dwarfs were being gruffly assigned their tasks, he edged his way towards a shelf of stoneware. At its end stood a tall jug. Kalgeck shot an anxious look at the crewman's back. Then he reached up and swotted the jug off its shelf. It went down with a crash, and shattered.

Silence fell, and the crewman spun round, looking furious. He strode to Kalgeck, red-faced.

'What the hell you playing at?'

'It was an accident. I—'

'Accident? You clumsy little swine!' He took a swipe at Kalgeck, landing a meaty smack. 'I'll give you accident!' The blows continued to rain down on the dwarf's head and shoulders.

While everyone was distracted, Spurral quickly palmed the knife and slipped it up her sleeve. It had a short blade, but it was razor sharp, and the coolness of the steel against her skin had a reassuring feel to it.

Kalgeck was still being clouted by the swearing crewman, and his arms were raised as he tried to protect himself. Spurral had a flash of regret at having involved him, and wondered how far the punishment would go. It crossed her mind to intervene and use the knife now. But no sooner had the thought occurred than the human, fury spent, ceased his pounding. He replaced it with even more colourful invective as he ordered Kalgeck to clear up the mess.

Down on hands and knees, gathering the pieces, Kalgeck caught Spurral's eye and gave her a wink.

Their group was set to washing dishes, carrying and fetching, bringing firewood from the hold to feed the kilns, and a variety of other duties. But nothing that involved anything sharp, such as preparing food. The galley crew took care of those tasks themselves, and Spurral feared they might notice a blade was missing. When there was no outcry she concluded they weren't methodical enough to realise.

The morning progressed in a grinding routine. One menial, back-breaking job after another was assigned, with the dwarfs spurred on with curses if they were lucky, kicks and punches if they weren't. At around noon all the captives were allowed out on deck to be fed. As usual, the fare dished up for them was even worse than the crew's own lacklustre chow. But the dwarfs, their appetites sharpened by the ceaseless labour, bolted it anyway.

Slumped on the sweltering deck, waiting for their short break to be rudely ended, some of them catnapped. Others exchanged whispers under disapproving gazes, or simply lounged, exhausted. For Spurral and Kalgeck, sitting with their backs to the rail, it was the first time they had a chance to confer since Kalgeck's earlier hiding.

'You all right?' she asked from the corner of her mouth.

He nodded. Though his developing bruises seemed to tell a different story.

'Sorry I got you into trouble,' she added.

'Don't be. It was worth it.'

'Yeah. We got our first real weapon.'

'And I pilfered these.' He discreetly opened his hand. In his cupped palm were four or five objects that looked like pegs, made of wood with metal tips.

'What are they?'

He smiled. 'Don't know much about seafaring, do you? They're kevels. You use them to secure ship's ropes. They'll make good shot for the slings.'

She was impressed. 'Smart thinking.'

'When do we act, Spurral? Everybody's ready. Well, ready as they'll ever be. They're just waiting on your word.'

'We have to pick the right—'

Kalgeck kicked the side of her leg and nodded up deck.

Salloss Vant had appeared. It was the first time they'd seen him since the day before. He was accompanied by a couple of particularly rough-looking henchmen, and he didn't look happy. Moving in the peculiarly slinking, almost feline manner that struck Spurral when she first saw him, the Gatherer captain positioned himself before them. As he did, other crewmen placed themselves around the captives.

'*On your feet!*' he barked.

The dwarfs reluctantly rose.

'Someone here has betrayed my trust,' Vant said.

'What trust?' Spurral remarked under her breath.

'When I took you aboard I asked you to surrender to your fate,' he went on. 'It seems not all of you saw the wisdom in my advice.' He regarded them with a baleful glare. 'A knife has gone missing.'

Spurral could have kicked herself for assuming she'd got away with it. 'Looks like you'll get the word sooner than you thought,' she whispered to Kalgeck.

His eyes widened. He began stealthily slipping a hand into his partly open shirt, seeking a weapon.

Spurral was aware that some of the dwarfs nearby were surreptitiously glancing her way.

'Is anyone going to own up to it now and take their punishment?' Vant demanded. Nobody spoke or moved. 'So you're cowards as well as fools. Just what I expected from inbred scum. You'll *all* be flogged for your insolence. Those assigned to the galley this morning, stay on your feet! The rest of you, back on your arses!'

'Here we go,' Spurral muttered.

She, Kalgeck and the five or six others in their group were left standing. They were more or less bunched, like a cluster of corn in a field otherwise flattened by a storm.

Vant scanned them. His malevolent eye fell upon Spurral and Kalgeck. 'You two,' he rumbled ominously. To his crew, he snapped, 'Bring them here!'

The nearest pair of sailors headed for those still standing. They didn't bother to draw their weapons, taking it for granted there would be no resistance.

One of them made straight for Spurral, approaching with a merciless smirk on his grizzled face. She had her arms behind her back, out of his sight, and let the stolen knife slide down her sleeve and into her hand.

'Move, bitch,' he grated.

Spurral swung round the blade, fast and hard, and buried it in his midriff. For good measure she thrust it into him twice more. The man looked as much bewildered as pained, staring down at the widening crimson patch with a bemused expression. Even as his legs buckled and he started to fold, she grabbed the hilt of his cutlass and dragged it from its scabbard. He was hitting the deck when she turned on the second man. This one appeared dumbfounded, too. She took the benefit of his slow reaction and drove the blade into him, putting all her force behind it. He went down.

A pall of silent, disbelieving shock descended. Everyone, captives and crew, seemed spellbound. For one stomach-churning moment Spurral thought she was alone, that none of the others would move to support her.

Then Kalgeck shouted, 'Now! *Now!*'

There was an explosion of movement and sound.

Dwarfs and men were shouting. Some screamed. Spurral saw three dwarfs piling into a crewman, pummelling him with their improvised hatchets. Somebody tugged free the man's sword and turned it on him. Another crewman staggered past with a female dwarf clinging to his back, repeatedly stabbing him with a seized dagger. Yet another was borne aloft by half a dozen captives and hurled, yelling, over the side. One of the hench-men beside Salloss Vant took a faceful of slingshot. He sank, writhing, to his knees. Everywhere there was chaos.

Kalgeck had got hold of the cutlass from the second man Spurral downed. He was no master with a sword, but the energy of his rage made up for the lack. Bellowing inarticulately, he laid into a knot of crewmen already besieged by his fellow islanders. Forced back to the rail, they were desperately trying to fend off their attackers.

Taken unawares, the Gatherers were faring badly. But Spurral knew the element of surprise wouldn't last long, and if the dwarfs didn't capitalise on it straightaway, they never would. Vant was wading into the dwarfs, swinging his sword like a madman. Spurral determined to settle with him.

She hadn't gone six paces when one of the crew blocked her way. He was armed with a cutlass and bent on stopping her. Spurral would have been happier meeting him with a staff, but she was as comfortable with a sword as just about any other weapon. And now the bloodlust was on her. She charged.

He was strong. When their pealing blades collided it sent a jolt through her. The blows they exchanged were harsh, like rock on rock and just as unyielding. Despite her strapping dwarfish build, Spurral was nimbler, which kept her from reach. But her opponent was the single-minded sort and came on relentlessly. He was good at blocking her thrusts, too, frustrating every attempt at breaking his guard.

They were close to stalemate when chance intervened. Spotting a crewman in the rigging, several dwarfs targeted him with their slingshots. The stinging bombardment made him lose his grip. Screaming, he plummeted to the deck, landing with a bone-shattering crash just behind Spurral's foe. It was enough of a distraction to make him turn, simultaneously dipping his guard.

Spurral didn't hesitate. She ran at him, cutlass at arm's length. The momentum took the blade deep into his chest. He went down heavily, falling backwards, the force of his collapse whipping the sword out of her hand. Thudding her boot on the corpse, she wrenched it free.

She straightened, panting, with sweat trickling from her brow. When she looked up, Salloss Vant was standing in front of her, bloody cutlass in hand.

He wore a demonic expression. His eyes burned like searing coals. When he spoke, he struggled to get the words out through his choking wrath. 'You . . . are going . . . to . . . *die*.'

'You can try,' she replied, trying to keep the foreboding out of her voice.

Done with words, he bellowed and came at her.

20

Vant's rage swamped any finesse at swordplay he might have possessed. He hurled himself at Spurral like a maddened bull. And now she saw that in addition to his cutlass he brandished a long-bladed knife. He swung the weapons like some kind of demented juggler, smearing the air with a metal haze.

Spurral hastily withdrew, trying to stay supple and anticipate where and how he might strike. An impossible task when facing someone as crazed as Vant, she soon realised. All she could do was keep moving. It was a strategy with limited value; inevitably he closed in on her and she was forced to engage.

The impact of the first blow she blocked had her staggering. The second came close to putting her down. She retreated once more, just a few steps this time, then feigned going in again. It was intended to wrong-foot him. Instead, she had to quickly duck as his blade whistled over her head.

A cacophony of yells, screams and clashing blades served as background. All around them, dwarfs and Gatherers battled. The surprise element had more momentum than Spurral guessed, and the islanders were driving home their advantage. Taken unprepared, dead and wounded crewmen littered the deck, or fought desperate rearguard actions. Some of the crew, those from the night watch, were sleeping when the rebellion broke out. Their awakening was rude.

Not that the dwarfs had it all their own way. They were

facing hardened brigands and, as proof, the bodies of their dead and wounded were nearly as plentiful.

Avoiding two blades wielded by someone demented with fury was taxing Spurral. Already she was less light on her feet, and her arms were starting to feel leaden. Taking the offensive, she opted to rush Vant, sweeping her sword like a scythe. It was his turn to swerve. He moved just fast enough to elude her low swipe. His anger further heightened, he was back on the offensive without pause. Another round of battering followed, rattling Spurral's bones.

It was shaping up as less than an even match, and Spurral knew she had to find a different strategy or lose. The thought occurred that if she couldn't change the *way* he fought, perhaps she could change *where*. She turned and ran. Bellowing, he dashed after her.

She headed for one of the few parts of the ship she was familiar with. That meant leaping over corpses and skirting fights. At one point a Gatherer tried to bar her path. She deflected his cutlass on the run, and left him to cope with a trio of dwarfs closing in at his rear.

Spurral arrived panting at the galley door. It was half open. She kicked it in, Vant close behind. Inside, she was relieved to find the place empty, and raced to the interior. A second later he crashed in behind her.

'You little freak!' he screamed, lips foaming. 'Stand and take what's coming!'

'You want me,' she hissed, 'you come and get me.' It was a bold challenge; he was between her and the only way out.

Her hope was that the restricted space would cramp his movements and perhaps give her, with the smaller frame, a slight edge. A bonus was that there were plenty of potential weapons in the galley. Or rather, missiles. She grabbed an iron cooking pot and lobbed it at him. It fell short, clattering at his feet, and Vant furiously kicked it aside. He began to advance. Spurral took to bombarding him with anything that came to hand. She threw kettles, pans, a wooden mallet, skillets, flagons, trenchers and a heavy ladle. Several of the objects struck him, but he seemed oblivious to any hurt they might have caused. The only obvious effect was that his vehemence rose to even greater heights. She started to wonder if anything would stop him.

There being nothing else within easy reach to throw, she braced herself for his onslaught. Oblivious to the broken crockery and utensils underfoot, Vant stormed her way. She stood her ground. There was little choice; the narrow, window-less galley's farthest wall was no more than ten paces behind her.

Spurral had to hold her sword two-handed to hang on to it, such was the energy of the pounding he delivered. She managed, just, to stop any of his passes getting through, but her every attempt at turning her defence into an attack was thwarted. He staved her off with almost contemptuous ease. Despite her resolve to stand firm, the sheer power of his pummelling was forcing her to retreat. And she knew that if her back touched the wall her chances of survival would be vanishingly slim.

Desperation breeds ingenuity. Or insane recklessness. Some-thing she noticed out of the corner of her eye, and the idea it gave her, could have fallen into either category. They had drawn level with the two largest kilns. Their fires had recently been banked, and the water in the massive cauldrons they supported was boiling vigorously. The clouds of steam they gave off misted the room. Condensation ran down the walls and dripped from the ceiling.

What Spurral had in mind was potentially as harmful to her as Vant, and she wasn't sure if she'd be nimble enough to steer clear of injury. But she did it anyway.

She swung her sword as hard as she could, not at the captain, but at one of the cauldrons. As it struck, she flung herself backwards. She hit the floor at the same time as the cauldron toppled from the oven, drenching Vant in scalding water.

He screamed in agony. Letting go of both his blades, he sank to his knees, a cloud of steam rising from his sodden clothes. His skin was already raw and blistering. A few drops of the boiling water had splashed on Spurral, and stung like hell. She could hardly imagine how it felt for him.

His screams cut through her like a knife, and she was sure they could be heard throughout the ship. Then he collapsed completely to writhe on the floor moaning.

She got to her feet and looked down at him. A quantity of the water had hit his face, inflaming it to the point where it was almost unrecognisable. There was an odour of seared flesh.

Spurral didn't know if the burns were severe enough to kill him, but if they were, it would evidently be a lingering, painful death. As much as she had grown to hate Salloss Vant and all he stood for, as much as she resented the humiliation he had heaped upon her, it wasn't in her to be sadistic.

Somehow she had been parted from her cutlass. It was by the kiln, whose fire had been extinguished by the cascade of water. The sword's blade was broken in two, presumably from when it struck the iron cauldron. She picked up Vant's long-bladed knife.

He was squirming, and perhaps trying to speak, or curse, but the sounds were strangled and unintelligible. His eyes, though glazing, still had a spark of malice. If he recognised Spurral as she leaned over him, he gave no sign.

She lifted the knife high, two-handed, and plunged it into his heart.

Once the deed was done, the wider world seemed to re-establish itself. For the first time she noticed the fusty smell from the quenched fire. Again she was aware of noises from the rest of the ship; distant cries, running feet, chiming blades.

The door flew open. Several figures barged in. She snatched up Vant's cutlass, then realised it was Kalgeck and two or three of the other dwarfs.

They stared at Vant's gently steaming corpse, and at Spurral. Their saucer-eyed expressions mixed disbelief with admiration.

'My gods,' Kalgeck whispered. 'You all right, Spurral?'

She nodded. 'How's it going out there?'

He tore his eyes away from Vant. 'We've managed to deal with most of them. Some are holding out.'

'They'll lose heart quick enough when they know their chief's dead. Let's get him to where he can be seen.'

They dragged the body out to the deck. It left a wet trail, and they dumped it in plain view, the knife still jutting from its chest.

There was a stand-off. The majority of the Gatherers who hadn't given up were occupying the bridge. But possession of the wheel meant nothing when the dwarfs had mastery of just about everything else, and most importantly, the rigging. Without control of the sails, the ship was going nowhere.

When the hold-outs saw Vant's corpse their resolution crumbled. The dwarfs gave them assurances that they wouldn't be harmed. Whether they believed it or not, the crewmen had little option but to surrender.

The islanders found themselves with getting on for twenty able-bodied prisoners and about a dozen wounded. They herded them below decks to the prison hold they'd had to endure.

As they watched them descend, Spurral remarked, 'Looks like you have your own slaves now.'

'That's not our way,' Kalgeck told her.

'It's to your credit that it isn't. Hostages, then. To deter the Gatherers from raiding your home again.'

'I was thinking we might be able to trade them for some of our kin who got taken.'

'Good idea.'

'If we can find out where they are, of course. Which might not be easy.'

'I know. But you could see this as an opportunity.'

'To do what?'

'To venture out from your homeland. You've got a whole

193

world to explore. Fear has kept you prisoners on your island as surely as the Gatherers held you captive on this ship.'

He hadn't looked at it that way. 'Yes,' he replied thoughtfully, 'maybe we could.' The sound of a splash turned their heads. Dwarfs were pitching the bodies of dead humans overboard.

'I can't believe we beat them,' Kalgeck said. 'It seems . . . unreal.'

'We did it because they didn't expect it of us. It's a good lesson. Remember it.'

'We did it because of you. If you hadn't—'

'You did it yourselves. You just needed to know you had it in you. That you could overcome the fear.'

'At a price.' He nodded towards a line of dwarf bodies, covered in blankets, laid out on the deck.

'Freedom always has its price, Kalgeck. I hope you'll come to believe it was one worth paying.'

'What do we do now?'

'We sail this ship back to your island.'

'How? I mean, we know a bit about seafaring, but we've only ever really done close-to-shore stuff, like canoeing.'

'We'll manage. If we have to, we'll get some of those humans to help us.'

'Would they?'

'What's their alternative? Drifting out here with us for ever? We'll make 'em think their lives depend on it, if need be.'

He smiled. 'Right.'

'You're learning. Only let's get underway soon, shall we? There's somebody whose company I've been missing.'

Jup had sunk into melancholy. He spent most of his time standing alone at the prow, searching for a sail or any other sign that might give him hope.

Stryke laid a calloused hand on his shoulder. 'There's no sense brooding.'

'There's little else to do.'

'Take a turn on the oars when we change over. Work off some of those worries.'

Jup smiled wryly. 'That's what I like about you orcs. You see everything so . . . *direct*. But some feelings can't be got rid of that easily.'

'You'll snap out of it when we catch the Gatherers.'

'You think we will?'

'Whatever it takes.'

'Thanks.' The dwarf eyed his captain. 'Expect you think I've gone soft.'

'No.'

'We dwarfs tend to mate for life. So to win Spurral and then lose her . . .'

'I know how I'd feel if anything happened to Thirzarr, Jup, or the hatchlings.'

'She sounds a good sort, your Thirzarr. Wish I could have met her.'

'You'd get on. You've something in common.'

'What's that?'

'You're both stubborn as mules.'

Calthmon, one of the veteran Wolverine privates, called out from the oars, 'They're gaining on us!' He pointed at the mysterious ship stalking them.

'He's right,' Pepperdyne confirmed. 'They're putting on some knots.'

Stryke hailed the second boat. 'See that?' He indicated the ship.

'We noticed!' Coilla yelled back. 'What do we do?'

'Row double-time and put some distance between us.'

'Run?' Haskeer exclaimed. 'Since when did we dodge a fight?'

'If it's the same lot who ambushed us in Acurial,' Stryke told him, 'I don't want to face their magic in open boats. Now up the pace!'

All hands to the oars, the boats increased speed, and at first, they widened the gap.

'They're catching up!' Dallog warned.

Pepperdyne looked back. 'At this rate they'll be on us in no time.'

'There's no way of outrunning them?' Stryke asked.

'Not with the wind-power they've got. Only thing I can suggest is we take our boats on different courses. Spread the targets.'

Stryke considered it. 'No. If we have to make a stand we'll do it together.'

Sails billowing, the ship came relentlessly closer. Finally it slowed and was looming over them. Seeing no point in wasting the rowers' muscle power, Stryke ordered the oars to be drawn. But he passed the word that they should be ready to resume at short notice.

'Now what?' Jup wondered, staring up at the massive wooden wall overshadowing them.

Figures appeared at the ship's rail and looked down at the boats. They were of diverse species, and familiar to the orcs.

'It's them all right,' Dallog said. 'The bunch from Acurial. And there's that elf who leads them.'

'*Attention, Wolverines!*'

'What the hell?' Jup exclaimed.

'*This is Pelli Madayar.*'

'How is her voice that . . . *loud*?' Dallog said.

'It's being amplified in some unnatural way,' Pepperdyne reckoned.

'Must be magic,' Stryke agreed.

'*Hear me, Wolverines! We have to talk.*'

'About what?' Stryke yelled.

'*The topic I broached with you in Acurial.*'

'She's on about the stars again,' Jup said.

Stryke nodded. 'You've had your answer on that!' he shouted back. 'Nothing's changed!'

'*I have to insist that we negotiate. Heave to and board our ship.*'

'No way!'

'*Would you prefer that I came down to you? To show good faith.*'

'You don't get it, do you? There's nothing to talk about!'

'*Refusal isn't an option, Captain Stryke. If you won't negotiate, I must demand that you hand over the artefacts.*'

'Demand be fucked!' Haskeer thundered loud enough for all to hear.

'Who the *hell* do they think they are?' Coilla added, enraged.

'Steady!' Stryke cautioned. To Pelli Madayar he bellowed, 'You were told before: we don't take kindly to demands!'

'*Then we cannot be held responsible for the consequences of your obstinacy.*'

'Why can't she talk plain like everybody else?' Haskeer grumbled.

'Pass on the word to be ready to move,' Stryke told Dallog under his breath.

'*This is your last chance, Wolverines,*' Pelli warned. '*I strongly advise you to lay down your arms and parley with us.*'

'Go!' Stryke roared. '*Move!* Get those oars moving!'

The boats glided away, the rowers straining. Stryke was no seafarer, but he knew a sailing ship couldn't set off from a standing start the way his boats could. He just hoped they'd get enough of a head start to stand a chance.

But the Gateway Corps had no need of pursuit.

The orcs had barely escaped the shadow of the ship when the air crackled. A blinding luminous beam struck the short stretch of water between the two boats. More shafts of incandescent light, red, purple and green, immediately followed. All came close to the vessels, but like the first, punched the ocean. Where they landed, the water boiled and gave off clouds of steam.

'Are they warning shots?' Pepperdyne wondered.

'Either that or they're lousy at aiming,' Stryke came back.

No sooner had he spoken than a fiery bolt struck the craft Coilla commanded. It wasn't a direct strike; the beam sliced into the rail and clean through one of the oars, neatly severing it. The impact was enough to rock the boat.

'To hell with this,' Stryke cursed. 'If one of those hits dead-on we're done for.'

'So what do we do?' Jup said.

'Give 'em something back.' He yelled an order stridently enough that it could be heard on both boats.

Stryke had had the foresight to place a more or less equal number of the band's best archers in each vessel. The order he issued, using phrases that meant nothing to outsiders, told them which strategy to use.

They plucked prepared arrows, with tips wrapped in tar-smeared windings. Sparks were struck, igniting the bolts. Then, at Stryke's signal, they were loosed in the direction of the ship; not at any of the beings on board, but at the sails. Most of the viscous, flaming missiles found their target, igniting the sheets. In seconds, several patches were ablaze. Figures could be seen running about the deck.

'Now let's move!' Stryke shouted.

The boats pulled off again. To their rear, the sails were well alight. Several more energy beams flared from the ship, but they were wide of the mark.

'That'll give the bastards something to think about,' Jup commented.

'For now,' Stryke said. 'But I don't think they're the sort to give up too easily. *Come on, rowers! Put your backs into it!*'

It didn't take them too long to put a respectable distance between themselves and the burning ship. Nevertheless, Stryke didn't let the boats slacken their pace. He wanted to get as far away as possible.

'What do you reckon to the damage on the other boat?' he asked Pepperdyne.

'Hard to say without actually being over there. But it doesn't look too bad from here. It's not been holed, that's the main thing. We should be able to patch it up soon as we get the chance.'

'Good enough.'

Throughout the whole episode Standeven had done exactly what they expected of him; he kept low and cowered. Now he rose and gingerly made his way to Stryke and Pepperdyne.

Seeing him approach, Stryke said sarcastically, 'Come to help, have you?'

'No,' the human replied soberly, as though it was a genuine question. 'I wondered . . .'

'Spit it out.'

'I wanted to be sure the instrumentalities were safe.'

Stryke glared at him. '*What?*'

'They're secure, right?'

'What the hell's that got to do with you?'

'It concerns all of us. They're our only way to—'

'They're just fine.' Despite himself, Stryke's hand instinctively went to the pouch.

'You're sure that they—'

'Why the interest? What business is it of yours?'

'Like I said—'

'Ignore him, Stryke,' Pepperdyne intervened. 'It's just his weak-minded fear talking.'

Standeven shot him a venomous look.

'Well, he can keep his fears to himself in future and let me look after the stars.'

'Of course, Captain,' Standeven said, oozing with sycophancy. 'I wouldn't have it any other way.' He turned and picked his way back to his seat.

Stryke glanced at Pepperdyne. The human didn't meet his gaze.

21

Jennesta enjoyed few things more than a spot of mayhem and arson.

Having relished the former, she brought about the latter.

The surprise attack, using overwhelming forces and aided by her magic, had succeeded. Now the settlement burned. Some of the creatures fought on, as she fully expected their kind to do, but the pockets of resistance were isolated. And as the camp was on the small side there were few of them to defend it; even she might have hesitated before venturing into one of their more densely populated regions.

She had given strict orders about which of the creatures her followers were to search for, and that they were on all accounts to be taken alive. The rest she had no concern for.

But now she was growing impatient. The ones she sought had not yet been found. Her underlings would rue the day if she had to take a hand herself. It was true that many of them were unnerved by the crossing, but that just made them weaklings in her eyes, not needy. She filled her time with some creative thinking about the form punishments would take.

Her reverie was broken by the arrival of a nervous officer. In the best tradition of those who wish to keep their heads, he broke the good news first. Their principal quarry had been caught, albeit at the cost of several of Jennesta's followers' lives and only by using an awe-inspiring number of troops. The less than good news was that the two other targets, the younger ones, had got away.

She expressed her anger at the less than perfect outcome, but it was really just a matter of giving the officer what he expected of her. In truth she was content. She had the important one.

The prisoner was brought to her. It was chained and well attended, yet still needed several of her undead guardians, including Hacher, to keep it in check. The creature was haughty, and when Jennesta approached, it spat at her face. She had it beaten for that.

Once the beast was further secured, and as fire and bloodshed held sway outside, Jennesta set to work.

Spurral was right. The Gatherer prisoners had seen the futility of not cooperating and helped the dwarfs with the ship, though they weren't allowed any leeway that might permit them to cause trouble. No one doubted the prisoners agreed in the hope of lenient treatment. But the boost to the dwarfs' confidence in having their tormentors in their power was considerable. Relations between the surviving Gatherers and their one-time captives were hardly cordial, but so far there had been no serious discord.

As the ship headed back to the dwarfs' island, something like normality was imposed.

Spurral and Kalgeck stood on the bridge, watching dwarfs and Gatherers trim the sails.

'But *why* do we have to slow down?' Spurral asked, irritated at the prospect of delay.

'Because of what the Gatherers told us,' Kalgeck explained, 'backed up by these.' He slapped his hand on Vant's charts spread out before them. 'Right now we're in deep water. Very deep. But soon it gets shallow. There's a reef or something down there, and we have to steer a careful path through it.'

'Why can't we just go round?'

'That really would add to the journey, and we'd have to pass through waters with treacherous currents.'

'Great,' she sighed. 'So what do we do, exactly?'

'Slow to a crawl and measure the depth. Look.' He pointed down at the deck.

A group of dwarfs were at the rail. They had a large coil of rope with a lead weight at its end. Knots in the rope marked out the fathoms.

When the ship was little more than drifting, the measuring line was lowered over the side. They played out almost its entire length before bottom was reached.

'How deep's that?' Spurral said.

'Getting on for fifty fathoms,' Kalgeck replied. 'No danger to us there.'

The ship crept on as the sun made its lazy way across the azure sky. Measurements were taken at regular intervals, but showed practically no variation.

Spurral grew more impatient at the sluggish progress. 'Are we ever going to get to this shallow patch, Kalgeck?'

'According to the chart, we're already in it.'

'Somebody should tell the sea.'

'These maps aren't always exact. Least, that's what the Gatherers say.'

'Well, I hope we're going to see some—'

There were shouts from the measuring team.

'Now what?' Kalgeck wondered.

'Let's see,' Spurral said, heading for the ladder that led to the deck.

When they reached the measurers, one of the dwarfs held up the end of the rope. It was severed and the weight was gone.

'What did it?' Spurral asked.

'Don't know,' the young dwarf with the rope told her. 'But whatever it was happened at about twelve fathoms.'

Kalgeck examined the rope. 'Looks like it was cut, or . . .'

'Or what?' Spurral said.

'It probably just got caught on something down there.'

'So let's try again.'

They brought another coil of knotted rope and fitted a new weight. It was fed overboard, and a dwarf was set the task of calling its progress.

'One fathom . . . two . . .'

'This should sort it out,' Kalgeck offered.

'Yeah, most likely,' Spurral replied, though there was a jot of uncertainty in her voice.

'. . . four fathoms . . .five . . . six . . .'

'I expect it's just a fluke.'

'Hmm.'

'. . . eleven . . . twelve . . . thirteen . . .'

'Seems it's all right this time,' Kalgeck announced.

'. . . fourteen . . . fifteen . . .'

'Good. Now maybe we can get on and—'

The line suddenly went taut. Then it began playing out at a rapid rate. The end of it would have disappeared over the side if several dwarfs hadn't grabbed hold of it. But they struggled, and the rope was sliding painfully through their hands. Kalgeck, Spurral and the others joined in, and still they fought to keep a grip.

'We're going to lose it!' Spurral warned.

'It must be snagged,' Kalgeck reckoned.

'Then why's it moving about so much?'

The rope was going from left to right then back again, and it was twisting in their hands. Kalgeck called for help. Three dwarfs ran to them and seized the rope. Now there were no less than nine of them clutching the line, but the bizarre tug of war went on.

It ended abruptly. Without warning, the line went slack. The release was so sudden it put them all on their backs. Scrambling to their feet, they quickly hauled the rope in. This time there was no resistance. Again, it had been severed.

'What the hell's going on?' Spurral said.

Kalgeck was blowing on his reddened palms. 'Maybe it got caught on a sunken wreck.'

'That's *moving about?*'

'The currents that deep can be strong. Maybe if—'

A weighty thump echoed through the ship. It originated somewhere far below. A second later there was another impact, louder and more powerful. The ship bobbed, tilting the deck and making the dwarfs' footing unsure.

Someone yelled and pointed. No more than an arrow's flight away a large segment of sea bubbled and boiled. The churning water was white with foam.

'What the hell is *that?*' Spurral exclaimed.

One of the Gatherer prisoners, working on some tedious chore nearby, had abandoned it and come to the rail. He stared at the seething mass of water with a fearful expression.

'Do you know what it is?' Spurral asked him.

He nodded, but seemed unable to speak.

'Well?' she insisted.

He whispered, '*The Krake.*'

'What's that?'

The human gave no answer. She looked at the others. Kalgeck had gone pale, and the other dwarfs in earshot looked just as drained of colour.

'Kalgeck?' she appealed. '*Kalgeck!*'

He tore his eyes from the restless water. 'We've heard the stories. The Krake are lords of the deep. Some say they're gods. They can crush any size of ship, or pull it down into the abyss.'

'To do that they'd have to be . . . gigantic.'

'Bigger than islands, they say.'

'But you've never actually seen these things yourself?'

'Not . . . until now.' He was staring over her shoulder.

She turned.

Something was rising from the angry water. At first, with

spray and mist obscuring the view, it was hard to make out what it was. As it continued to rise it became clearer.

It was an appendage, a tentacle with the girth of a temple pillar. Like a blind cave worm it was greyish-white, and its gristly skin was dappled with thick blue veins. Soon it had risen to the height of the ship, and was still growing.

Another tentacle erupted from the water, much closer to the vessel; near enough to rock it and send a wave over the rail. Soaked and dazed, the dwarfs retreated.

Shouts and screams had them turning to the opposite rail. On that side, too, tentacles were rising. The dwarfs stood transfixed as more and more emerged. In minutes the tentacles, swaying grotesquely, stood taller than the mainmast. All around the ship the water frothed wildly.

One of the tentacles came down, striking the deck a tremend-ous, sodden blow. Another swept in horizontally, demolishing the rail and causing dozens to duck. When a third crashed into the bridge, the dwarfs snapped out of their stupor.

They set about attacking the odious limbs with cutlasses and axes. The rubbery flesh proved resilient. Blows glanced off, and only continuous hacking made any impression. When blades did break through to tissue they released copious amounts of a glutinous ochre-coloured liquid. Its disgusting stink had them reeling.

The tentacles weren't just causing damage to the ship. Some-how sensing the dwarfs and humans, they slithered at remark-able speed to entwine any they could catch. Screaming victims were hoisted into the air and over the side.

Encircled by a muscular tentacle, the mainmast snapped like matchwood and toppled, pinning dwarfs and humans alike. So dire was the situation that even the Gatherers joined the effort to repel the Krake. They were using improvised weapons, or snatching up swords and axes dropped by dwarfs that had been taken. In the face of disaster the slavers and their one-time captives made common cause. Not that it made much difference.

'This is hopeless!' Spurral yelled as she battered at a writhing tentacle.

'We'll have to abandon ship!' Kalgeck returned. He was smothered in the foul-smelling yellowish-brown life fluid.

'I wouldn't give much for our chances on the open sea!'

'What, then?'

'Just keep fighting!'

A bellowing human was dragged past, a tentacle wrapped around his legs. Spurral and Kalgeck tried to hack him free, but their blades made practically no headway. The unfortunate Gatherer was whipped over the rail and disappeared.

Ominous creaking and rending sounds came from the ship's bowels. Above deck, tentacles ripped through timber as though it were parchment. Planks buckled, the remaining masts shuddered, canvas fell.

The ship lurched violently. Then it began to descend.

'We're going down!' Kalgeck shouted.

Water began pouring over the rails and swamping the deck. It was ankle deep in seconds, then knee and quickly waist-high. Panic broke out.

Spurral felt as much as heard the hull crushing. Dwarfs and humans were swept overboard. She looked around for Kalgeck and saw him being carried over the rail by a torrent of water.

There was a dizzying drop as what remained of the ship was pulled beneath the waves.

Spurral was immersed. Underwater, all was chaos. The sinking craft, with fragments shedding. A jumble of barrels, chests, ropes, scraps of sail, struggling bodies, twisting tentacles.

Just briefly she glimpsed animate forms, deathly white and grotesque in appearance. They were of enormous bulk, and their repugnant flesh pulsated horribly. She saw gaping, cavernous mouths lined with fangs the size of broadswords. And she caught sight of a single massive eye, unblinking and afire with greedy malevolence.

Then mercifully, total darkness closed in on her.

22

Once the ship they set on fire was out of sight, the Wolverines inspected their second craft. According to Pepperdyne, the only one with any real knowledge of boats, the damage was worse than he first thought.

'That magic beam punched through the hull in a couple of places,' he explained. 'Kind of sprinkled it. Look, you can just see the burn marks around the holes.'

Stryke leaned and nodded. 'And?'

'It left us with a number of leaks. Small and slow, but a nuisance. We can patch them up, and get somebody bailing.'

'So what's the problem?'

'I don't know how much the timbers might have been weakened by the hit. It could get worse, and we don't have what we need for a major repair.'

'What can we do?'

'Stop at the next island we come to and hope it's got trees.'

'We'd have to change course. That'd slow us.'

'We'll slow a damn sight more if we sink. Where is the nearest island?'

Stryke took out the chart and unfolded it. 'There,' he said, jabbing at a spot.

'I'm not sure if this boat would make that.'

'Great,' Stryke sighed. 'Any ideas?'

'When this sort of thing happened back in Trougath we'd lash the boats together.'

'If this one sinks won't it take both boats down?'

'You have to look at it the other way round. The buoyancy of the good one keeps them both afloat. It's not ideal, Stryke, but it should get us there. Though joining the boats will slow down our speed, of course, and it'll steer like a cow.'

'With that Pelli Madayar after us, this isn't a good time to fetter ourselves.'

Pepperdyne shrugged. 'Only other thing I can come up with is abandoning this boat and squeezing everybody into the good one. Mind you, *that* would slow us down a lot too. Not to mention things would be kind of crowded.'

Stryke considered it. 'No, we won't do that. It'd cramp our style too much if we have to fight. Take as much help as you need and see to the lashing. But do it fast; I feel like a sitting target.'

'Right. Jup'll have to be told about the delay.'

'I know, and he's not going to like it. You get on here. I'll tell him.'

The boats were already linked by a couple of lengths of rope. And they were near enough to each other that he could easily step over.

Jup was at the prow of boat one as usual. He was leaning over the side and stretching his arm to get his hand in the water.

'What you doing?' Stryke asked.

Jup straightened and wiped his wet hand against his breeches. If anything, the sombre expression he'd worn since they set out was more intense. 'I was trying farsight.'

'I thought this much water stopped it working.'

'It does, mostly. I'm . . . I wanted to do *something*, you know?'

Stryke nodded.

'And I picked something up,' the dwarf added.

'You did?'

'A life force. Or maybe a whole lot of them clustered

together. Really massive. Big enough to counter a lot of the water's masking effect.'

'Any idea what it is?'

'No. But it's got an . . . atmosphere that I don't like. Definitely didn't feel friendly.'

'How far away?'

'Hard to say. The amount of energy it threw out, it could be a long way off. But my guess is that it isn't too far.'

'Is it a threat?'

'Who knows? But like I said, it didn't come over as pleasant.'

'We'll be on our guard.' He considered his sergeant. 'There's nothing to say it's anything to do with Spurral.'

'No. Not directly. But knowing she's out there with . . . whatever isn't a good feeling.'

'We've got to detour, Jup.'

'*What?* Why?'

'Pepperdyne says the other boat might sink if we don't find an island and fix it.'

'Shit' He looked over at boat two. Pepperdyne and several Wolverines were starting work. 'What're they doing?'

'Lashing the boats together.'

'Doesn't that mean if one sinks—'

'I thought that. Pepperdyne says no.'

'Damn it, Stryke; first that elf tries to fry us and now this. Am I ever going to get to Spurral?'

'I'll make it as quick as I can. We'll be working all out.'

'I'm counting on it.'

'Meantime, you keep doing whatever it is you do with the farsight. We could use a warning if what you picked up comes our way.'

'Sure. But if what I sensed comes our way a warning's not going to help much.'

It didn't take long to get the boats secured and plot a new course. The two-boat behemoth they created was ungainly and difficult to manoeuvre, but Pepperdyne maintained it would get them to land.

After a faltering start, due to how cumbersome the vessel had become, they got the hang of handling it. They rowed hard, and there was enough of a prevailing wind to make it worth raising the small sails.

Those who weren't on rowing duty speculated on the mystery of Pelli Madayar's group. Some looked forward to tangling with the Gatherers by recounting previous battles, as orcs were wont to do, and garnished their tales with some light boasting. A few concentrated on sharpening their weapons. Jup stayed at the prow, looking grim and occasionally dipping his hand in the water. Standeven continued to occupy his lonely place at the stern. He seemed restless, and Pepperdyne, too busy to spend time with him, nevertheless noticed that his one-time master's eyes were rarely off Stryke.

They quickly fell back into toiling at the oars combined with breaks for rest and bluster. A couple of hours into this routine, with the sun well past its highest point, a lull developed. Wheam tried filling it.

He stood and cleared his throat. No one paid any attention. He cleared his throat again, louder and theatrically. Two or three heads turned but most ignored him.

'Comrades!' he declared. '*Shipmates!*'

Haskeer groaned.

'It occurred to me,' Wheam said, 'that this could be the perfect time to give you all the first taste of the epic ballad I've been composing.' He pointed a proud finger at his temple. 'In my head.'

'You haven't got your lute,' Coilla reminded him desperately.

'It doesn't matter. All good verse should be as powerful whether spoken or sung.'

'How powerful is it if you keep it to yourself?' Haskeer said.

Wheam ploughed on. 'This particular extract is about what we're doing right now. It goes:

> *'They were cast upon the briny deep*
> *for their solemn oath they would keep*
> *to rescue a lost comrade true*
> *from the sea so very blue!*

> *'Ooohh they battled magic mean and nasty*
> *and their victory was proud and tar-sty . . .*

'That should be tasty. I need to work on something else that rhythms with nasty.'

'End my life,' Coilla pleaded, 'Now.'

'Tasty?' Haskeer murmured, baffled.

'We could throw him overboard,' Stryke said with no trace of humour.

'Anyway,' Wheam continued, 'the next bit is a kind of chorus. Feel free to join in.

> *'They fought the elf*
> *they fought the witch*
> *one was a pest*
> *the other a bitch!*

> *'Raise your flagons*
> *raise your trumpets*
> *the Wolverines*
> *are no dunces!*

'Things get really gripping now, In the next thirty verses—'

'*Land ahoy!*'

It could have been a lie. A frantic attempt by a tormented grunt to ease the pain. No one cared.

In reality, land was in sight. The dark, bumpy outline of an island could be seen on the horizon.

Haskeer raised his eyes heavenward and muttered, 'Thank you, gods.'

'How we going to handle this, Stryke?' Coilla wanted to know. 'If it's inhabited, that is.'

'Choices?'

'The usual. Sneak, full frontal or parley.'

'Nothing special in mind?'

'Not knowing what the hell we'll face, no.'

'We'll try parley. After scouting the lay, of course.'

' 'Course.'

'If it's inhabited and they're hostile,' Dallog said, 'what then?'

'Friend or foe, we'll get what we need,' Stryke vowed. 'We've no time to waste.'

When they got nearer and the island's features became clear, they saw that several ships were anchored in its largest bay.

'So it is inhabited,' Coilla said. 'Or at least somebody's visiting.'

'I'd say there's a settlement,' Stryke reckoned. 'Look. Just by the tree-line there. Those are some sort of buildings, aren't they?'

She squinted. 'Yes, I think they are.'

'Then we'll circle from a distance and see if there's somewhere quiet we can land.' He turned and shouted, *'Get those sails down, now! We don't need spotting!'*

When they got round to the island's far side they could see no signs of habitation. They headed for a small, deserted cove, and managed to land on its sandy beach. Stryke ordered the twin boats to be hauled ashore and into the trees, then had them camouflaged. Four privates, including Wheam, were assigned to guard the boats. Standeven was told to stay, too, though he uncharacteristically tried to object. Stryke led the rest of the band into the interior.

'Why are we going inland anyway?' Jup asked. 'Don't we have what we need where we landed?'

'Not really,' Pepperdyne answered. 'We could use good seasoned timber for the repairs, and there's nothing suitable. Some serious tools would be handy too.'

'And our food and water are running down quicker than I thought they would,' Stryke admitted. 'That settlement we saw seems the best place to restock. Maybe we can pick up news of the Gatherers there, too.'

The island's heart was dense with jungle, and hacking their way through was inevitably a slow job. Anxious to speed things, Jup had suggested taking the much less obstructed coastal route. Stryke thought that would leave them too exposed and vetoed the idea.

But the island was small, certainly compared to the dwarfs' homeland, and the sun had still to set when they arrived at the beachside settlement. They surveyed it from hiding places at the jungle's edge.

There were around half a dozen dwellings of various sizes. An odd feature was a largish pool that had been dug in the clearing in front of the buildings. It was fed with salt water by channels connecting it to the sea, and there was a stout wooden barrier all around it. There were creatures of some kind splashing about in the water. They were of a fair size and dark skinned, but it was hard to make out what they were.

Other beings were present, and obviously in charge. These were instantly recognisable to the orcs.

'Fucking goblins!' Haskeer growled.

'I gather they're not one of your favourite races,' Pepperdyne said.

'We've had run-ins,' Stryke told him.

'Maybe they're different here,' Coilla ventured.

'Yeah, right,' Haskeer came back acerbically.

Pepperdyne was curious. 'So what is it about them?'

'They're ugly, back-stabbing, two-faced, mean, greedy, underhand, stuck up, cowardly, stinking bastards.'

'Those are their good points,' Coilla added.

'Given what we've known of them in the past,' Stryke said, 'we'll forget the parleying. Now let's get some scouts out.'

When the pathfinders had left, stealthily blending into the

jungle, the others settled to watch what was happening in the encampment.

After a while, Coilla said, 'Those creatures in the pool; I reckon they're horses. Or maybe ponies.'

'Why would goblins keep horses in a salt-water pool?' Jup reasoned.

'I think Coilla could be on to something,' Stryke said thoughtfully.

'You reckon they're horses? What are the goblins trying to do, teach them to swim?'

'No, not horses. Not exactly. And if I'm right, they wouldn't need teaching.'

'So what do you think they are?'

'I want a closer look to be sure. Let's think how we can do that.'

Zoda, one of the scouts he sent out, returned at that point. 'Chief, you better come and see what we've found.'

Stryke beckoned Coilla, Jup and Pepperdyne to accompany him. He left Haskeer in charge.

They followed Zoda into the jungle. It took just a few minutes to reach a clearing, an area where the vegetation had been trampled flat and several trees bodily uprooted. Gleadeg, one of the other scouts, was waiting for them. He wasn't alone.

Stryke took one look and said, 'I was right.'

The creature before them did look like a horse, but not entirely so. It was about the same size as a pony, but much more muscular and powerful looking. With the exception of its mane, which was dark grey, it was completely black with no markings of any kind save a little patch, again grey, about its eyes. Its skin wasn't like a horse's at all; it was smooth and oily in appearance, resembling a seal's coat. There was a very unusual aspect to its mane, too; it exuded a steady trickle of water, as though it were a gently squeezed sponge. The water ran down the creature's shiny flanks and fell in drops.

'You're a kelpie?' Stryke asked.

'I am,' the water horse replied, its voice low and throaty. 'And you are orcs.'

'You know us?'

'I know of your race.' He looked to Jup, 'And I have communed with dwarfs.' The kelpie bobbed its great head in Pepperdyne's direction. 'And I am more than familiar with his kind. Unhappily so.'

'I can vouch for this human. He means you and your kin no harm.'

'That's hard to believe of his race. But he hasn't yet struck me down or tried to enslave me so I must take your word for it.'

Pepperdyne looked embarrassed.

'Your kind are rare where we come from,' Coilla said. 'They say it's wise to keep away from you, that you lure hatchlings to watery graves so you can eat their hearts. It's even said that you're really the spirits of evil creatures who have died badly.'

'Many untrue things are said about orcs too,' the kelpie replied. 'Do you eat your young? Are you the twisted offspring of elves? Do you murder the innocent for the sheer pleasure of it? Like you, we kelpies are subject to hatred and fear simply because we are different and prefer a solitary path.'

'Well said.'

'There is one true story told about us, however. Above all else we value our freedom.' The subject was painful enough to mist the kelpie's startlingly blue eyes. 'To us, enslavement is worse than death.'

'Yet it looks like that's been your fate,' Stryke commented. 'Why are you here?'

The kelpie looked to Pepperdyne again. 'Because his folk brought us here by force, as they have since time out of mind.'

'Why is no one ever pleased to see me?' Pepperdyne asked.

'Now you know how we feel,' Coilla told him.

'The ones who brought you here,' Jup said, 'are they called Gatherers?'

'Yes,' the kelpie confirmed.

'So how do the goblins fit into this?'

'The Gatherers are the catchers of slaves. The goblins buy. A few for themselves, but mostly to be sold on in turn. They stand between the slavers and their prey's ultimate masters. Their role is to match suitable slaves to the tasks they will undertake. So it's trolls or gnomes for islands where mining takes place, elves and brownies for houses of pleasure, gremlins for the drudgery of scholarly work. Even orcs, to provide bodyguards for petty tyrants. Though they are notoriously hard to break, you'll be proud to hear.'

Coilla frowned. 'There are islands here where orcs live?'

'Oh, yes. None near to this one, however, and even the Gatherers hesitate to try plundering them.'

'And what about kelpies? What sort of so-called owners are found for you?'

'We are in demand on many islands.'

'You have special skills?'

'No. It seems we make good meat.'

The silence that followed was broken by Jup. 'How did you escape the goblins?'

'Purely by chance. A rare lapse of attention on their part let me seize the opportunity to get away. I believe the only reason they haven't mounted a search for me is because, as my kind counts time, I am old. Very old. My flesh would be too tough!' He gave a watery, snorting laugh. 'There's no profit to them in wasting energy on me. Particularly as they are presently small in number.'

'How small?' Stryke wanted to know.

'Barely two score. Normally there are many more present, but the rest are away delivering the latest batch of . . . *goods*. That's why there are only kelpie prisoners here at the moment.'

'Why haven't you tried to overcome them yourselves, while their numbers are low?'

'We are hampered in two ways. First, we have no leadership.

It's not our way. We are a fiercely independent breed.' He sighed. 'And look where it's got us.'

'And second?'

'Can you who dwell solely on the land imagine what it is to be dependent on water? We have to wallow in its life-giving essence several times a day. Our lives depend on it. A kelpie deprived of water dies a horrible and lingering death. We can hardly mount an uprising when weighed down with that necessity. I myself have to visit the shore daily to bathe. I don't doubt they will catch me there one day and kill me.'

'No they won't. We're gonna help you.'

'You are?'

'You bet,' Coilla said.

'Definitely,' Pepperdyne and Jup chorused.

The kelpie was taken aback. 'The human too? What have we done to deserve this?'

'Let's just say we're like you; we value freedom,' Stryke said. 'Do you have a name?'

'Of course.'

'What is it?'

'It would do you no good knowing, unless you're able to talk under water.'

'Er, no. That's not one of our skills.'

'Just call me the kelpie.'

'You have our protection. Come with us. You could probably use something to eat. What *do* you eat?'

'Not the hearts of hatchlings. Our appetites are wide-reaching, but given the choice we favour fish.'

'We'll see what we can do.'

On their way back to the others, Stryke asked Jup how he felt.

'I'm fearful of Spurral falling into the hands of scum like these goblins.'

'So take it out on them until we find the Gatherers.'

'I intend to.'

'Good. I knew that'd cheer you up.'

They waited for dark.

Under cover of night they positioned themselves around the goblin compound. Stryke had sent for the five guarding the boats, to up the numbers. But he kept Standeven well out of things, and relegated Wheam to a back-up.

There were perhaps a dozen goblins visible. Most of them bore the metal-topped trident spears they favoured, but also carried blades. The rest of the goblins were either in the various buildings or on the beach near the anchored ships.

'We keep this simple,' Stryke whispered to Coilla. 'Get in fast, kill 'em.'

'So how's that any different to what we usually do?'

'Ready?'

She nodded.

He signalled, and it was passed on.

The first move was down to the archers. They shot bolts into the compound that dropped five or six of the goblins before the others caught on. The next volley was of flaming arrows aimed at the buildings' rush roofs, for chaos' sake.

The blazing arrows were the signal to charge. Out of hiding, the Wolverines swept in from all sides. The goblins who survived the arrow bombardment were recovering their balance, and the ones in the now-burning buildings had spilled out. Those on the beach, alerted by the fires, were hurrying back.

So the orcs faced the full complement, and relished it.

Stryke lashed out at the first goblin he met. His blade severed the sinewy neck, sending its head bouncing across the sand. The next took steel to its guts. He disarmed a third by simply doing just that; he lopped off the creature's sword arm, then ran it through.

For Coilla, the lure of her throwing knives had proved too strong. Plucking them from the holsters strapped to her arms, she lobbed in rapid succession. A goblin fell with a blade in its eye; another stopped one with its back. Spotting a goblin rushing at her, its trident levelled, she struck it square to the chest. Yet another caught a knife in what would have been its privy parts, if it had had any.

Pepperdyne had the by now familiar experience of confronting foes surprised to be facing a human. For the goblins, he guessed, humans meant Gatherers and grubby mutual interest. They were stunned to be attacked by one. Their initial hesitation was a bonus he seized. His sword hewed wiry flesh.

Haskeer, battling nearby and trying not to admire the human's style, spat on subtlety, as usual. He brought down the first goblin he came across with bare fists, then snapped its curved spine over his knee. The one after that he eviscerated.

All acquitted themselves well, even the seasoning tyros. But Jup outshone. He fought with a ferocity to equal the matchless orcs. Spurred by frustration and fury, drunk on bloodlust, he gave no quarter. Armed traditionally with his staff, and having a long-bladed knife to hand, he thundered into the goblins like a pint-sized tsunami. He shattered skulls and ripped through throats. Landing a particularly vicious blow, he propelled a goblin over the fence and into the kelpie's pool. They put paid to it with thrashing hooves and snapping teeth.

The moment arrived, as it does in every battle, when it dawned on the victors that there was no one left standing to fight. A quick search of the buildings that escaped the fire, and the surrounding area, confirmed it.

The kelpie prisoners were liberated. They scrambled from the pool and shook themselves. Some pawed the ground, as though that was a pleasure they had long been deprived of.

Stryke got his officers together, and the ageing kelpie joined them.

'We've got to make a choice,' Stryke told them. 'Either we push on to the Gatherers' island or we stay here in the hope that Spurral and the slavers turn up. You should have first say on this, Jup.'

'I . . . I honestly don't know, Chief. My instinct is to go on. Then again, knowing this is where the slaves are brought . . .'

'It's one place they are brought,' the kelpie corrected. 'This isn't the only island where goblins, and other races, collect slaves.'

'Shit. So Spurral might not be brought here?'

'Don't despair. This is the most likely place. But your mate has not arrived yet, which given when she was taken, makes me think the Gatherers are sticking to their pattern.'

'What do you mean?'

'The time when they come has never been predictable, but the *order* of their coming is always the same. The Gatherers next port of call after raiding the dwarfs' island is invariably our own. Take us to our island, Wolverines, and there's a chance this Spurral of yours can be found. There's nothing here for us. We want to go home.'

'What do you think, Jup?' Stryke asked.

'Gods, this is getting so complicated. But it seems to make sense.'

'You're forgetting that we've only got two small boats,' Coilla reminded them, 'and one of those damaged.'

'And you're forgetting those,' the kelpie said. 'He tilted his head to indicate the beach and the anchored craft. 'Why use a boat when you can have a ship?'

'I'd feel a damn sight better in one of those,' Haskeer announced.

Stryke turned to Pepperdyne. 'Could we handle one of those goblin ships?'

He took a look. 'I reckon so.'

'All right then. We leave at first light.'

The kelpie nodded contentedly. 'Good. I can assure you of a warm welcome. Few are as hospitable as the kelpies.'

23

The darkness dissolved, to be replaced by a blinding light.

Spurral was on her back, staring up at the sun. She turned her head to avoid its punishing glare. There were fiery floats in her eyes and she blinked to rid herself of them. She had no idea where she was. As the floats faded and her faculties returned, so did the memory, of the ship, the Krake and what had happened.

She became aware of the sound of pounding waves, and when she reached out a hand it came into contact with wet sand. Water was lapping at her feet and thighs. Her sodden clothes were steaming gently in the heat.

Slowly, painfully, she got up and tried to make sense of her surroundings.

She was on a long, golden beach. Wreckage and general debris was deposited along the shoreline, including a couple of large sections of ship's decking. She guessed that she had probably clung to one of them, although she had no recollection of it.

Behind her, the beach stretched back a long way until it met a jumble of palm trees and other vegetation. Above the trees she could see the peaks of several small mountains of greyish rock, gleaming in the sunlight. There was no sign of habitation.

She stilled. Mixed in with the crash of waves and shrieking gulls there seemed to be something else. It took her a moment to realise it was someone shouting. As she attuned herself to it she grasped that there was more than one voice.

Looking along the beach to her left, she saw nothing. It was a different story to her right. In the far distance she could see figures. There appeared to be seven or eight of them. They were humanoid in shape and looked as though they were waving. As she watched, trying to make out who or what they might be, it became obvious they were heading her way. Spurral hesitated for a moment. Then, spurred by hope, she began to run towards them.

It felt as though it took for ever to cover the expanse of beach between her and the approaching figures. As she moved, her legs growing leaden with the effort of running through the obstructive sand, she became conscious of how much she ached. The battering she had taken when the ship went down, and presumably afterwards when she was at the mercy of the tides and drifting flotsam, was starting to make itself felt. Her elbows were grazed, there was a dull pain in her back and she noticed large blue-black bruises coming up on her pumping arms. But the prospect of someone else being on an island she thought deserted kept her going.

When she finally got close enough, she saw that the figures were dwarfs. Closer still, she recognised Kalgeck among them. Then they met and she was hugging him, relieved and frankly amazed that her friend had also survived the catastrophe. His companions, five males and two females, all young, clustered round joyfully.

'Are you injured?' Kalgeck asked, surveying her.

'I was lucky. Just a few knocks. How about all of you?'

'Fortune smiled on us, too. Our injuries are slight. It was a miracle.'

'It's hard to argue with that. But. . . are you all there is?'

His expression turned solemn. 'As far as we can tell. We've not been looking for too long, but apart from each other, and now you, we've seen no one else.'

'You couldn't have looked everywhere. It could be survivors have washed up elsewhere on this island, or even other islands.'

'Yes, we'll have to hope for that. But it does seem a mockery by fate if my kin should beat the Gatherers only to perish because of the Krake.'

'It would,' she agreed glumly. 'How about the Gatherers? You've not come across any of them?'

Kalgeck shook his head. 'But most of them were imprisoned below decks, remember.'

'Yes, of course. I could almost feel sorry for them.'

'It's hard for us to think that way about them. They caused us so much misery.'

'I know, and I can't blame you for it. Still, it's possible some of them might have made it here. We should take care.'

'What do we do now?'

'Do you know where we are? Or anything about this island?'

'No.'

'All right. So let's find out if it's inhabited; and if it is, whether the natives are friendly or not. But first we ought to look through the wreckage for anything useful, like provisions.'

'I already found this.' He held out a water flask.

'Oh, great. Can I? I'm parched.'

As she drank, Kalgeck said, 'It doesn't look like there's a lot else, though.' He was staring at the wreckage she washed in with.

That proved almost right. In fact they were lucky enough to find another flask, containing coarse brandy this time, though it was only half full. A nip each raised their spirits a little. They also scavenged some chunks of timber that would serve as clubs. Nothing else was of much use. But a couple of the dwarfs had managed to hang on to weapons from the ship; a Gatherer knife and one of the wooden hatchets the captives had made clandestinely.

They set off inland. Just inside the tree-line they came across bushes with a crop of yellow, spiky fruit about the size of apples. They were unfamiliar to Spurral but the dwarfs knew them and were delighted. Once the tough skin had been peeled off the sweet, juicy white flesh proved delicious. They ate their fill and then some.

'Right,' Spurral said, licking her fingers, 'let's see what else this place has to offer.'

Fortified, they continued their journey.

The jungle was thick and difficult to get through. After they'd trekked for some time, with Spurral in the lead, hacking at foliage with the knife and stumbling on vines, they were beginning to wonder if it was worth going on. Then she stopped, raising a hand for the others to be quiet. There was an extensive clearing just ahead. There seemed to be nobody about, so they gingerly stepped into it.

Trees had been felled, or more accurately uprooted, and dragged to form several heaps at the glade's edge. The undergrowth was trampled flat. In the centre of the clearing was a sizeable pool.

Spurral cupped her hand and tried the water. She spat it out. 'Salt. Must be fed by the sea.' Looking round, she added, 'Nothing here is natural except the pool. Somebody cleared this area.'

Kalgeck held a finger to his lips and pointed. There was a rustling in the undergrowth. They raised their meagre weapons. More rustlings came, but from several directions. The dwarfs drew themselves into a protective circle, eyes peeled.

Some kind of creature crashed through the vegetation, then several more. They were big and black.

'Horses?' Spurral exclaimed. As soon as she said it she saw her error.

The creatures entering the clearing looked superficially like horses but with important differences. Their skin was wrong, resembling a seal's, and their luxuriant manes oozed water. They were much more muscular and robust looking than commonplace horses. Above all, they had eyes that betrayed far greater acumen than any steed.

Kalgeck confirmed it. 'They're not ordinary horses. They're—'

'Kelpies,' one of the creatures grated, trotting forward. 'And we would like to welcome you to our island if we were sure you meant no harm.'

'We don't,' Spurral replied, recovering her poise. 'Do we look like raiders?'

'No, you look like bedraggled dwarfs. And as there is no ship off our coast I assume the sea cast you here.'

'Yes. We survived a wreck.'

'Then you are most fortunate, given some of the perils in these waters.'

'We met one of them.'

'Doubly fortunate then.' He surveyed the dishevelled group. 'You must forgive our suspicion. We have few visitors, and those who do come are usually unbidden and mean us no good.'

'You wouldn't be talking about humans, would you?'

'They can be among the worst of races, as you dwarfs must surely know.'

'You mean the Gatherers.'

'That's a name reviled by my kind. Even more so now, as we believe a visitation from them is due. And that always means pain and grief.'

'I can set your mind at rest about that. They went down with the ship we were on.'

'*Truly?*'

'Yes.'

'And their vile captain?'

'Salloss Vant? Dead.'

'You're sure?'

'I saw it.'

'Spurral's being modest,' Kalgeck interjected. 'She's the one who killed him.'

Insofar as they could read the kelpie's expression, he looked impressed. 'We have been in hiding, hoping against hope that the slavers might pass us by this time. Now you bring us this glad news. Come, your injuries will be tended and you can rest. Then there will be celebrations and feasting in your honour.'

'Now you're talking,' Spurral told him. 'We've had nothing but gruel for days. But tell me, what do we call you?'

'Before I can answer that question,' the kelpie said, 'I have one for you. How good are dwarfs at talking underwater?'

By the time Pelli Madayar's group put out the flaming sails, the Wolverines had made their getaway. She ordered a clean-up and went to her cabin.

The nature of the magic she used to communicate with the Gateway Corps' homeworld was such that it utilised any suitable medium. Sea water was the simplest, most plentiful and by far the most effective channel. She stared into a large bowl of it. The application of certain compounds to make it more receptive, followed by a gestured conjuration, sparked the enchantment.

The water simmered and ran a gamut of colours before settling down. At which point Pelli found herself looking at an image of Karrell Revers, human head of the Corps.

'I hope you have more cheering news for me this time,' he said without preamble.

'We've had our second engagement with the orcs.'

'And it wasn't a success. I can tell from your expression, Pelli.'

'They *are* a prime fighting unit.'

'So are you. Or you're supposed to be.' His tone had been much more prickly of late. The strain was telling on him. 'Could it be that your failure to overcome the warband is due to you exercising too much restraint?'

'It's true I began by trying negotiation, but—'

'This situation requires a remedy, quickly and decisively. You should have known better than to try parleying with orcs. Force is what they understand.'

'I thought we were supposed to stand for moral principles.'

'There'll be no principles, moral or otherwise, if instrumentalities fall into the hands of orcs, or worse.' Revers softened a little. 'I'm sorry, Pelli, but the gravity of what's going on makes it vital that we draw this to a close quickly. Forgive me for saying this, but the impression I have is that things are getting beyond your control there.'

'They're not,' she assured him, though she didn't entirely believe that herself. 'I intend to clear this matter up.'

'Then you'll follow my earlier advice.'

'Sir?'

'Use the special weapons.'

'That could involve the loss of innocent life.'

'Not if you proceed with caution when you use them. You've had no luck taming the Wolverines. This could be the only way you'll triumph over them.'

'I'll give your advice serious consideration.'

'Do it. Pelli.'

Without further word his likeness faded and disappeared.

She sighed and got up.

Out on the deck, her second-in-command, Weevan-Jirst, was gazing at his open hand. He held a palm-sized gem of fabulous rarity. Its iridescent surface flashed a series of images.

'Traced them yet?' she asked.

'I think so,' he rasped. 'They have altered their course, but their destination is predictable.'

'Then we'll continue the pursuit as soon as we can.'

He looked up from the gem. 'You look troubled. Can I ask the outcome of your communication with our leader?'

'We take the gloves off.'

24

Stryke didn't choose the biggest goblin ship. He thought that might stretch the ability of his band to crew it. Pepperdyne would effectively be commanding the vessel, and he agreed.

At first light they loaded whatever provisions they could forage from the ruins of the goblin encampment, got the freed kelpies aboard and set off. The journey, their new allies assured them, would not be lengthy. For Jup, wracked with anxiety and unusually distant, it couldn't be fast enough. He kept himself to himself, and the others mostly let him be.

The ship ploughed on uneventfully until well into the day. During all that time Pepperdyne was up at the wheel, with Coilla beside him.

'You really look in your element,' she said.

'It's the first thing I've got real pleasure out of since we set off on this crazy escapade.' He gave her a sideways glance. 'Apart from the few chances we've had to talk, that is.'

She smiled. 'Yeah, I've enjoyed that too.' She broke eye contact and said, 'This ship's certainly much faster than those dwarf boats.'

'That's the power of sail.' He nodded at the billowing sheets. 'And we've been lucky with the wind so far.'

'This must be like old times for you.'

'Sort of. Though on Trougath we lived more like the dwarfs do here. Coastal sailing mostly. But we had ships too, of course, for trade.'

'So you've captained one this big before?'

'Well . . . not quite. But don't tell the others.'

They laughed conspiratorially.

'The principles are more or less the same though,' he continued. 'Sailing's sailing.'

'We couldn't have done this without you, you know.'

'I think you could. If there's one thing I've learnt about the Wolverines it's that you're resourceful.'

'We've had to be. But whether it runs to commanding a ship . . .'

'It's easy. Here, try.'

'Really?'

'Sure. Come on, take the wheel.'

He stepped aside and she grabbed hold.

'Wait a minute,' he said, and moved behind her. Arms round her, he took her hands and guided them to a slightly different position. 'That's the best way. And don't grip so tightly. Relax. A light touch is best.'

'This is fun.'

'If you did it long enough you'd get a feel for the vessel. I mean, a *real* feel for it. Those who do this all the time can sense the mood of the ship.'

'Ships have moods?'

'Oh, yes. They're like people. Sorry. They're like people or orcs or . . .'

She smiled. 'You don't have to keep correcting yourself, Jode. I know what you mean.'

'Maybe it's because I find it easy to forget our differences.'

'We are different.'

'In how we appear, sure. But there are deeper things; ways in which all races share certain similarities. That's another thing I've learned during our time together, and I'm grateful for it.'

'But you're from Maras-Da— Oops. Now I'm doing it, aren't I? You're not from there, are you? Not in the way I mean.'

'No. Same world, different part. The area you come from was

always shrouded in mystery for the rest of us. It was a forbidden place. Only when I got there did I realise how many different forms life takes. *Whoa!* You're letting her drift a bit.' He corrected the wheel. 'When I said a light touch I didn't mean *that* light. You have to keep in control or she'll start to rove.'

'That's something I've never understood.'

'What is?'

'Why ships are *her* or *she*. Is it because males build them?'

'I hadn't really thought about it. Maybe.'

'So it's to do with males seeing females as something they own and can control?'

'I like to think it's because a ship has grace and charm, like a female.'

She grinned. 'Quick thinking.'

'It was rather, wasn't it?' He had to smile too. 'I can never imagine anybody controlling you, Coilla.'

'Gods help the male who tried. What about you?'

'How do you mean?'

'Was there a *her* or *she* for you in Trougath?'

His smile went away, and it was a moment before he answered. 'Once.'

'And?'

'Like my nation and my previous life, she was . . . swept away.'

'Sorry. I didn't mean to dredge anything up for you.'

'That's all right.'

'I won't ask anything about—'

'No. What's done is done. I'm not one for dwelling in the past.'

'I understand. You know, your story, your people's story, isn't that different to ours in a way. We lost our birthright too.'

'I know. But not the details. You've never told me how your band came to leave Maras-Dantia.'

'It's a long story.'

'I'd like to hear it some time.'

'Sure. Though you might find it a bit boring.'

'I doubt that.'

They heard footfalls on the ladder leading to the wheel deck. Stryke appeared. Pepperdyne quickly stepped away from her.

'What's going on here?' Stryke said, seeing Coilla at the wheel.

'Nothing!' the two of them replied simultaneously.

'That is,' Coilla elaborated, 'Jode's giving me a lesson in seamanship.'

'Maybe that should be seaorcship,' Pepperdyne suggested. He and Coilla sniggered.

'Yeah, right,' Stryke replied, failing to see the joke. 'You've been at that wheel quite a while now, Pepperdyne. Got anybody to relieve you?'

Pepperdyne took back control of the wheel. 'Hystykk and Gleadeg had a turn earlier. They seem to have the knack. But I'm fine for now, Stryke.'

'Sure?'

'It's a long time since I did anything like this. I'd like to savour it a bit longer.'

'Suit yourself. Just shout when you want a break. I'm going back to the others.' He started to leave.

'I'll come with you,' Coilla told him. She flashed Pepperdyne a quick grin and followed.

Down on the main deck, out of earshot, Stryke said, 'You seem to be growing very friendly with him.'

'We get on.'

'That might not be for the best.'

'What do you mean?'

'Do I have to remind you about the way humans are? Getting close to any of them—'

'Jode's different.'

'Is he?'

'He's helped us. He's helping us *now*. Not to mention I owe him my life a couple of times over. I reckon that entitles him to a little of my time.'

They came to a row of barrels standing by the rail. Stryke stopped and sat. Coilla lingered for a moment, considering the unspoken invitation, then sat down herself.

'I'm only saying this for your good,' Stryke assured her. 'We know that as a race humans can't be trusted.'

'Hold it right there. We came on this mission because of a human. Serapheim, remember? How's he different?'

'He saved us in Maras-Dantia.'

'And Jode saved some of us in Acurial, like I said.'

'Serapheim gave us the means to help the orcs in Acurial, and to get our revenge on Jennesta.'

'And how's that worked out? All right, we aided the Acurial rebels, but there's been precious little in the way of a reckoning as far as Jennesta's concerned. And we wouldn't be in the fix we're in now if it hadn't been for Serapheim.'

'You could always outargue me,' Stryke admitted. 'But I stand by what I said about humans. You've only got to look at the other one, Standeven, to see how low they can get.'

'We're not talking about *him*. Jode's out of a different mould.'

'We aren't going to see eye to eye on this, are we?'

'Nope.'

He reached into his jerkin and brought out a flask. 'Drink?'

She smiled and nodded.

Several healthy swigs of brandy mellowed them both.

'Talking of Serapheim,' Coilla said, relaxing, 'do you ever question why he sent us on this assignment?'

'We know why. To help fellow orcs and for revenge on Jennesta.'

'Think about it. Why should he care about orcs? And Jennesta's his own daughter, don't forget.'

'Being his flesh and blood might be more reason for wanting to punish her. He feels disgraced by her evil, and wants to atone for it by taking away the life he sired.'

'And us orcs?'

'He said he was ashamed of what his race was doing to ours in Acurial.'

'Ah, so the nasty humans *can* act nobly.'

Stryke said nothing. He had another drink.

She went on, 'There's something about all this, Stryke . . . I don't know; it doesn't ring true somehow. I mean, his servant turning up in Ceragan with a knife in his back; what was that about? Who killed him? Why? Come to that, how did Serapheim himself survive the collapse of the ice palace in Ilex?'

'That's an awful lot of questions.'

'Here's another one. How come Jennesta's still alive after going through the . . . What did they call it? The vortex. Not only didn't die but ends up helping to run a human empire. How did that happen?'

'I don't know, Coilla. And I *do* dwell on these things. But sometimes I think there are some mysteries we'll never solve.'

'Perhaps.'

He stood. 'I need to check on Jup.'

'What's he doing?'

'Trying to use his farsight. Remember that big life force he detected? I thought it'd be a good idea to have some warning if we're going to run into it.'

'Has he seen anything?'

'Not so far. But Haskeer's been needling him again, and it throws him off. That's what I need to check on.'

'All right. I'll be with the kelpies if you want me.' She nodded to the far end of the deck where the sea horses were herded together. A bunch of grunts with buckets on ropes were hauling up water to douse them with.

He finished by telling her, 'You remember what I said about Pepperdyne.' Then he turned and walked away.

He passed a stack of chests stowed nearby. What he didn't notice was Standeven sitting on the deck behind them, chin resting on raised knees, listening.

The rest of that day and most of the next passed without incident.

They were into the afternoon when land was spotted. The kelpies grew excited in their rather stately way, and the band prepared to disembark.

When they were close enough to see the island in detail, the old kelpie who first befriended them was puzzled.

'My folk are on the beach,' he rumbled.

'What's strange about that?' Stryke asked.

'You don't understand. My kin shouldn't be cavorting openly in the sea, and certainly not in the daytime, for fear of the Gatherers.'

'Could they have come and gone?' Jup wanted to know, his heart sinking.

'If they had, you can be sure kelpies wouldn't be enjoying themselves in broad daylight.'

As they nosed in and dropped anchor, things became clearer. The kelpies on the beach were joined by a group of two-legged beings, waving frantically.

'They're . . . dwarfs,' Jup whispered, not daring to get his hopes up.

He didn't wait for the gangplank. Tossing a length of rope over the side he agilely shinned down it. Splashing knee-high through water, then onto the flaxen sand, he saw someone running towards him.

Spurral flew into his arms.

The following hours were filled with explanations and renewed camaraderie, for orcs and kelpies alike. At one point, Haskeer marched up to the couple, slapped Spurral heartily on the back and bellowed, 'Well done! Always knew we'd find you.'

Jup watched open mouthed as he swaggered past.

'Maybe he's not so bad after all,' Spurral said.

Haskeer barged his way to Stryke and asked, '*Now* can we get out of this place?'

'Soon as we can.'

'Good. Ceragan's starting to look really good compared to some of the places we've been.'

'Yeah, well, hold on. The stars didn't get us there last time we tried. We have to work that problem out.'

'That must have been something you did wrong, Stryke.'

'If I did, I did it wrong a lot of times.'

'So how we going to sort *that* one?'

'I don't know. Maybe—'

'Excuse *me*,' Spurral interrupted, 'but what about these dwarf survivors?' She waved a hand in their direction. They were sitting morosely by themselves further along the beach.

'What about 'em?' Haskeer said.

'We've got to take them home. Back to their island.'

'Shit, can't somebody else do that?'

'Who? The kelpies aren't a seafaring race. And even if the dwarfs thought they could crew a ship, what would they do for one once we've gone?'

Coilla nodded. 'She's right.'

'Yes,' Stryke agreed. 'We take them back. Then we'll think about the stars.'

'But we won't think about them tonight,' Spurral announced. 'The kelpies are laying on a celebration for everybody, and they're keen on celebrations, I can tell you.'

'And to spice it up a bit,' Coilla added, 'I've got a little something here I found in a cabin on the goblins' ship. Didn't mention it before; thought it might be a surprise.' She took out a small black pouch, loosened its strings and poured some of the contents into her hand.

The others crowded round and instantly recognised the heap of tiny pinkish crystals.

'Pellucid,' Haskeer all but drooled.

Coilla clamped her hand shut. 'But only with the permission of our captain, of course.'

'What do you say, Stryke?' Spurral wanted to know. 'Do we deserve a little relaxation after all we've been through?'

'There were a couple of times when crystal led us to some bad outcomes,' he replied stern faced. A smile cracked it. 'But I don't think this is going to be one of them.'

25

The celebration was good. It must have been, because most of those present would never be able to remember it.

There was drinking, feasting, boasting and inane giggling. The latter was due to the pellucid, which bathed the proceedings in a dreamy, kaleidoscopic haze.

A high point, for Wheam if no one else, came when the tyro, sober and without the benefit of crystal at that juncture, came to them excitedly. He was holding something.

'Look what I found on the ship!' he exclaimed.

'What'd ya say?' Haskeer mumbled, his eyes red pinpoints.

'I thought that if Coilla found that crystal lightning on the ship there might be other things of value. And I found *this*!' Beaming, he held up the object.

'Whassit?'

'A *lute*! It's not like any I've seen before, it's a goblin one I suppose, not that you'd think those creatures would appreciate music, but you never know, do you, anyway it's more or less the same as the sort I'm used to, so I thought—'

'*Aaarrghh!* Talk plain. And slow.'

'Ah. Yes. I found this lute.' He held it aloft once more, and wobbled it. 'It'll replace the one I lost. I can sing my ballads again.'

'If I could get up, I'd kill you.'

'So you don't fancy hearing anything now then?'

They say that even when Wheam started to run, Haskeer was still crawling after him.

There were a lot of thick heads the next morning, and Dallog was kept busy tending minor wounds inflicted during the horseplay. But the band was accustomed to quick recoveries after revelry, and dunkings in the tepid brine, voluntary and otherwise, sobered the majority.

Anxious as everybody was to be off, the kelpies insisted on a prolonged farewell ceremony complete with rambling speeches and numerous toasts. Though Stryke ordered that the latter should be in coconut milk as opposed to alcohol.

They finally shipped out mid-morning.

The journey back to the dwarfs' island was without event, which at least gave the band a chance to fully recover. Jup's spirits had soared. Not that much was seen of him and Spurral during most of the voyage. The only damp blanket was Stand-even, unsurprisingly, who continued to brood when he wasn't dogging Stryke's footsteps.

At first, their arrival caused something of a panic. The islanders assumed that the advent of a three-master meant another visitation by Gatherers. Once that was sorted, and it soaked in that the slavers had been defeated, there were joyful scenes. The Wolverines, partied-out, accepted the accolades with fixed, clenched-toothed smiles.

As soon as they could, Stryke and his principal officers slipped away. Pepperdyne accompanied them, and Standeven tagged on, like a dependent cur. They made their way up to one of the dead volcano's lower ledges.

Stryke surveyed the view. 'Seems fitting that we should leave this world from the place where we entered it.'

'And good riddance,' Haskeer offered.

'Oh, I don't know,' Coilla said. 'Just look at it. There are a lot worse places.'

'To hell with it; I want to get back to Ceragan.'

'We're assuming we *can* get back. I mean, we didn't intend being here.'

'Remember what the kelpies said?' Spurral reminded them. 'About there being islands occupied by orcs? If the stars let you down maybe you could make a life here. Perhaps we could even find an uninhabited island and—'

'You're forgetting something,' Stryke said. 'Some of us have mates and hatchlings in Ceragan.'

'Sorry. Of course you have. I was being thoughtless. But . . . and don't take this the wrong way; there should be a fall-back plan if the stars don't get you home.'

'But we won't know that until we try them,' Coilla reminded her. 'And if they take us somewhere other than Ceragan, what's the odds they'd bring us back here?'

'It's a good point, Stryke,' Dallog reckoned. 'Surely the only real decision is whether we try using the stars or not.'

'I know. My head's full of it. But my instinct *is* to try. I want to do all I can to get back to my brood.'

'I can understand that,' Jup said.

'It gets my vote,' Haskeer chipped in.

'I think you might have been right about me making a mistake, Haskeer,' Stryke admitted. 'I must have set them wrong.'

Coilla nodded. 'And no wonder, given how rushed we were.'

'Think you can get it right this time, Stryke?' Standeven wanted to know.

'What's it to you?' Haskeer sneered.

'I just want to be sure we do it properly this time.'

'*We?* What makes you think *you're* included?'

'You can't just leave us here!'

'Why not? We're not your mother!'

'We've been through all this,' Stryke returned sternly. 'We've already said we'll take the humans back to Maras-Dantia. I gave my word.'

'What are we now,' Haskeer grumbled, 'wet nurses?'

'I'll have no more argument. It's decided.'

'Well, sorry to go on about it,' Jup put in, 'but did we ever really resolve what happens to Spurral and me?'

'We said you'd be welcome in Ceragan,' Coilla replied.

'Yeah, and we appreciate it,' Spurral responded. 'But with respect, I don't know if we want to spend the rest of our lives in an orcs' world.'

'And you haven't changed your minds about being in Maras-Dantia? You don't want to go back?'

Jup and Spurral exchanged a look. They shook their heads.

'Why can't they stay here?' Haskeer wanted to know, jabbing a thumb at them. 'This is a place for dwarfs.'

'It isn't a dwarfs' world,' Spurral explained, as though to a hatchling. 'It's a . . . dumping ground.'

'Let's stick to what we agreed,' Stryke decided. He indicated Pepperdyne and Standeven. 'We take these two back to where we found 'em, in Maras-Dantia. Jup and Spurral can come with us to Ceragan.'

'Then what?' Jup wanted to know. 'For me and Spurral, I mean.'

'We can try to figure out the stars, and the amulet. Maybe—'

'Maybe we can find a way to send them to a dwarf world?' Coilla finished for him. 'It's a long shot, Stryke. What if we never—'

'Can you think of anything better?'

'No.'

'Then that's what's on offer.'

'This is all moot if we've no way of knowing the stars work,' Pepperdyne said. 'There's no point going round in circles.'

Stryke nodded. 'You're right. We all need to cool off, and I need to think. We'll try the stars again, but a bit later today, after I've had a chance to study them and you've all cooled off. Anybody object to that?'

Nobody did.

*

When everyone had dispersed, and Stryke had gone off somewhere quiet to try figuring out the instrumentalities and the amulet, Coilla and Pepperdyne found themselves alone.

'This is a rare thing,' he remarked.

'It is unusual not to be part of a mob, isn't it?'

'While it lasts. What's the betting somebody's going to barge in on us any minute?'

'We could avoid that.'

'How?'

'These volcanoes are supposed to be riddled with caves. And the view from up there must be quite something. Fancy exploring?'

'I'm game.'

The climb was actually very gentle, so they went as far up as they could reach, reasoning that the higher they were the less likely they'd run into anybody else. Before long they found a cave and seated themselves just inside its mouth.

Pepperdyne expelled an appreciative breath. 'It's pleasantly cool in here.'

'Said it'd be good, didn't I?'

'What's really good about it is having the chance to spend some time with you. You know, without anybody wanting something carried or trying to kill us.'

She smiled. 'And I've got something that should brighten things.' She pulled the small black pouch from her pocket. 'I kept some of this back.'

'The crystal?'

'Yeah. I noticed you didn't have any last night.'

'I've never had any. I've heard about it, of course, but never really saw the need.'

'It's not something you need; it's just nice now and again. You're in for a treat.' She began filling a clay pipe, then stopped. 'If you want to, that is.'

'Why not? And I'd rather do it without a crowd watching my first time.'

She got the pipe going, took a lungful and passed it to him. They felt the effect almost instantly.

After a little while she asked, 'How is it?'

'Not how I imagined.'

'Is that good, bad . . . ?'

'Mellow. Relaxing.' He took another pull on the pipe, held it, let it out. 'So . . . ges, yood. Uhm. I mean, yes . . . good.'

'Your face!' She started to giggle.

'What about it?'

'Just looks funny, that's all.'

'You look pretty comical yourself.' Then he caught the giggles too.

They laughed until they shook, then fell back and sprawled helplessly on the ground.

When the laughter subsided a tranquil mood came over them. They lay staring at the cave's roof, admiring the patterns reflected sunlight made on the soft stone.

At length, Coilla said, 'After today . . .'

'Yes?'

'It looks like we might not see each other again.'

'I was trying to put that out of my thoughts.'

'Me, too. But it keeps creeping back.'

'Mind you, if Stryke can't make the stars behave maybe you will be stuck with me. Somewhere.'

'I know Stryke. Somehow he'll make them work. Even if it takes a hundred tries. He's stubborn.'

'A hundred different worlds like the ones we saw before? Doesn't bear thinking about.'

'But if he does make them work, that's it. You'll be in Maras-Dantia and I'll be back in Ceragan.' She turned her head and regarded him. 'I'll miss you. You've been a good comrade in arms.'

'Coming from an orc, I take that as a high compliment.'

'It's meant to be. We fight well together. That's important to my kind. Particularly for a—'

'For a what?'

'Nothing. Tongue running away with me there. Expect it's the crystal.'

'Is it?'

'Would you do something for me, Jode?'

'What?'

'Scratch my back. It's itching like hell in this heat.'

They laughed.

'Sure,' he said. 'Give it here.'

She sat up and he commenced scratching.

'Hmmm, that's good. This isn't something you can get just anyone to do, you know.'

'Then I'm honoured.'

'Bit higher. Yes, there. Aaaahh. Nice.'

The scratching turned to a gentle massaging. The massage became a series of caresses. She turned her face to his.

They kissed.

26

It was nearly evening when Stryke emerged from the longhouse the dwarf elder had put at his disposal. He had ordered the band to gather on the beach, ready for what they hoped would be an initial hop to Maras-Dantia. But when he got there not everyone was present.

'Where's Coilla?' he asked.

'No idea,' Jup reported. 'Pepperdyne and Standeven are missing, too.'

'Words I've been longing to hear,' Haskeer said.

'Don't start that again,' Stryke told him.

'Well, if the pair of 'em got left behind it'd be no great loss.'

'But it's not like Coilla to miss a roll call.'

'To be fair,' Jup said, 'I don't think she's been seen since we were all together earlier. Chances are she didn't know about your order to be here now.'

'Anybody seen Coilla lately?' Stryke wanted to know. None of them had. 'Give it a couple of minutes, Jup, then start the roll call. If she's not here by the time you're done I'll send out a search party.'

Jup nodded and set to getting the ranks into order.

Not far off, on the other side of the volcano, Coilla and Pepperdyne were climbing down from the cave. They turned a corner on the narrow path and saw the beach.

'Shit,' she said. 'Looks like Stryke's mustered the band. They must be getting ready to leave. He'll kill me for missing the roll. Come on!'

'Wait!'

'What is it?'

'Down there.' He pointed to a spot further along the beach and just round a bend. 'That's Standeven.'

'What the hell's he doing sitting out there?'

'Who knows? He's been behaving very oddly lately.'

'Doesn't he always?'

'Not usually this much.'

'You know, Jode, this could be a golden opportunity for you to dump him.'

'What, leave him here?'

'Doesn't he deserve it?'

'Well, yes. But . . . No, I can't do it.'

'Really?'

'No. I mean, how could I inflict him on those innocent dwarfs?'

She laughed. 'That's what I like about you, Jode; you've got values. Even if they are wasted on a rat like Standeven.'

'You get to the band. I'll go and fetch him.'

'Don't be long. There are some who'd like to see you two left behind.'

'Would Stryke allow that?'

'Don't look so alarmed. Of course he wouldn't. Just don't keep him waiting.'

'I'll drag him there if I have to.'

'Right. Hey, before you go.' She leaned over and kissed him, then they dashed off in opposite directions.

Standeven was sitting by the shore, throwing pebbles into the waves.

Pepperdyne arrived, panting. 'What are you doing?'

'Nothing.'

'The band are gathered up the beach there. I reckon they're getting ready to leave.'

'So what?'

'*So what?* You want to be left behind?'

'Hardly seems to matter.'

'Are you insane? Stryke's going to take us back home.'

'Maybe he's going to *try*.'

'You're scared of the transition, is that it?'

Standeven flared indignantly, 'How dare you imply—'

'Oh, stow it. You've hardly proved yourself a hero on this little jaunt, have you? Cowardice's a fair assumption.'

'It's not that.'

Pepperdyne doubted it. 'What, then?'

'Suppose he does get us back. We'd be no better off, Hammrik's going to be on our trail again, and Stryke will still have the instrumentalities.'

'That again, is it?'

'What do you mean?'

'The stars. You've become obsessed with them. We can sort out the situation with Hammrik, if only by getting as far away from him as possible, but you have to have the stars. Is there a limit to your greed?'

'It's not that.'

'What, then?'

'I just think . . . I think they'd be better with me.'

'The instrumentalities would be better with you,' Pepperdyne repeated incredulously.

Standeven nodded.

'You have gone crazy.'

'It's hard to explain. I—'

'Don't even try. We've no time for your ravings. On your feet.'

He stayed where he was.

'If we don't get to the band right now,' Pepperdyne warned him, 'we're going to spend the rest of our lives in this place.'

'Suits me. But then, you wouldn't be with your little friend, would you?'

'What?'

'Coilla. Grown close, haven't you? But you should have a care. The others don't like it. Stryke's certainly not keen. Do you think he might have ambitions in that direction himself? After all—'

'Right, that does it.' He grabbed hold of his one-time master and bodily hauled him up.

'Take your filthy hands off me you—'

Pepperdyne punched him in the solar plexus, hard. Standeven doubled, gasping. Pepperdyne took hold of his arms and began frogmarching him along the beach.

Jup was just finishing the roll call when Coilla turned up. She was breathless.

'Where've you been?' Stryke demanded.

'Sorry,' she gasped. 'Didn't . . . know we . . . were supposed . . . to be here.'

'You would if you'd stuck around. Where were you?'

'Just . . . taking a walk.'

She got some odd looks for that.

'Picking wild flowers?' Haskeer mocked.

Coilla glared at him. 'I was taking a last look at the island. That all right with you?'

Haskeer shrugged.

'You seen the humans?' Stryke asked her.

'Jode and Standeven?'

'Know of any others tagging along with us?'

'Oh, right. No. Er, yes.'

'Which is it?'

'I saw them back there. Just briefly. They're coming.'

'They'd better be quick.'

'Here they are!' one of the grunts shouted.

The pair of humans were hurrying their way. Pepperdyne was no longer propelling Standeven, though the latter was limping and looked rough.

'Sorry, Stryke,' Pepperdyne said.

'Let's do this, shall we?' He took in their expectant, and in some cases apprehensive, faces as he dug out the instrumentalities and the amulet.

'Try to get it right this time,' Haskeer muttered.

Stryke shot him a murderous glance. 'I've been studying the markings for most of the day. It'll be done right.' He started to assemble the stars.

Everybody gathered round and watched him carefully slot together all but one of the artefacts.

'Right,' he said, 'brace yourselves.'

Coilla and Pepperdyne exchanged a furtive look. Jup and Spurral linked hands. Dallog gave Wheam's trembling shoulder a supportive squeeze. Standeven wore an expression similar to a cornered rodent's. Everybody tensed.

Stryke began easing the fifth and final star into place.

There were shouts and screams. Along the beach, dwarfs were scattering in panic. The source of their terror was a ship that seemed to have appeared without any of the band noticing.

'Ah, fuck,' Haskeer cursed, 'not again!'

Stryke stayed his hand.

'Do it!' Haskeer urged.

Stryke removed the fifth star.

'What you doing?'

'We've got company.' He nodded at the ship.

'You mean *they* have.'

Stryke glanced at the running dwarfs. 'We don't abandon comrades.'

'For the gods' sake, Stryke!'

'We're *not* leaving. Not till we know what this is.'

'Recognise that ship?' Pepperdyne said. 'It's the same bunch that attacked us earlier.'

'Remember what they did to us last time, Stryke,' Coilla warned. 'They've got strong magic.'

'Still,' he replied calmly, 'don't you want to know who they are?'

'No!' Haskeer protested.

'Just because you want to dodge a fight—' Coilla began.

Haskeer bridled. 'Who you accusing of—'

'*Button it,*' Stryke growled. 'This isn't the time.' He put away the stars and stuffed the amulet back down his shirt.

Kalgeck arrived at a sprint. He made straight for Spurral. 'Is it them? Have they come back?'

'The Gatherers?' she said. 'No, it's not them. You know it can't be. But they're as deadly in a different way. Get your kin clear of the beach.'

'They're already doing that. I want to fight.'

'Not this time, Kalgeck. 'We're facing something too powerful.'

'Then why not use the trebuchets?' He pointed to the volcano.

'Of course!' Coilla exclaimed. 'The catapults. Stryke?'

'It's a good idea. Let's get up there.'

'Catapults ain't going to dent those bastards,' Haskeer grumbled.

'*Come on!*' Coilla yelled.

'You get to cover!' Spurral sternly instructed Kalgeck.

The band dashed for the path leading to the ledge on the mountainside. All but Standeven, who under cover of the uproar slunk away.

When they got to the line of catapults they immediately began to prime them, working with an efficiency born of much experience.

'We don't know how far their magic can reach,' Dallog said. 'We could be sitting targets up here.'

'All weapons have a limit,' Stryke reminded him.

'Even magical ones?'

Stryke ignored that and continued barking orders.

The ship was at the shoreline when the first volley of heavy rocks was unleashed. All fell short, but close, making great splashes that swamped the ship's deck. The next battery was better aimed.

A rock crashed into the side of the ship, demolishing a large section of the rail. Seconds later, another struck one of the masts, neatly severing it. Timber and sails fell in a jumble.

Something like a slow lightning bolt issued from the ship. Purple and crackling, it flashed to one of the catapults and blew it to bits. Orcs were thrown back by the impact.

'*Casualties?*' Stryke roared.

Dallog dashed around checking. '*Nothing bad!*' he yelled back.

The arms of several catapults went up and over, launching another cascade. They were all misses, some very near, others soaring over the ship and splattering down on its far side.

This time, there was a different response from the ship. What emanated from it was a sort of pattern, similar to ripples in a pond, only travelling through the air. Like the lightning bolt it travelled fast, but not so rapidly that the band didn't have the chance to flatten themselves. The ripples, alternately black and glowing gold, wiped out all of the catapults, shredding them to splinters in a deafening cacophony.

'So much for being out of range,' Haskeer complained.

Coilla pointed. 'Look! They're coming ashore!'

A small flotilla of boats was heading for the beach.

'It's fight or run time,' Stryke announced.

'We don't do run,' Coilla reminded him.

'So let's meet 'em, shall we?'

He gave out a battle cry and they followed him down.

27

If the Wolverines thought they would engage the strangers conventionally they were soon disabused of the notion.

Even before the group of boats hit the beach their multi-race occupants were on the offensive. Variously coloured beams of intense energy flared. Bolts struck the sand, throwing up clouds and gouging deep pits. They seemed to be shots designed to get the firers' eye in. The next round came a lot closer to the band.

On Stryke's order they ran to shelter behind a scattering of large rocks occupying the space between beach and island proper.

The Wolverines replied with arrows, some flaming. They were sticks against a hurricane. Some of the bolts were obliterated by piercing energy shafts. Others simply evaporated before they got near their targets. The orcs saw that this was because an almost invisible energy shield of some sort shimmered around the beings wading ashore.

'We're not touching 'em,' Coilla said.

'At this rate we'll be overrun,' Dallog warned. 'What'll we do, Stryke?'

'Maybe we'll have better luck hand to hand with them.'

'Dream on,' Haskeer growled. 'Those wizards are too powerful for steel to make any headway. Use the stars and get us out of here.'

'No. Even if I wanted to, the band's scattered all over the place. We'd leave half our strength behind.'

'Here they come!' Coilla shouted.

A good dozen of the attackers were drawing close. Pelli Madayar was at their head. Behind her tramped a colourful assortment of elder races.

'There's a couple of fucking goblins with 'em!' Haskeer exclaimed.

'Should have known those bastards would have something to do with this,' Jup snapped.

The advancing party was still spraying the area with their magic beams.

'Ready to engage!' Stryke ordered.

Orcs drew second weapons, nocked bows and primed slingshots.

When they were no more than ten paces distant, Pelli Madayar held up her hand. The group stopped, as did the bombardment.

'We don't have to do this, Stryke!' she called out.

'She knows your name,' Coilla said. For some reason she found that especially disquieting.

A chill had gone up Stryke's spine on hearing it too, though he would never have admitted it. Ignoring the others' gestures to stay put, he stepped out from behind the rock.

'Who are you? What do you want?'

'We're not your enemies, whatever you think. You know what we want. The instrumentalities, that's all.'

'*All?*'

'You can save yourselves further grief very simply. Just hand them over.'

'Like hell we will.'

'You have no right to them.'

'And you do?'

'Morally . . . yes.'

'Fancy word from somebody who just tried to kill us.'

'We weren't trying. Look, if you're worried that giving up the artefacts means we'll leave you stranded here, don't be. Maybe I can arrange to have you sent to your home world.'

'Maybe? That doesn't sound too promising to me.'

'I have to consult a higher authority.'

'This is my higher authority,' Stryke told her, holding up his sword. 'And it says *no*.'

'Be sensible. What you've just seen is only a taste of the power we command. If we turned it on you full force you wouldn't stand a chance.'

'We'll play those odds.'

Pelli sighed. 'This is so pointless. Why are you so intent on wasting your lives for the sake of—' She stopped, as though hearing a voice no one else heard. Then she turned to look out to sea.

A small armada of ships was making for shore.

All of the strangers turned to look, contemptuous of offering their backs to the Wolverines. The band, too, came out from their shelter and stared.

'This place is as busy as a whorehouse on pay day,' Haskeer muttered.

It was obvious that the arrival was as much of a surprise to the strangers as it was to the orcs.

Feeling as though he'd been virtually dismissed, Stryke backed off and rejoined his crew.

'Who the hell's knocking at the door now?' Coilla said.

'I don't know. More Gatherers?'

'No,' Pepperdyne told them. 'Definitely not Gatherers. Look!'

One of the fleet of five ships was engaging with the strangers' vessel. And it was doing it magically. Vividly hued beams shot from craft to craft.

Seemingly having forgotten the Wolverines, Pelli and her ill-assorted group began jogging towards the shoreline. Before they reached the waves they were sending out shafts of their own.

'What the *fuck* is going on?' Haskeer demanded.

'Looks like our enemy has an enemy,' Stryke replied.

'Which would be fine,' Jup pointed out, 'if our enemy's enemy wasn't our enemy too.'

'What the hell are you talking about?'

'Take a look at that ship coming into shore, the leading one. It's prow-on. See? Now do you notice somebody standing there, right at the front, bold as shit?'

'Yeah,' Haskeer said, blinking and with a hand shading his brow.

'Recognise who it is?'

It was Coilla who answered. 'Jennesta,' she whispered.

28

'I thought the stars were supposed to be incredibly rare,' Coilla said, 'but it looks as though everybody's got them.'

'Maybe we've just run into everybody who *has* got them,' Pepperdyne suggested.

Down on the beach, the magical battle raged. The new arrivals had sent in boats of their own. They were running a shuttle, dropping troops off in shallow water and going back for more. The soldiers were Jennesta's human followers, along with a much smaller number of her zombie personal guard. But they seemed no more able to overcome the strangers' magic than the orcs were. That was for Jennesta. Ashore now, and sweeping majestically up the beach, she was essentially waging the war single-handed and, considering her opponents' might, making a good job of it.

Stryke figured that if they couldn't fight the strangers' magic, they could fight Jennesta's army. As there was no way to escape, he argued, they could at least kill something.

At first, it went well. They charged into the fray and gave a good account of themselves, downing troops and hacking zombies to pieces. But it didn't take long for both Jennesta and the strangers to notice them. A bombardment of enchantments forced the band to retreat. Though Stryke wasn't alone in thinking that, vicious as their magic was, neither side was actually trying too hard to kill them.

The band pulled back to the edge of the beach and the shelter of rocks.

'The stars!' Haskeer pleaded. 'Use 'em now!'

'Lay off!' Stryke snapped. 'Coilla! Are we all here?'

'No. We're missing Dallog, Wheam and a couple of the other tyros.'

'Bloody typical,' Haskeer moaned.

'I'll go and look for them,' Stryke decided.

'I'll come with you,' Coilla told him. 'No, no argument. You'll need somebody to watch your back.'

'All right.'

'Me too.' Pepperdyne said.

'No.'

'Going to stop me?'

'If I have to. But better that you stay here and help hold our position.'

'But—'

'Do it, Jode,' Coilla said. 'I'll . . . We'll be fine.'

'If you're going,' Haskeer grated, 'you better get a fucking move on.'

Stryke tossed his head. 'Come on.'

They ran towards the scrum.

The bodies barring their way were all human or zombie. The wizardry was taking place further down the beach, at the water's edge. But soldiers and the undead were still a formidable obstacle.

Stryke and Coilla hacked, slashed, stabbed and battered their way through them. They had a few errant energy bolts to dodge on the way. Some of Jennesta's horde weren't so lucky.

'I see 'em!' Coilla yelled. She pointed.

Dallog and a couple of tyros were slugging it out with twice their number of soldiers.

Coilla and Stryke fought their way to them.

Their blades quickly turned the tide. A bloody exchange saw the attackers overcome.

'Where's Wheam, Dallog?' Stryke asked.

'Down there!'

Further along the beach, Wheam was trying to hold off a pair of zombies. He had his new musical instrument strapped to his back, and looked more worried about protecting it than himself.

'I'll get him,' Stryke said.

'We'll come!' Coilla and Dallog chorused.

'*No*. I'll not have the band scattered again. Get yourselves back to the others. *Now*.'

They left reluctantly. He plunged back into the fray.

Coilla, Dallog and the tyros had as tough a path to travel on the way back as she and Stryke had on the way out. The troops seemed to be everywhere, and none left them unchallenged. By the time their goal was in sight, their blades ran with gore.

'Can you make it alone from here, Dallog?' Coilla said.

' 'Course.'

'Get on then.'

'What about you?'

'I'm going after Stryke.'

'But he said—'

'Just get these two back, all right?' She ran off.

Stryke came at one of the zombies from the back and ran it through. True to experience it hardly registered the blow. So he took to chopping at it, as though he were felling a dead tree. When enough major damage had been inflicted the armless creature hopped on its one leg for an instant then collapsed. The second zombie Stryke simply decapitated, sending its head bouncing in the blood-soaked sand.

'Am I glad to see you, Captain,' Wheam panted.

'I'm going to get you out of here. Stay close.'

Before they could move, Coilla arrived.

'I thought I told you—'

'You need me,' she said. 'Look around. Somebody's got to cover your back.'

'All right. Let's go.'

It was getting harder to steer a way that didn't have troops in it. So they were compelled to carve a path. But still the increasing opposition made them take a different route back. It took them past a large outcropping of rock.

It was only very shortly after what happened next that Stryke started to think they'd been deliberately herded that way.

Jennesta stepped out from behind the rock.

The trio stopped in their tracks.

'Run, Wheam!' Coilla pleaded. 'Get out of here!'

The youth fled.

Jennesta laughed, disturbingly. 'It seems not *all* orcs are courageous.'

Stryke and Coilla rushed her as one, their blades levelled.

She made a swift hand gesture. The pair instantly froze in their tracks, rigid as statues.

Strangely, the fighting seemed to have frozen too. Or at least the sound and sight of it had. It was either more of Jennesta's magic, or her followers had fallen back, reinforcing the suspicion that it had been a set-up.

'Now that I've got you nicely calmed,' Jennesta said, 'we can have a civilised conversation.'

Stryke and Coilla were helpless. They struggled to move or make a sound but couldn't.

'When I say conversation, of course, that doesn't imply that you'll be taking part in it. Actually, Stryke, I've got someone here who knows you. Or did.' She snapped her fingers loudly.

Two zombies lumbered into sight. They walked on either side of somebody.

It was Thirzarr.

Stryke's mate showed no sign of recognising him. She looked healthy enough, apart from a few bruises, but seemed to be in a light trance or coma.

'Surprised?' Jennesta mocked. 'I thought you might be. She isn't fully undead, like my servants here. She's . . . let us say she's in the stage before that, and could go either way. A zombie or back to how she was. You can decide which.'

For all his torment, Stryke couldn't break through her enchantment.

'My proposition is straightforward,' she informed him. 'I'll free your mate if you and your band surrender yourselves to me. Just the orcs; I've no need for the other types you have hanging on. Do that, Stryke, and you'll not only free Thirzarr, you'll also be part of a wonderful enterprise. The Wolverines will form the nucleus of my zombie-orc army. Quite a combination, yes? Unquestioning obedience coupled with your peerless fighting skills and robust fitness. A great improvement on the present sort.' She indicated her zombie slaves with a casual flick of the hand. 'Think of it, Stryke. You'll be able to fight and conquer to your black heart's content. Not just in one world, but many. *All* of them. With the instrumentalities turned out on a mass scale . . . Oh, yes. That's how I come to be here. I copied yours. And now I know I have the means perfected, I can start to build an army of totally compliant orcs to conquer . . . well, everywhere really. Anyway, that's the proposition. I'm going to sever the bonds holding you now so you can give your answer. One move and you'll go back to helplessness.' She gestured with her hands again.

Stryke thawed. Despite his rage and anguish he fought back the urge to leap for her throat. He knew it would be futile, and he needed to bide his time. If he had any. He kept his bile for words. 'You stinking bitch! What have you done to Thirzarr? And what about our hatchlings? Where are they?'

'You don't expect me to tell you, do you? Your brats are not the issue. Your mate or your band. What's your answer?'

'I can't agree, not on behalf of the others. They fought hard for their freedom. I can't be the one to make them forfeit it.'

'Then your mate becomes a mindless slave. Perhaps you'd *like* a mindless slave for a mate. I could see it might have some advantages. Is that it, Stryke?'

'If you'd only face me one to one, in a fair—'

She burst out laughing. 'Oh, *please*. As if I'm going to do that. But perhaps there's another way of resolving this.'

'How?'

'If you won't capitulate, then settle it in a way more to your liking. In combat. If my champion wins, you succumb. Well, you'll be dead actually, but you would have conceded defeat. You win, you have your mate back, good as new.'

Coilla struggled against her invisible bonds futilely.

'Who's your champion?' Stryke said.

'She's standing right next to me.'

'*Thirzarr?* I won't do it. She wouldn't either.'

'Really?' Jennesta waved a hand at Thirzarr.

She seemed to come alive, yet not quite.

'Fight him,' Jennesta ordered, 'to the death.' She handed Thirzarr a sword.

She snatched it and immediately made for Stryke. He stood stupefied for a second, not believing his eyes. Then he had to move fast to evade her singing blade.

Stryke twisted and turned to avoid the rain of blows she sent his way. He only reluctantly raised his own sword when he had no other way of fending her off. Every move he made was defensive. Her every stroke was calculated to kill.

It was getting desperate. Stryke was being driven to up the ante in the face of her inexhaustible attack. He dreaded his instincts taking over and, Thirzarr or not, striking back in like kind.

Suddenly Wheam reappeared. He popped from behind the outcropping. Of all the things he might have done next, Stryke would never have guessed the one he chose.

He threw a rock at Jennesta. It struck her on the shoulder and she cried out, more in injured pride than hurt.

The unexpectedness of the attack broke her concentration and whatever mental power she exercised to maintain her enchantments.

Coilla unfroze. Thirzarr stopped, lowered her arms and dropped the sword. She seemed to have re-entered the state she arrived in.

As Jennesta raged, and presumably struggled to re-establish her hold, Coilla grabbed Stryke and began pulling him away. He struggled at first, wanting to go to Thirzarr, but even in his frenzy he saw that was hopeless. He let Coilla and Wheam guide him.

They ran. Something like a thunderbolt followed them, but boomed harmlessly overhead.

The fighting had died down considerably, and although they faced opposition, which fell to Coilla to deal with, they got back to the others unscathed.

What had happened was quickly relayed to the band. Most took the news in dumb silence.

Coilla said, 'Take us to Ceragan, Stryke. We'll raise an army and come back here to kick Jennesta's arse so hard—'

'We don't know if the stars would get us there. But there's worse.'

'How could it be worse?' She had an icy churning in the pit of her stomach.

'Don't you see? Jennesta must have been there, to get Thirzarr. And Thirzarr wouldn't have come willingly. No orc would. They would have fought. It wouldn't be beyond Jennesta to wipe out every orc there if she could manage it. Coilla, we don't even know if Ceragan still exists.'

Acknowledgements

Of all the unsung heroes of publishing, translators play an especially important role. The success of a foreign edition of a book stands or falls on the expertise and sensitivity of its translator. So I'd like to take this opportunity to acknowledge my enormous debt to all the translators of the many editions of the Orcs series that have appeared around the world. In particular, my gratitude is due to Isabelle Troin in France, Juergen Langowski in Germany and Lia Belt in Holland as peers of their profession.